Mostly Happy

Mostly Happy

PAM BUSTIN

thistledown press

Library and Archives Canada Cataloguing in Publication
Bustin, Pam, 1965-
Mostly happy / Pam Bustin.
ISBN 978-1-897235-39-3
I. Title.
PS8603.U828M68 2008   C813'.6   C2008-900073-0

Cover photograph ©Josef Scaylea/CORBIS
Author Photo: Debra Marshall
Cover and book design by Jackie Forrie
Printed and bound in Canada

Thistledown Press Ltd.
633 Main Street
Saskatoon, Saskatchewan, S7H 0J8
www.thistledownpress.com

Canada Council   Conseil des Arts
for the Arts   du Canada

Canadian   Patrimoine
Heritage   canadien

We acknowledge the support of the Canada Council for the Arts, the Saskatchewan Arts Board, and the Government of Canada through the Book Publishing Industry Development Program for our publishing program.

ACKNOWLEDGEMENTS

It's been a long, wild, ride to get here. I'd like to thank Leon Rooke for accepting the first Bean story, odd as it was, for publication. Much thanks to the Saskatchewan Arts Board and the Canada Council for their support — I hereby send a big hug to those who sat on the peer juries and dug Bean enough to want to hear her story told. Thanks to Rod, Connie, Byrna, Sylvia, and Di for their early and ongoing support; to Isabel, Verlie, Wendy and Duncan for the beauty of Mulligan's Bay to dream on; to Patti for the trip to the desert. Special thanks to Suzanne and Mansel for their careful reading and comments on an early draft and their continued support as I wrestled with rewrites. Heaps of gratitude to Robert, who read it and read it and read it again. Your clear eye, ear for dialogue, and fearless questioning are invaluable to me.

I cannot think of any words big enough to express my thanks to Harriet Richards, who met Bean early on, accepted an excerpt from the book for publication in *spring* magazine, and then asked to see the completed manuscript. Thank you Harriet — for your patience, your support over the years it took me to get to a draft I felt good enough about to let you read, and your vigilance and skill as an editor in helping me tell the story clean.

Thanks to my mother, my sister, aunts and cousins, and my amazing friends who surround me always with love.

Mostly and always — thanks to Kathryn, who once shared a chocolate bar with me and whose letters keep me sane; and to Mansel, who loved Bean the first time he met her and said, "She's the one. Tell me her story."

Here it is.

Hope you like it.

Pam Bustin, Saskatoon, 2007

For Mansel and Mr. G

Life's a tightrope, baby. Don't look down.
— Gustave Peterson

Prologue: Running

I left the suitcase with Goose and I went to the desert.
All I took with me was my guilt.

The suitcase: A Samsonite Saturn. Red.
The contents:

A paper napkin with a lipstick kiss

A dog tag

Two wedding announcements

A turquoise earring

Four rocks

A torn Camp Mihkwaw T-shirt

Two hospital bracelets

An old purple bottle

A broken bobble-head dog's head

A bullet

A blue marble

A collapsible tophat

Six books, one hand written

Three concert ticket stubs

A stick a stone a feather and a bone wrapped in red felt

A few theatre programs

A ring in a black bag filled with salt

A plastic troll

Some letters

A chipped jade Buddha

A small leather pouch

A church pamphlet

A postcard from Paris

A purple scarf

A piece of wedding cake

A Shazam comic

A red rubber ball

Photos: a girl with an eye patch, a guy with a fish and two babies

A stone goose

A matchbook

A birth announcement

A ripped piece of cardboard from a Ouija Board

A funeral announcement

A child's plaster handprint

Forty-six days later, I called Prissy from Cheyenne Wyoming.

One

nostalgia *n* homesickness; the desire to return to some earlier time in one's life, or a fond remembrance of that time, usually tinged with sadness at its having passed. [Gr *nostos* a return, and *algos* pain]
— *The Chambers Dictionary* (Standard)

PRISSY'S KISS

Prissy Fallwell smoked Player's Plain, played crib for money, and drank Wild Turkey when she was between men. She worked as a waitress up at the Husky in a uniform that was just a little too tight across the hips. Prissy twirled among the truckers with steak and eggs, tuna melts, and all the coffee they could drink. She called everybody Honey. She laughed at their jokes, smiled over pictures of their kids and touched them softly when their hearts got broke. Prissy had the sad eyes of an angel.

I sat at the counter and watched Prissy work. I was *refining my voice-over.* I squinted my eyes and turned the world to black and white. Prissy was the smart-talking heroine and I was the precocious kid who saved the day. I stuck to long shots — like

Prissy showing a boy how make a spoon stick to his nose. Close-up, Prissy looked tired.

It was a good movie. We were happy.

We'd just moved in to a new place out by the Husky and I'd gone to register at school all by myself that morning. Prissy kissed a napkin for me, folded it up and tucked it into my jean jacket pocket with the letter from my last school. "There. Now I'm with you." It wasn't her fault she couldn't come with me. I had to be brave. She straightened my collar. "Sorry, Kid"

I held my hand over the pocket that held the napkin. "Don't worry. I'm OK."

She hugged me, and I knew she was giving Carl, her boss, a look over my shoulder. He snorted. "Too busy, Edith. Sorry." Carl called my mom Edith, even though her nametag said Prissy. Edith was her old name. Edith Marietta Fallwell. She liked Prissy better. It was her nickname. Her whole family had nicknames, but Prissy was the only one who liked her nickname better than her real name. She changed it officially when she was twenty-two. She changed my name then too. Not my first name — my last.

Prissy swung by to drop off some dirty dishes. She came and gave me a hug. "How'd it go, Kid?"

"Good. I found the office easy and told the principal you would call him tomorrow. I gave him the letter from Cawanas and he put me in a grade three/four split."

"That's 'cause you're a smarty." She mussed up my hair. "Snack?"

"Grill cheese please!"

"Any homework?"

"A math sheet." I always had a math sheet. I was the spelling-bee champion in every school I went to, but numbers messed me up. Subtraction was the hardest. I always ended up with one too many because I counted the one I ended on. Five minus three was three — Five — Four — Three — where I ended up. The teachers told me to use my fingers.

Prissy brought me my grill cheese and a coke. She swept the hair out of my eyes and kissed me on the forehead. "I love you, kid. A bizillion times a million."

"I love you too, Mom."

"You happy?"

"Y'betcha." I never let Prissy wipe her kisses off. I never threw out her napkin kiss, either. I put it in my collection. I kept all my treasures in a shoebox, so I knew where they were and they never got left behind when we moved. I had to be choosy though. Prissy said she didn't wanna live with no damned pack-rat.

Me and Prissy travelled light.

WEDDING ANNOUNCEMENT: PRISSY AND RITTER

I started my collection when I was about three years old. The first thing I put in the box was Prissy and Ritter's wedding announcement. I wasn't born yet, when they got married, but I'd heard the story a million times.

Prissy Fallwell was sixteen years old when she married Ritter Eberts. He was twenty-two, loved sardines, Colt cigars, and Johnny Cash. Ritter had the overcooked left arm of a full-time cabbie and drank — too much.

When Prissy said, "I'm pregnant." Ritter said, "Guess we'd better get hitched then."

Ritter found out before the wedding that his other girlfriend, Rita Schmidt, was pregnant too. "Too late, sweetheart," he said. "I'm already on the hook."

Prissy told me that I was *conceived* in the back seat of an off-duty cab and born six months after the wedding. The Beatles' "Ticket to Ride" was number one on the charts and Elvis was at thirty-seven with "Crying in the Chapel".

Ritter's the one that named me Bean. He said that's what I looked like when he first saw me — a little red Kidney bean. He also figured with a name like Bean, Prissy's family couldn't give me some crazy nickname.

Prissy gave me my middle name — E.

She said, "Elvis".

Ritter said, "Aron?" — which is Elvis Presley's middle name and at least sounds like a girl name.

Prissy said, "E." And so it was.

Me and Prissy stayed with Ritter for just about six years.

Me and Ritter knew how to have a good time. We watched Red Skelton, in our pjs, while Prissy was at bingo. We'd eat spaghetti with butter and salt and laugh our heads off. Ritter'd have a few ryes and I'd practice my impressions of Clem Kadiddlehopper. When we heard Prissy's key in the lock, I'd beat it down the hallway, jump into bed, cover up my head, and pretend to be asleep.

We never got away with it.

"Hey, Honey," Ritter'd say. "You win?"

Prissy'd toss her bingo bag on the coffee table with the dirty plates and Rye. "You kept her up again."

Ritter would sigh.

"How am I supposed to get her up in the morning if you keep her up all night?"

"It ain't all night, and what the hell does she have to get up for?"

"She gets cranky."

"So let her sleep."

"She doesn't fucking sleep, that's the problem."

That was true. I didn't sleep much. I listened. To make sure the fights didn't get too crazy. Prissy and Ritter fought all the time. The after bingo fights were never very serious. They were just *spats*. I covered my head up and hummed to myself. I didn't have to hear every word. I just *monitored the tone*.

I had to pay more attention when they were both drinking. I sat underneath the kitchen table and read. I could read by the time I was three. I couldn't write until I was six, and even then I couldn't figure out p's, b's, d's and g's. Took me years to get q. I heard a lot under the kitchen table: stuff about Rita Schmidt, about how we didn't have enough money to cover rent, the ongoing battle over who was better singer — Elvis or Johnny Cash. Prissy and Ritter always forgot I was there, which was perfect. I was out of sight, but close. If I heard them getting too sad or mad, I'd jump up and make them laugh with a skip/trip, "ring-a-ding-ding" — Red Skelton style.

I like making people laugh, especially if it distracts them from hurting each other. Ritter called me his little *comedabean*. Prissy called me a *laugh riot* when my jokes made her laugh. When they didn't, she just called me a smart ass.

HOSPITAL BRACELET: RITTER EBERTS

Staying close usually worked. Unless it didn't.

Like when Ritter hurt himself.

It was my fault. I wasn't listening.

I was under the table with my Dr. Seuss books, trying to draw a Sneetch. It was hard. I had to concentrate.

Prissy and Ritter were playing crib and drinking Five-Star. Ritter got up and walked over to the counter. I watched his feet.

His left big toe was all black from where he'd dropped a wrench on it a few days earlier. Prissy said that toenail was going to fall right off. I checked it every night, before bed, to make sure it was still hanging on good.

He reached up. I thought he was going for the box of chips on the counter. Old Dutch Salt and Vinegar. My favourite. He wasn't. He picked up the big butcher knife and stuck it in his stomach. Twice.

Prissy started screaming.

Ritter plopped on the floor. Two red flowers on his belly. He saw me under the table. "Hey, Bean, where y'bin?"

The knife was sticking right out of him.

I took a breath. I swallowed sour. I banged my head getting out from under the table. I shoved a chair over to the phone, and called the ambulance. I didn't cry. It was very calm inside my head. Calm and quiet.

But Prissy was screaming.

I couldn't hear what the ambulance lady was saying. I covered the phone and I told Prissy to shut the hell up. She did. The lady told me not to touch the knife but to *apply pressure* to the other hole he made. I used a clean tea towel. I sat between Ritter's legs and pushed on his belly, hard as I could. I sang to distract him. I sang his favourite Johnny Cash songs.

Ritter passed out, but I kept singing.

I didn't hear the ambulance.

Two men came in. They stopped when they saw me and Ritter. "Jesus," one of them said. I thought it was on account of all the blood. There was an awful lot of blood. The man kneeled beside me. He smelled like Old Spice aftershave and cinnamon gum. He asked me how old I was.

I told him I was almost four and that my arms were tired.

Me and Prissy rode along in the ambulance. The siren was on. Prissy sat beside Ritter and cried. I just watched him breathing. He had a mask over his face, and it made a hissing sound when he took a breath. I watched his chest move and listened to the hiss. We stayed at the hospital until the doctor said Ritter was OK, then we called Grandpa Tom and he came and took us home.

Prissy was shaky. I put her to bed and brought her a sleeping pill and some water. I crawled in with her until she fell asleep. She looked pale, but pretty; like a fairytale princess.

I couldn't sleep. I walked out onto the porch and looked up at the Lady on the Moon. I started shaking, and I got real cold. I cried. Ritter could've died. I had to pay better attention. I vowed on the Lady's face to take better care of him and Prissy.

They kept Ritter in the *Munroe Wing* for two weeks.

"It's a place for resting," said Prissy.

"It's a place for Nutters," said Grandpa Tom.

GT's Dictionary

Grandpa Tom was Prissy's dad. He had two dogs, no teeth and was the best swearer on the prairies. My personal favourites were the ones with a bit of *alliteration*. "Coddling Crapsucker!" Monkey lovin' mooselicker! Jesus H Christ in a Cadillac, on a cracker, a crumpet, a cruise. He lived in a little grey house near the railroad tracks. He had the best yard on the whole block. There was a big old ash tree in the front, and the backyard was full of stuff we'd rescued from the Nuisance Grounds.

Grandpa Tom could fix anything: radios, fridges, even the broken lamps Ritter was always dragging home. Ritter liked lamps. When people couldn't pay for their cab ride, Ritter marched straight into their house and took a lamp. We found him some great ones at the Nuisance Grounds too.

I loved the Nuisance Grounds. I loved the name. Most people called it "the dump" but Grandpa Tom always said, "The Nuisance Grounds". I didn't know what nuisance meant, so I tried to look it up. Grandpa Tom caught me kneeling under the kitchen table with his dictionary and my face all scrunched up. He asked what I was looking up.

"Newsince grounds."

"Try n-u-i," he said. "N-u-i-s-a-n-c-e." I felt stupid. I hated misspelling words, but Grandpa Tom said that's how you learn. If you misspell a word, it takes you forever to look it up. But once you find it, you never forget the spelling again. He was right. I spent a lot of time looking things up. I like words.

I read the entry out loud. "Nuisance. Noun. 1: anything that annoys bothers or irritates; a cause of trouble or vexation." I sat back on my heels. "What the hell's annoying about the Nuisance Grounds?"

"Don't swear."

I crawled out from under the table. "I don't get it."

"Things that are broken annoy people, so they chuck 'em out."

"Why don't they just fix them?"

He sighed. "Sprout, most people would rather just throw a broken thing away. They don't want to take the time to figure out how to fix anything." Grandpa Tom always called me Sprout. I called him Grandpa Tom or GT.

GT was the giver of nicknames. He had three daughters. Prissy was the oldest, then Molly and Auntie Lip. Auntie Lip's birth certificate said Erica Louise Fallwell. Molly's real name was Dora.

I got confused the first time I heard someone call Molly *Dora*. It was GT's friend, Gerard Glatt. Gerard was kind of fancy. He called everyone by their real names. "Dora's the one to do it," he said. "She's familiar with the business from sorting out your taxes. I'd let her handle the insurance as well. Must be nice to be able to trust a daughter with all your accounting worries."

I crawled out from under the table, tugged on GT's sleeve and whispered, "Who the hell's he talking about?"

"Your aunt Molly—and don't swear."

I crawled back under the table. When Gerard left, I asked GT why Dora had two names. That's when I found out that Prissy's real name was Edith and Auntie Lip's name was Erica. I thought a minute, and then felt really stupid again. "Shoog ain't a real name either, is it?" I asked. That's what we all called Dora's husband. "That's just short for Sugar, isn't it? What the hell is *his* real name?"

"His name is Ralph and stop swearing or your mother'll cook my G.D. giblets for me."

"How come everyone's got a nickname?"

"Suits 'em better."

"But why?"

"Your Grandmother named those girls and then she left." That was the first time I'd ever heard about a Grandmother Tom. "Prissy was always fussy about her clothes as a girl, Molly was a whiner and Lip — well, Lip is self-explanatory."

I thought a bit. "I don't get Molly."

"Look up *mollycoddle*," he said and walked away. That was the end of that conversation.

GT's nicknames weren't always nice.

Molly wanted me to call her Dora. Auntie Lip didn't care much either way.

I called Lip *Auntie* and I didn't talk to Dora much.

MOON ROCK

Sometimes GT called me Moony. It wasn't really a nickname —
more of a poke for when I looked distracted or dreamy. He said
I thought too much. People laughed when he called me Moony,
but I didn't really mind. I liked the moon. GT read me stories
about sailors and adventures on the high seas. The moon was
magic. The way it grew and shrunk. The way it pulled the tides.
I couldn't wait to see the ocean and watch the tides shift.

I dreamed of living all alone on an island. I'd build a hut and
live on coconuts and rainwater. I'd have animals for friends and
I wouldn't miss people at all. Well, maybe I'd miss a few people,
but it would be quiet there. No one would be yelling. And I
would have a monkey named Fred.

When the moon was full, I saw a face. It was a lady's face, not
a man's like everybody else said. I talked to her sometimes. I
called her *The Lady on the Moon*. I felt her pull. I felt her pulling
inside me. My best friend, Goose, told me that the body is over
75% water. The moon pulled my watery innards. My blood. I
could feel it.

I watched the Americans land on the moon. July 20, 1969. I
made Prissy and Ritter take me over to GT's, because he had the
best TV. I sat right in front of the set. It was still light outside,
and I could see my face floating on top of Knowlton Nash and
Walter Cronkite. When they cut to the moon coverage, I put my
hand onto the screen. I couldn't believe it. *The moon*, I thought.
*A man is on the moon. The moon is over two hundred thousand
miles away from the earth. It has no air.* A big ghosty-looking
man in a space suit stepped off the ladder and onto the moon.
Neil Armstrong. The image was blurry and his voice was crackly
as he talked about the powdery surface. I traced him on the

screen. I wondered how the Lady on the Moon felt about Neil Armstrong stomping all over her.

The grown-ups missed the whole thing. They were out in the kitchen, drinking. I yelled for them to come and look. They didn't. I went into the kitchen to get them.

GT sat in his usual spot at the end of the table, drinking coffee and smoking. Prissy told me GT drank *like a fish* when she was a kid, but I never saw him drink anything but Maxwell House. She also told me that he used to beat the snot out of her with the big wooden flyswatter that still hung by his chair.

Prissy and Ritter were arguing about whether or not it was good thing for Elvis to do the Vegas show. I stood there a minute and listened.

Prissy said she wanted to go.

"Are you mental?" Ritter said. "No goddamned way I'd haul my ass to Vegas to watch a man make a fool out of himself. You mark my words, if he goes to Vegas, he may as well flush his career down the crapper. Vegas ain't ready for Rock and Roll."

"How the hell would you know?" Prissy sounded slurry.

I leaned in. "The Eagle has landed."

Ritter took a swig of his drink. "I know what I know, and I sure as shit know that Vegas is no place for Elvis."

I took a step closer. "We landed on the moon."

"You know what you know. Jesus. You don't know much — that's what I know." Prissy slammed her hand on the table.

"We landed on the effing *moon!*"

Prissy's head swiveled. "I'll wash your mouth out."

"Sorry." *Look down. Be repentant. Wait for the smack.*

Ritter shifted. "You better be sorry."

"Yes sir." I chance a quick look. They're good. *Sir* almost always works. "Could I have some Tang?"

Prissy waved her hand. "In the fridge."

"I'll spill." *Shh. Careful.* I was pushing my luck.

GT stood up. "I got it." He poured the Tang into my favourite cup. GT always used my favourite cup. He had a favourite cup too. He never let anybody wash it.

"NASA invented Tang," I whispered.

GT put his hand on my head. "They sure did, Sprout." He topped up his coffee and then raised his cup in a toast. I moved beside him. I cleared my throat to get Prissy and Ritter's attention. "A-HEMMM! A toast," I said. "To the moon!"

They raised their glasses and we all clinked, "To the moon!"

I guzzled my Tang and went outside.

It was quiet. No traffic. No kids screaming up and down the alley. I stood on the back steps and looked up. It was still too light out to see the moon.

I went to visit Floke. Floke was GT's old hound dog. He had runny eyes and a house big enough for both of us. I spent a lot of time in there. It helped me think. I told Floke all kinds of secrets. He was an excellent listener.

GT's other dog was a border collie named Tate. We didn't like each other much. Tate had a smaller house on the other side of the yard. She barked at me when I walked toward Floke's house. I chucked a rock at her. Just a little rock, and I aimed wide. *Yappy mutt.*

Floke was lying in his house. He thumped his tail when I walked over, but he didn't bother getting up. I crouched down and took his droopy head in my hands. "Floke, my dear, we have stepped on to the moon. The world will never be the same."

Floke sighed and blinked.

"It's true." I sat on the ground. "Everything will be different now."

Floke put his head in my lap.

"They don't even care. They just sit there arguing about stupid Elvis. Who cares if stupid Elvis plays Vegas? Who cares if he plays freakin' Tisdale?"

Floke woofed.

"Well, yeah, Tisdale might be cool. We could actually go to Tisdale." I flapped my hand in the dirt and smacked it on a pointy black rock. I picked it up, looked at it awhile, and then showed to Floke. "See these sparkles?" The rock held flecks of shattered silver. "I'm gonna say these sparkles are moon shine. I'm gonna keep this rock forever, to remind me of the *giant leap for mankind*. I'm gonna mark this day."

Floke sniffed the rock and then licked it.

I touched my own tongue to the rock. It was salty, like potash. I stuffed the rock in my pocket, crawled into the doghouse, wrapped my arms around Floke, and fell asleep.

We woke up to Prissy yelling, "Bean E. Eberts, get your butt home!"

Floke scrambled up, woofing.

I crawled out of the doghouse. "I'm right here." *Stop yer screeching.* It was dark out.

"Jesus Christ on a stick," Prissy said patting at her heart. "Scared the crap outta me. I told you to stay away from that mangy mutt." Prissy swore a lot too, but her swears were nowhere near as good as GT's. "C'mon," Prissy said, "We're goin'.

Dog's Head

We should've slept over.

We'd moved to Moose Jaw for a change of scenery after Ritter stabbed himself. It was late and Ritter'd been drinking all day. When we hit the highway, it started to rain. We were in Ritter's cab, a big old blue Pontiac. I was sitting up front in the middle. We were singing "Ring of Fire". Ritter was smiling at me, doing the Tijuana trumpets "whoot do-dit-do-dit doo doo doooooo!" Then the world went sideways and everything slowed down.

Prissy's mouth stretched wide but no sound came out. Something was roaring in my ears. Prissy's mouth was huge. *Tangerine 005*. New lipstick. *Avon*. Bought from Marge. Marge was the new Avon Representative. She had her own car. Prissy reached for me through the spinning. I went into her arms, and she tucked me under the dash. She was wearing her favourite blue dress. She had nylons on. Her legs smelled of Jovan Musk, cigarettes and Rye. I closed my eyes.

I woke up in the hospital. Auntie Lip was beside my bed. She smiled. "Welcome back, Kiddo." I had a Band-Aid on my elbow. I was dizzy. "Good goddamn thing you guys were in the Pontiac and not the Bug."

"The Bug's broke down."

"Good goddamned thing. The cops said you rolled three times. You'd have been flattened for sure."

I tried to get up. "Where's Prissy? Ritter."

"They're fine, Kid. Relax."

Prissy's arm was broken and she had cuts on her face. She had to stay overnight *for observation*.

The nodding-head dog me and Prissy gave him for Christmas bit a big hole in the back of Ritter's head while we were spinning. He was hurt bad. He didn't wake up for three days.

The dog's head was beside my bed when I woke up. Auntie said they had to pry it out of my hands when we came into the hospital.

I still had the moon rock in my pocket. I saved them both.

I must've banged my head in that accident.

Next thing I knew, me and Prissy were living at GT's and I was starting kindergarten with Goose. It was a confusing time.

I don't remember when we left Ritter, or why.

I was four and we landed on the moon.

Then I was five and my new name was Bean E. Fallwell and me and Prissy were living at Grandpa Tom's.

Goose's Aggy

Prissy called GT's place a regular circus. There were always people around: family, guys who worked with GT, friends, and neighbour men who popped over for a yack with GT. Prissy was the Chief Cook and Bottle Washer. She was always making coffee, cooking food and doing the dishes. She said she was run ragged.

GT told her to *like it or lump it.*

I liked it at GT's. Nothing really bad ever happened there. Nobody shoved a knife in their guts. Nobody hit anybody. Not really. Prissy might give me a smack on the head, or something, but she never got carried away at GT's. There was always someone to say, "Enough."

My favourite thing about living at GT's was that Goose lived right down the street. Goose is my best friend. We met when we were real little — way back before the moon landing even. He was the first kid I ever saw with glasses.

I was playing hopscotch and this funny looking kid was hanging over his fence, watching. "Hey," I yelled, "You wanna play?"

He ducked.

I went over for a closer look. He was sitting on the grass. We looked at each other awhile. His hair was white and fluffy, like the feathers coming out of GT's favourite pillow and he had little tiny glasses on. I asked him if he wanted to play hopscotch.

"I don't mind."

"Does that mean yes or no?"

"It means yes."

"Well, c'mon then," I said. "I'm Bean E. Eberts. That's my Grandpa Tom's house. I'm three and a half and I can read."

He walked along the inside of the fence to the gate. "You can not."

"Can too. I've been reading for years."

"I can print my name," he said.

"Go ahead and print it. I'll read right out."

"I don't have any paper."

"Use this." I held out the rock I'd been using to draw my hopscotch.

"That's a rock."

"Yeah."

"You can't write with a rock."

"Can too." I drew a happy face on the sidewalk. "My Grandpa says there's chalk in some rocks. You just gotta try 'em."

"Who's your Grandfather?"

"Tom Fallwell." I swung my head over toward GT's place.

The kid giggled. He sounded like a *lunatic*.

"What's funny?"

"He swears."

"Betcher hairy ass he does. C'mon."

The kid giggled again. I saw the curtains in the kitchen window twitch. Lace curtains. It was a nice house. The grass was all green and short, and there was no junk lying around. There was even flowers up by the house. Red ones.

"What kind of flowers are those?"

The kid shrugged. "I don't know."

"Hmm. They look nice."

"I guess." He came out from behind the fence. He took my rock, squatted down and wrote his name on the sidewalk. I squatted beside him and read it out loud, "Goose-tave Wilson Peterson? What the hell kinda name is that?"

He stuck his chin out. "What the . . . heck kind of a name is Bean?"

"Good question," I said and stuck out my hand to shake. "Glad to meet ya, Goose."

"It's Gus," he said and stood up. "Pleasure to make your acquaintance, Bean E." We shook hands, grinning.

He looked at the rock. "Chalk in a rock. I'll have to tell my father. He likes to know these sorts of things." He brushed at his knees even though he hadn't even touched them to the ground. "You like going to the picture show?" he asked.

"The what?"

"Films. Movies?"

"Sure."

"My mother calls them picture shows. We go every Saturday. I just saw *Jungle Book*."

I brushed my own knees off. They were dirty from kneeling to draw my hopscotch. "Me Prissy 'n' Ritter mostly go to the Drive-in. Not every Saturday though. You're lucky."

"Who are Prissy and Ritter?"

"My mom and dad. Mother and Father." I liked the way Goose talked. Not really fancy, but . . . nice. He talked nice.

"Why do you call them Prissy and Ritter?"

I shrugged. "That's their names."

He handed me my rock and walked up the street towards the gravel lane that ran parallel to the railroad tracks. "What's the Drive-in?"

"The Cinema Six. They show movies up on a real big screen and you sit in your car and watch."

"Can you buy popcorn?"

"Sure and cokes and hot dogs even."

"How do you hear the movie?"

"Little speakers that hang on your window."

"Oh." He looked sad.

"What's the matter?"

"I've never been to a Drive-In."

"Where you see movies then? On TV?"

"No. At the Metropolitan Theatre."

"Where's that?"

"Downtown."

"Well, I ain't never been there — so we're even."

"You've never been to the Metropolitan?" He was *amazed*. He told me all about it while we walked down the alley. Goose could only go one block from home, so we walked up and down the alley a few times, while he told me about the theatre and all the movies he'd seen. The Met was Goose's favourite place in the whole world. It had red velvet seats and the ceiling was so high you could barely see it. They had kiddy matinees every Saturday. He'd seen twenty-two movies already. He promised to take me with him to the next one. I promised to ask Prissy if we could take him to the Cinema Six to see *Planet of the Apes*.

"You know what?" he said.

"What?"

"Porcupines float in water."

"Really?"

"Yep. My dad told me." Goose's dad told him all sorts of weird stuff and Goose remembered it all. He reached in his pocket. "Here."

"What's this?"

"It's my favourite marble." It was blue and clear with little bubbles trapped inside.

"It's beautiful."

"It's an aggy. I want you to have it."

"I can't"

"Why not?"

"I don't have anything for tradesies"

"We don't need to trade. It's a gift."

I gave him my chalk rock.

From then on, me and Goose were *fast friends*. I went over to his place every time we came to visit GT. Goose wasn't allowed to hang around Grandpa Tom's on account of GT swearin' so much. I didn't care. I liked hanging out at the Peterson's. Goose had Weebles, Rockem-Sockem Robots, a Fisher-Price village with a castle, and tons of Lego. We played in the basement, or outside if Goose's dad was home. Mr. Peterson worked at the Steel Plant. Sometimes he worked all night and then slept all day. I could never be quiet enough.

Outside, we played *Spy* from Goose's garage roof. Nobody ever looked up there. We mostly spied on teenagers — sneakin' smokes or makin' out — but sometimes, we saw grown-ups doing stuff. We knew that old man Schaeffer kept his dirty magazines in a Coca Cola crate at the back of his garden, Marietta Doona was sneakin' around with Harold Potts, and Mrs. Mullen cried a lot in her kitchen while she was doing the dishes.

Goose said we could only use our *furtively gathered intelligence* if one of us was in *dire straits* — meaning we were about to get pounded by some older kid. We'd never squeal; we just let it be known that we had all sorts of secrets worth squealing about.

I was real happy that I got to go to Goose's school for the start of Kindergarten. Maybe that's why I didn't miss Ritter much. I didn't think about it.

Prissy missed Ritter. I heard her crying sometimes, at night, when she thought me and GT were asleep. I also caught her kissing Alden and Gerard.

Alden Bellamy worked with GT fixing furnaces and cleaning chimneys. He had curly brown hair, straight white teeth, and he could do a Tom Jones dance like nobody's business. Alden stayed for supper a lot. He was a bachelor. Prissy was always telling me not to bug him, but Alden didn't mind me hanging around. I helped him clean the chimney sweep brushes and he taught me how to dance.

One night, he stayed over. I saw his shoes when I went to the bathroom. I checked the couch. He wasn't there. He was in Prissy's room. I didn't say anything, in the morning. But then Prissy pissed me off, so I called her an awful name and ran like hell before she could catch me. I climbed up the old Ash tree in the front yard and stayed up there all day.

I spent a lot of time up that tree. Prissy and GT couldn't climb it, and it was in the front yard so they couldn't even cuss me out too bad when I was up there. Unless they were mad enough not to care what the neighbours thought.

Prissy didn't yell at me that day. She just said, "Come down." I wouldn't. She tried to bribe me with cookies for lunch, but I didn't budge. I was *stewing in my juices*.

When Alden and GT got home, Alden came out and sat under the tree. He didn't say anything; he just sat there.

Let him sit, I thought. *I don't care. Let him sit there all night. I don't care.* He sat a long time. Finally, I asked him what he was doing.

"Sitting," he said.

"Why?"

"It's nice out here. You want me to go?"

"Do what you want. I don't care." So we sat.

After a while, he got up and stretched. "You coming in for supper?"

"No."

"You must be hungry." I knew Alden could climb straight up that tree if he wanted. He could drag me right the hell down if he wanted. "It's getting cold out." It was too. It felt like it might snow. We'd had snow at Halloween, but it melted. GT said we were having an *Indian summer.*

"Prissy's mad at me."

"No she isn't."

"Shows what you know."

He sat back down, cross-legged, on the grass and looked up at me. "What happened?"

"I called her a hooer."

"Why'd you call her that?"

"You stayed here last night."

"Yes, I did."

"I saw her kiss you this morning."

"Yes."

"Well, you're both hooers — dirty rotten hooers — that's what I know." *There. Now he'll go. Now he will leave and he will not come back.*

He took a deep breath. "Bean," he said. "Do you know what a whore is?"

"A what?"

"A hooer."

"Why'd you say hor?"

"That's how you say it, it's w-h-o-r-e, whore."

"Oh." *Shit.* I hated mispronouncing words. It was embarrassing. Maybe it was a different word. "I dunno what a *whore* is, but I sure as hell know what a hooer is."

"What is it?"

"Somebody that does bad stuff."

"Like what?"

"Like stealing."

"Ah." He nodded. "So. What did Prissy steal?" *God men are so stupid!* "What did *I* steal?" *Stupid.* "Bean?"

"Nothing." *None of your beeswax, Stupid. If you don't even know then you are just a big fat loser head and it doesn't matter anyhow.* "Nobody stole anything. I'm just mad."

"Because Prissy kissed me."

"No." *Shut up!* "Whaddo I care if you wanna kiss? I don't care if you wanna be stupid kissy facers."

"OK then."

"OK."

"You coming down now?"

"Not if Prissy's mad I ain't. She'll skin the tar offa me."

He smiled. "Nobody is going to skin you."

"Yeah, right."

Alden went in and Prissy came out, wiping her hands with a dishtowel. "C'mon in, Honey," she said. "I made mashed potatoes."

Alden stayed for supper.

That night, I looked up *whore* in GT's dictionary.

Whore *n* A prostitute. *v* **whored, whoring,** *v.i.* 1. To have illicit sexual intercourse, especially with a prostitute.

What the — ? That didn't sound right. I thought whore meant *stealer*. That's how people used it. Prissy and Auntie always said, "The stupid hooer took my . . . whatever." I looked up *prostitute, harlot, concubine* and *strumpet*. They were all about sex. I wished people would use words *properly*. How are kids supposed to figure anything out if grown-ups go around using words wrong?

Prissy found me and asked what I was looking up. I slammed the book closed. "Nothin'." She told me to put the dictionary away and get ready for bed. Her and Alden tucked me in. Prissy sat on the bed beside me and asked me if I was happy. I liked it when she did that.

"Y'betcha." I smiled and closed my eyes. "Hey, Prissy?" I said before she left.

"Yeah?"

"How come we say *Indian Summer* when it gets warm again in the fall?"

She shrugged. "Ask Goose," she said. "He'll know."

Alden slept over again that night. They probably smooched. I didn't mind anymore.

I did mind when Prissy smooched Gerard Glatt. He gave me the heebie-jeebies. Gerard always wore a suit, reeked of *Hai Karate*, and had the shiniest shoes I'd ever seen. Prissy said Gerard was "a friend of the family". I didn't get that. Far as I was concerned, everybody who came to visit was friend — else why'd they come to visit in the first place? Prissy and the aunts all had a crush on Gerard. Not me though. Those shoes made me nervous.

When I saw Gerard kiss Prissy, I almost gagged. He put his tongue all over her mouth and it looked really sloppy and gross. I couldn't believe that she didn't just start choking with that fat old tongue going down her throat. He squished her boob too. It didn't look very romantic. When Auntie Lip came in from outside, Gerard just about jumped out of his suit to get away from Prissy — like it was some kind of secret. I didn't like that. He was probably kissing Auntie too. He flirted with everyone. *Charming* they called him. I just thought he was a *snake in the grass*.

Prissy told me that Alden and Gerard were her friends. "We all need friends," she said. "You've got Goose, GT's got Mr. Quint, I've got Alden and Gerard."

"But aren't they GT's friends?"

"You can have more than one friend."

"Yeah, but — "

"Yeah but nothing. Don't be such a Nosey Parker."

"What does that even mean?"

"What?"

"Nosey *Parker*? Who's this Parker and why is she so nosey?" That made Prissy laugh. I didn't ask her why she had to smooch her friends. I figured it was grown up stuff. I couldn't quite let it go, though. "Are they your best friends?"

"What?"

"GT says everyone needs a *best* friend. Someone they can tell everything to."

"Like you and Goose?"

"Yeah." I squirmed a little. I didn't tell everything to Goose. The only person I told everything to was old Floke — and he wasn't even a person — *technically*. "Or like GT and Mr. Quint."

GT was comfortable with Mr. Quint. They hung out every day. When other men came over, GT would stop what he was doing and talk. When Mr. Q showed up, GT just carried on working 'til he was finished and then he'd say, "Feel like a snort, Q-ball?"

Mr. Q would do this funny inhaled "Yuh-yuh-yuh" thing and say, "Guess I could have a wee short one." They'd sit at the kitchen table, talking and sipping their Maxwell House. GT always poured a shot of rye into Mr. Q's cup. They mostly talked about work.

GT was a Chimney Sweep and Furnace Repair Man. Sometimes kids wanted to shake hands with GT so they could get some luck off him. I didn't really believe that *chim-chimeny* stuff, but I still shook GT's hand on test days, just in case. GT had a tophat that squashed flat. He got it at a chimney sweep convention. He let me wear it sometimes. He even taught me how to pop it open with a snap of my wrist.

Mr. Q worked as a *commissionaire* at a big building downtown. He had a hat too. It was like a cop hat, nowhere near as cool as GT's. Prissy said being a commissionaire meant that Mr. Quint wore a uniform and sat behind a desk, but I knew what he really did. I sat under the table and listened to them talk while they had their coffees. Mr. Quint was in charge of that whole building. It was an important job.

Goose was my best friend because we were comfortable together and I told him almost everything. I thought Ritter was Prissy's best friend, but now that he was gone, Prissy was lonely. "Who's your best friend?"

She thought a bit. "You."

"Aw, Mom. I don't count."

She smiled and stroked my hair. "OK. Then . . . Spuddy, I guess."

Prissy met Spuddy Maxwell before I was born, so her and Uncle Slim were always around. I came up with their nicknames. Spuddy was big and round and comforting, like a potato, and

Slim was skinny as a rail. They lived over on the East Side in a house that was packed to the roofters. Spuddy collected salt and pepper shakers. Uncle Slim collected tin toys, wooden tools, flashlights, furniture built without nails, and a whole bunch of other stuff. They'd lived in the same house for years. Slim built shelves and cabinets to display all their collections. He was an excellent carpenter. That was his job, building cabinets and things in rich people houses. *Fine woodworking*.

Aunt Spuddy had a lot of different jobs. She sold Tupperware, Regal, and Tri-Chem Liquid Embroidery. It was mostly about the Tri-Chem for Spuddy. She sold the other stuff to make money, but Tri-Chem was her *passion*. Spuddy was an artist. The walls in their house that weren't crammed with shelves were covered in her paintings. She was really good at blending colours.

Before we left Ritter, me and Prissy spent a lot of time at Spuddy and Slim's. We always went to their place for dinner on Sundays when Ritter was working. They said *dinner* like Goose's parents. We mostly said *supper*, like GT.

Spuddy's dinners were fancy. She made ham or roast beef or a whole chicken every Sunday, even when it was just her and Slim to eat it. There'd be green beans and corn and a salad and little tiny roasted potatoes. She always made desert.

I liked dinners at Spuddy and Slim's. They were quieter than suppers over at GT's. Whoever was over when GT started cooking got invited to stay. There was always lots of people and sometimes they fought. Not big fights, just arguments, but they still made my stomach hurt. Dinners were *civilized*. Suppers could get loud or scarily silent.

I leaned against Prissy. "I miss Spuddy."

"What?"

"We haven't been over there for a long time." *Since we left Ritter.*

"You're right, Kid. I'll call her up and we'll go over for dinner."

"Good. Best friends gotta keep in touch."

THE SAMSONITE

A few weeks later, Prissy brought me home a present. My first suitcase — a red hardbody Samsonite Saturn, from the Sally Ann. It had a key and everything.

I had a thing for Samsonites.

When we weren't watching Red Skelton, Ritter took me for ride-alongs in his cab. I sat up in the front, beside him, and tried very hard not to talk to the customers unless they talked to me first. That was the rule. I was to be *seen and not heard.* Ritter worked the Bus Depot — picking up people after their trips. Most of them had really beat-up luggage. Some even used garbage bags. Classy fares had Samsonites.

One day, we picked up an old lady with three Samsonites — all matching. I helped put them in the trunk. The lady said I was a very pretty girl and she gave me a green mint. It was sticky and covered with pocket fuzz, but I ate it anyway. She told me she'd gone all the way to Florida on the Greyhound to visit her daughter. That's far. It took her three days to get home.

I asked her if she liked riding on the bus.

She said that Greyhounds had comfortable seats and that they even have bathrooms — right in the back.

I told her I sure wouldn't want to pee on a bus.

She laughed and gave me another mint.

That night, I told Prissy about the old lady. "I'm gonna go on a big Greyhound trip one day."

"Yeah?"

"Yep. I'm going to buy a whole set of Samsonites and hit the road. I ain't using the bathroom though. I'll piss when the bus stops for gas."

Prissy gave me a smack. "Don't say piss."

"Pee then. I'll pee when the bus stops for gas."

"Where will you go?"

"Dunno yet." I sipped my Kool-Aid and thought. "Somewhere far — like a desert."

"Why a desert?"

"Never seen one."

"Why would you want to?"

"For an adventure. They seem clean — like the sand would blow you clean."

"Blow sand right up your arse, more like."

The Samsonite Prissy bought me was great. It was big enough for all my stuff. I tried it out right away. Prissy watched. Then she said, "Let's go. I've got a place for us to look at."

I locked the suitcase and hung the key around my neck. "What place?"

"A new place. For just you and me."

I squinted up at her. "We're not going back to Moose Jaw."

She stared at me with her mouth skrinched to one side.

I looked down. "What about Ritter?"

"What about him?"

I fiddled with the Samsonite latches. "Is he coming too?"

Prissy clicked her teeth. I hated that sound. Prissy got false teeth when she was real young. She was playing catcher in a softball game, and some girl struck out. The girl got so mad that she threw the bat and it hit Prissy right in the mouth and knocked her teeth right out. I hated it when Prissy clicked her teeth. I also hated it when she left them in a cup beside the bed. She looked scary without them. Not like Grandpa Tom. He didn't have any teeth either, but his mouth didn't go all cavy-in like Prissy's did when she left her falsies out. *Falsies.* That means boobs too. Fake boobs. Prissy had a pair of those, too. She put them in when she went out drinking with Auntie. *Falsies falsies falsies.*

"Bean!" Prissy barked. "Did you hear me?"

I didn't. Sometimes my mind just wandered off with me, especially if I didn't want to think about something — like getting a new place without Ritter. I hadn't been thinking about Ritter 'til right then. I was happy at Grandpa Tom's, like I didn't even care about Ritter at all. Ritter needed watching — maybe even more than Prissy did — and I hadn't thought about him at all. I didn't know if he was OK. I hadn't talked to him since we left. I couldn't even remember leaving. I knew he called sometimes. Prissy talked to him. She always made me go outside — every time. She even checked under the kitchen table when he called, to make sure I wasn't *skulking around*. I didn't know what was going on.

Prissy looked down at me and sighed. She sighed at me a lot. Sighed like she was so tired she could barely *exist*. Sometimes, I just wanted to punch her right in the face. "Don't be a retard," she said. I chewed my fingers. "We don't live with Ritter anymore."

"Why not?"

"Because he's an Asshole!"

I pulled my fingers out of my mouth. Prissy hated it when I chewed my fingers. "OK. OK Mom. It's OK." I didn't want her to get mad, especially when no one was around. "So, where's the new place?"

"Over by Auntie Lip's," she said. "You'll like it. It's close to the park."

So. We moved.

I filled the Samsonite with my clothes and books, and my shoebox of treasures. GT gave me his dictionary to keep me company. Alden gave me a fifty-cent piece, for luck. Me and Goose blew it on candy. We sat up on his garage roof and divided the spoils.

I was worried about moving away from Goose.

"It'll be OK," he said. "I'll still see you. It'll be just like before. It's not like you'll never visit."

"I guess." I was chewing my fingers. I had a plan, but I didn't know if Goose would go along with it.

"What are you thinking?" Goose always knew when I had something on my mind.

I pulled out a jackknife I'd lifted from GT's garage. "Will you do a blood swear?"

Goose looked at the knife. "Is that thing clean?"

I pulled out a lighter, flicked it and held the blade in the flame. "This is how Prissy sterilizes needles when she pulls splinters outta me."

Goose gulped, but he held out his hand. I handed him the knife. He nicked his thumb and handed the knife back. I nicked my own thumb. Didn't hurt. We pressed our thumbs together.

"I, Bean E. Fallwell solemnly swear to remain best friends with Gustave Wilson Peterson for better or worse, in sickness and in health, for ever and ever, amen."

Goose took the same oath.

We smiled and sucked on our thumbs to stop the bleeding.

"Hurts like a bitch," I said.

Goose giggled like a lunatic.

Stick Stone Feather and Bone

Spuddy and Slim helped us move.

We drove to Moose Jaw to get our stuff. Ritter wasn't home. We didn't take much. I grabbed some more clothes. Prissy took a couple of pots, her records and the big velvet Elvis we had hanging over the couch.

I wanted to leave a note for Ritter, but Prissy wouldn't let me.

"Can we take the shag lamp?" It was a big round orange plastic ball that looked like loopy spaghetti coated in cheese sauce. When Ritter brought it home, I licked it.

I broke my nose on that lamp. I was playing Supergirl. I ran with my hands stretched out in front of me, took a corner too fast, tripped over the lamp cord and lifted right off the earth — light and easy — like I suddenly remembered how to fly. I pulled a nice graceful arc and headed for the open window. Then I smashed into the floor. I was so surprised I didn't put out my hands to break my fall. I sat up, sniffing, and Prissy started to scream. I sniffed again, swiped at my nose, saw blood and passed out. When I came to, Ritter was carrying me into the hospital.

"Please, Mom. Can we take it? It's my favourite."

"Fine."

Slim took it down and packed it in a box.

"It's a *swag* lamp," Spuddy said.

I shrugged. "Ritter calls it a shag lamp." *Darn it.* I shouldn't have said that. It was OK if I got words wrong; I was just a kid. I hated it when people said that Prissy and Ritter got words wrong. They weren't dumb — they just talked different than some people.

"Swag, because it hangs from the ceiling and swags."

"What's *swag*?"

"Hangs in loops, drapes down . . . Swoops, like the cord was."

"What's *shag*?"

"Like carpet," Prissy said.

"Long tangled carpet," said Slim.

"So, the cord swags and the shade's shaggy — in a plasticky kind of way. It's a *shaggy swaggy* lamp."

Spuddy chuckled, and slipped a pair of salt and pepper shakers into the box.

I helped Slim tape the box shut.

Our house looked sad. All houses look sad when you're leaving.

Our new place looked great. It was a *semi-furnished apartment*. It came with a yellow plaid couch, an orange chair, a lumpy double bed, a kitchen table with two wooden chairs and a big wooden stereo.

Auntie was washing the living room floor when we got there. She was playing her newest album on the stereo and singing along with *Tony Orlando and Dawn*. She did a spin. "Welcome home!" Auntie was a great singer. She taught me all the words to her favourite songs. We did shows for Prissy. We sang "Little Arrows" by Leapy Lee, and "Daydream Believer" by the Monkeys. She even taught me to sing "Shitty Shitty Bang Bang". Prissy almost peed her pants laughing when we sang that one. "*Chitty*," she snorted. "It's Chitty!" Auntie was also an excellent cleaner. The place looked spic and span and smelled like lemons.

Spuddy and Slim gave us some stacking stools, a rollaway cot, some TV trays and a big painting of blue horses that Spuddy made. We hung the horses in the bedroom and the Elvis over the stereo. The apartment only had one bedroom and the bathroom was tiny, but we had a huge old clawfoot tub, and lots of windows. The bedroom was big enough for the two of us to share. Prissy got the big bed and I got the rollaway. The shag/swag lamp looked great over the orange chair.

Slim gave me a little wooden shelf he built. "For your books," he said. It was just the right size to sit on top of my Samsonite. It had two little legs on one end and then sloped down to an ell on the other end. It didn't have any nails in it. *Joinery,* he called it. I set it up right away.

"I have room for more books even." I gave him a hug. He blushed and chuckled behind his hand. My books were mostly from Spuddy and Slim. They always bought me books. I had twelve Dr. Seuss books and one book of Fairytales. I was getting a little old for Dr Seuss, but I still liked him. He was my collection. The Fairytales were from Auntie. *The Blue Fairy Book.* I loved Fairytales. I loved the magic words, *Once upon a time*; the way the stories took place in a world almost like ours, but not quite; and the fact that the good guys always won in the end.

It didn't take us long to unpack.

After everyone left, me and Prissy had a cup of tea. "Well, Bean," she said. "What do ya think?"

"Sure is quiet."

"Yeah."

"I've never lived in an apartment before, have I?"

"No."

"I like it."

She gave me a big hug. "Bath and bed," she said. "You must be tired."

The bathtub was big enough to swim in. I loved it. Prissy washed my hair and gave me a brand-new set of pajamas with horses on them, but I wasn't quite ready for bed. I lifted the shelf of books off my Samsonite and pulled out my treasure box. I opened it up and laid four things on the floor: a stick, a stone, a feather and a bone.

Prissy watched. "What the hell is that?"

"It's magic."

"Magic."

I took a breath. "You ever notice how no bad things can ever come into Grandpa Tom's yard?"

"Bad things?"

I hadn't told Prissy about the weird guy who followed me and Goose to school for a week and then called us over to his car and showed us his thing. We ran all the way to GT's and I made Goose come in the yard, even though he wasn't supposed to, because I knew the man would never follow us into GT's yard. I didn't tell Prissy about the weirdo because I knew she'd be mad at me for looking at his thing. She'd say that I should know better. I did know better. I wasn't a baby. Besides, Prissy had enough to worry about. "Bad things like . . . thieves," I said. "Or bad people who are gonna hurt somebody. Or bad dogs that wanna bite me."

"OK."

"Well, I think the yard is safe because of old Floke," I said. "Every day, when Grandpa Tom lets him off his chain, Floke circles the yard, all the way around, and he pees."

".Uh huh."

"Well, Goose says, that's old Floke marking his territory so other dogs and bad people can't get in."

"OK. But what's all this?"

"This," I spread my hands like a magician showing my wares, "is from Grandpa Tom's yard."

"Is this stuff covered in dog piss?"

I giggled. "No. Well, maybe. I dunno. It's just from the yard. GT's yard is safe and if I put these things around *our* place, it'll be safe too."

"OK."

"Really?"

"Sure. Need help?"

"Nope — but once I put the stuff you can't move it, OK?"

"OK."

"I need to use a stool."

"OK."

I started at the front door but, even with the stool, I couldn't reach the top of the door. Prissy came over to help. "On top there. In the middle."

"Do I have to say anything? Hocus Pocus? Alakazan Alakazoo?" She was joking. I was serious. She took the rock and placed it on top of the doorjamb. Then she helped me place the other things. A feather over a window in the living room, a stick over the bedroom window and a small, Floke-gnawed, bone over the back door.

"There," I said. "Now we're safe and sound."

Prissy smiled. "Thanks, Honey." Then she tucked me into my new rollaway bed. "Happy?"

"You betcha!"

She brushed the hair out of my eyes. "I love you, Kid. A bizillion times a million."

My sheets smelled Downy fresh. "I love you too, Mom."

"It's just me and you, now."

"We'll be OK, Mom. I promise. Just you and me, safe and sound."

We *were* safe and sound in that apartment, but we didn't stay there very long. That was around the time that Prissy took to drinking Wild Turkey, playing Crib and bringing home stray men. That's when me and Prissy started moving every few months.

I didn't mind moving. I liked picking out my room; finding the right place for my books. I liked the places best before we moved in, all bright and clean and empty, the beginning of a whole new story.

We always picked our new places together. Sometimes we looked at places just for fun. For *future reference*, Prissy said.

I became a bathtub *connoisseur*. I'd head directly to the bathroom, climb into the bathtub, close my eyes and see if it was a good dreaming place. If I walked out and said, "Nope," we'd leave. If the tub sucked, it didn't matter how great the *location* was, or how many plug-ins there were, or how new the fridge was. *Bad tub — no dealy.* You need a good tub. A good tub can make a rat-hole feel like a palace.

I performed the circle ritual every time we moved to a new place; convinced it would keep bad people out. I never thought about what would happen if one of us invited them in.

Prissy was always inviting them in.

PRISSY'S LUCKY BINGO TROLL

Prissy had bad luck with men, but she was a sorceress at bingo. She played thirty-six cards back before there were magnetic chips or dabbers. Back when the cards were cardboard not slips of paper. On Monday nights, she played down at the

Trianon Ballroom at the Legion. On Thursdays, she played at St. Mary's.

I liked the Trianon best. Prissy'd set up her cards and her lucky bingo troll and I'd head to the pinball room. I played pinball nearly as good as Prissy played bingo. Most nights I could make two quarters last me the whole night.

For a while, we lived on bingo winnings. We'd moved to a creepy little apartment above the Viking Laundromat. Prissy got fired from her waitressing job and we had to go on Welfare. I hated Welfare and I hated that apartment. It only had one door, and all the windows were painted shut. Only good thing about it was that it smelled clean — like laundry soap.

Prissy hated that apartment too, so we started hanging out downstairs in the Laundromat. We played crib and I started helping people fold their laundry. They gave me quarters to play pinball. Then I started watching people's clothes for them if they had to go somewhere while their stuff was in the dryer. Before I knew it, I had regulars that paid me two bucks to do their laundry for them. I did people's laundry, and Prissy played crib for cash. We used the money to go to bingo and the bingo winnings to *keep body and soul together.*

We had Welfare, but Prissy said it was worse than her paycheck used to be. Even when Prissy was working, we lived on bingo winnings and tips from truckers. Her actual paycheck was never very big. Truckers tipped big — especially the one's Prissy dated.

Prissy dated a lot of truckers.

They were all right. They took us out to eat, they didn't stick around long, and they always thought they might be back through — so they never got mean with Prissy or up to any funny business with me.

The guys Prissy brought home from the bar were a whole different breed.

Prissy and Auntie went out to the bars a lot.

I got to help Prissy gussy up. We'd pick out an outfit, and then I'd sit in the bathtub and watch her put her face on. Sometimes she tried to give me lipstick. I hated lipstick. I hated makeup in general. Prissy only wore it when she went out. One day, I told her that lipstick was made of fish scales.

She looked at me like I was a nut. "It is not."

"Well, most lipstick has fish scales in it. It's a fact."

"Goose tell you that?"

"Yes. He read it somewhere."

"That kid is weird."

"Bet that's what Mrs. P says about me."

Prissy laughed, blotted her lips on a piece of toilet paper and tossed it at me. "No doubt about it." I chased her out of the bathroom. When I caught her, she spun me around 'til we were both dizzy.

When we caught our breath, I smoothed her hair. "You look real pretty, Mom. Have fun."

I didn't mind when Prissy went out with Auntie. It made her happy. They'd come home late, wake me up and tell me all kinds of stories — like who asked Prissy to dance or how cute the drummer in the band was.

One time, Auntie threw herself across my bed and said, "It's hopeless Bean. I am a freak magnet." She turned to Prissy "We are never going there again!" Prissy was laughing.

I sat up. "What happened?"

"Well, as usual, your motherdear is dancing away with some hunka hunka burnin' love, and the only guy who asks me to dance, all night, is a big beer-gut slob with one arm and a huge belt buckle."

Prissy shook her head. "He wasn't the only one."

"He was!"

"What about Dirk?"

"Dirk's a jerk."

"Yeah, but he asked you to dance."

"Well, we are never going to the Little Bavaria again. Circle J, Scary Nights, even the friggin' Paddock if ya want — but I refuse to return to the den of the one armed man. The Pump. We can go to the Pump." Auntie kicked off her shoes. "Scootch, Kid, I'm sleeping over."

I didn't mind when Auntie stayed over.

I did mind when Prissy's men did.

The best nights were when Goose slept over and Prissy stayed home. She never went out when Goose was there. She promised his mom. Having Goose sleep over was a *privilege not a right*.

The Peterson's didn't really want me and Goose to be friends — at first. I was a girl and they wanted Goose to make friends with boys — which we thought was *incredibly* stupid. They also said I might be a *bad influence*. They thought I would swear like Grandpa Tom. Goose made me promise not to even say *shit* if I stubbed my toe. I made sure not to. I said *jumpin' jimeny* a lot.

I won over Mrs. Peterson pretty quickly, but Mr. Peterson was a tough nut. He never talked to me directly. Goose said he called me a *Hoyden*. We looked it up and found out it meant a country lout or heathen; or a girl or woman of saucy, boisterous, or carefree behavior. A tomboy.

"He could have meant either," Goose said. "You're a tomboy for sure, but I've heard him call you a heathen too. He thinks you're uncivilized, mostly because you're so freaking loud."

I didn't mean to be. The Petersons had the quietest house I was ever in. Even Spuddy and Slim usually had the radio playing or something. At Goose's, it was silent — especially if his dad was sleeping off a night shift. Sometimes, I thought I was deaf or that they communicated with *telepathy* or something. Me and Goose would be in the basement, playing with his Fisher Price Village, and suddenly he'd say, "Dinner's ready. Mom just called." I never heard Mrs. P call us, unless we were outside. Then, she could yell just as loud as Prissy.

Me and Mrs. P. got along great. I told her jokes and she fed me fish sticks. She was pretty and she always smelt like lilacs, even in winter. She had dark brown hair that she did up with curlers and she always had makeup on. Nice makeup, not going to the bar makeup. She had dark penciled-on eyebrows and red lips. She looked just like the ladies in the old black and white movies that me and Goose loved so much.

That was the best thing about Goose being able to stay over at my place; we got to stay up late, pop popcorn and watch old movies on channel nine. Old movies made us *swoon*. Our favourite was *Breakfast at Tiffany's*. We saw that about a billion times. We loved Holly Golightly best, but we loved all those old shows. We loved the men, all strong and safe, with their arms around the smart-talking women with the nice teeth. Sometimes, Prissy did her hair like Lauren Bacall, but Goose said she was really more of a brunette Marilyn Monroe. He said that Prissy was kind of *soft around the edges*. He figured that's why she was always hooking up with losers.

I didn't like it when he said that. I punched him right in the gut. He was right, though. Prissy did hook up with losers.

I only told Goose the funny stories about Prissy's men — the guy with the toupee that looked more green than blonde, the guy who stayed with us for a week and only ate cheese, the trucker who insisted on calling me *Scooter Magoo*. Goose never knew about the real losers Prissy brought home. The ones who only stayed one night, or part of a night. The ones who booked out as soon as they saw me, or just did it with her and then left Prissy at the table with a smoke and a plastic tumbler of Wild Turkey.

Those were bad nights.

I'd sit on the floor beside her chair and rub the silky material of her robe between my fingers. It had butterflies on it. "Monarchs fly all the way from Canada to Mexico," I'd say. "Every year."

She'd stare out the window.

I'd bring her the bottle of Wild Turkey.

I'd get myself a glass and the milk jug and we'd sit and drink 'til dawn. She drank the Turkey. I drank the milk.

Sometimes she'd cry.

Sometimes she'd talk. She'd warn me about falling in love. "It's just you and me, Bean. You're all I got. You be careful. You find a good man."

Prissy was never careful. She never said it, but I knew she thought that if she could find the right guy we would magically turn into some happily-ever-after Disney family. She wanted to find her Prince. I didn't much believe in princes. I was happily ever after enough with just me and Prissy Fallwell.

But Prissy got lonely.

She thought I was lonely too. For a while, she brought me home pets — strays she found, like that goddamned iguana she found wandering around the highway outside of the Husky. Prissy liked the baby animals best — kittens, puppies, anything cute and cuddly. Once they grew up a bit, she lost interest. I tried to take care of them, but they usually wandered off or died, or we had to get rid of them when we moved to a new place. I didn't get attached.

The men Prissy dated felt like strays too. Every few weeks, she'd bring home a new one. They stayed a few days or a few weeks. If they weren't truckers, they never seemed to have jobs to go to. They just hung around. Sooner or later, there would be a fight and a break up. Sometimes the guy would just disappear one day and never come back.

Ned Dacey stayed a few months. He didn't live with us, but he was at our place a lot. I didn't like him. He reminded me of Gerard Glatt, the guy who stuck his tongue down Prissy's throat at GT's. Ned did that too. He had shiny shoes, wore too much cologne, made me sit in his lap when I didn't want to, and pinched me, hard, when Prissy wasn't looking. I had bruises on my legs.

Prissy liked Ned because he worked in an office. She was all impressed that he wore a suit to work. She made me polish his ugly shoes when he slept over. He slept over a lot, but he kept his own place. He lived in a hi-rise downtown — a *real bachelor's pad*, Prissy said. I wouldn't know. I never got to see it.

Prissy seemed happy, with Ned, but nervous. He bought her fancy clothes and told her what to wear. She dyed her hair blonde and laid on the blue eye shadow. She started to fidget. She smoked more and more. Ned yelled at her if she took too long getting ready or her makeup wasn't right or her hair didn't turn out *just so*.

One time, I came home just as his car pulled away. Prissy was crying at the table. Her lip was bleeding. I got a facecloth, wet it in the kitchen sink and cleaned the blood off.

"It dripped on your new dress."

She took the facecloth and pressed it to the side of her mouth. "Doesn't matter."

"I thought you were going out."

She shook her head.

"Should I call Auntie and tell her not to come over?"

She nodded.

I told Auntie that Prissy was staying in because she didn't feel well. Auntie still wanted to come over, but I told her Prissy didn't really want any company that night.

After that, I stayed in the house when Ned was around. Prissy tried to make me go outside, but I'd just go to another room and sit and listen. They fought different than Prissy and Ritter had. I could never distract Ned. I couldn't make him laugh, at all. Prissy said that me hanging around made Ned madder, but I wouldn't leave her alone with him. I listened, and it made my stomach hurt. It was always the same. He'd get all cranky about something and the only way Prissy could head him off from a pout or a punch was to fuck him. Worked most of the time.

I told her to break up with him. But she wouldn't. He finally broke up with her. Like they all did.

"Good riddance to bad rubbish," GT said when he found out Ned was gone. I agreed.

Prissy was sad, but I patted her and said, "It's for the best," which made her smile.

Me and the girls threw a party to dye Prissy's hair back to brunette. Auntie and Spuddy said, "You deserve better." She did, too. Prissy Fallwell deserved the best.

We started looking for a new place the next day. A brand new start.

I went over to GT's and gathered up some new stuff to do my circle ritual. I took Floke for a walk around the yard, and I took the stuff he pissed on. We needed all the magic we could get.

BUDDHA

We moved across town — over to the Cathedral area. We got a two bedroom in the Beta Apartments. I was happy to have my own room. Sharing with Prissy got weird when she had guys over. I always tried to sleep on the couch and let them have the bedroom, but sometimes, Prissy wanted me to go to bed early, which meant the two of them were on the couch and I was trapped. I hated that. I needed to slip outside sometimes. Our place in Beta didn't have a back door, but there was a balcony I could shinny down from if I needed an escape route.

That apartment was lucky. The day after we moved in, Prissy got a job waitressing at the Quality Tea Room and we were off the Welfare. She met Keith at the Quality.

GT called Keith a crazy hippy, but I thought he was cool. He looked like Jackson Browne and he told us stories about playing in a band with Kenny Rogers. The only crazy thing about Keith was that he didn't eat any meat. I loved meat — especially steak, which we didn't get to have very often.

Things were mellow and easy when Keith was around. We ate a lot of lentil stew, burned incense, and wore cotton. Prissy let her hair grow out. She stopped wearing makeup, and her face got even more beautiful. She was calmer and gentler. When she came home from working at the Tea Room, Keith brushed out her hair and massaged her feet. He gave her a cup of tea and said, "You sit. I'll cook." Keith was a great cook. Our kitchen smelled like sautéed onions, garlic and curry. Me and Prissy would sit at the table and watch him chop stuff. "Like this," he'd say. "Keep the point of the knife planted. It's all in the wrist." Keith had strong wrists; he was a drummer.

After dinner, we'd go for a walk around the neighborhood. Prissy and Keith held hands. I wanted him to stay forever.

We played *Carnival*. Keith would give me under the pits airplane rides, wrist and heel heli-rides, horsey on his foot or back and he even had two rides he made up himself *Earthquake* and *The Flusher*. *The Flusher* was my favourite. Keith laid on his back with his knees bent. I sat on his knees with my feet on his belly. He held his hands up, bent at the wrist. He was *the throne*. His hands were the flushers. I'd smack a hand and wait to be flushed. I never knew which flusher would work. I'd smack and smack 'til he opened his legs and made a big flushing sound and I'd fall, laughing hysterically. Prissy just smiled and shook her head. I didn't like *Earthquake*. It gave me a stomachache.

When Prissy was at work, me and Keith took walks up to Wascana Park. One time, we played hide 'n' seek in the Legislative building. Me and Goose played in the Leg all the time, but we never told any adults. Keith was different. It was OK to tell him stuff. He never told me to smarten up or went tattling to Prissy.

I even took Keith to the museum and showed him the wolves. They were on the second floor. I used to sit and stare at them for hours. There were three Grey Wolves. It was winter and they'd just finished hunting. There was blood on the snow and the world was lit with blue. There was a button you pressed to hear them howl. I pressed the button the day I took Keith to meet the wolves. "The skinny one looks like the one in my dreams."

"You dream of wolves?"

"Just one. Sometimes she's a wolf and sometimes she's an old lady."

"What do you mean?"

I put my hand on the cool glass of the display. I hadn't told anyone about the wolf. "She comes to warn me."

"About what."

I didn't look at him. "Stuff."

"What kind of stuff?"

I pressed the howling button again. "Sounds lonesome, doesn't it?" He nodded. We stood, watching the wolves until the howling stopped. I turned away. "Let's go look at the dinosaur bones."

I didn't tell Keith any more about my wolf dreams. They were private. I didn't even tell Goose about them. I'd had them for as long as I could remember, but it had taken me a long time to figure out what they meant. I dreamed of the wolf the night before Ritter stabbed himself. I dreamed of her just before guys broke up with Prissy. The wolf came to tell me to pay attention.

Keith was with us for six months. One day, he said his feet were itching and he had to move on. Before he left, he gave me a green jade pendant of a fat man named Buddha.

I was mad at him for leaving. "Don't you love us?"

He hung his head. "I do, Bean." He looked at me. "I do love you, Bean."

"And you love Prissy."

"I do."

"Then what the fuck?"

He laughed. "Don't swear."

"Well?"

He just looked at me.

I tucked the Buddha into my Samsonite.

Me and Prissy went to the Bus Depot and waved goodbye as he rode off into the sunset.

Prissy cried a little after Keith left, but she also said she was relieved. When I asked her why, she said, "Because I could've loved him." That didn't make any sense to me.

Auntie said, "He scared her, Bean." That didn't make any sense either. Grown-ups are screwed.

When Keith left, Prissy hardened up again. She went back to *"You be careful,"* and *"It's just you and me, Bean."* I took care of her as best I could.

We started moving even more often. Prissy went back to drinking Wild Turkey and bringing home stray men. I made sure our new places had a back door.

Prissy cried at night, when she was alone. If it was a real bad night, I curled up beside her and sang "In the Ghetto", or "Puff the Magic Dragon", so she could cry real hard and get it out faster.

I hated Jackie Paper. One night, I asked Prissy if girls could play with Dragons. I told her that I hated Jackie Paper for abandoning Puff that way. She said, "He just grew up."

"Growing up doesn't mean you go . . . chuck your friends at the Nuisance Grounds."

Prissy thought awhile and then she said I was right and that Jackie Paper was an ass. She said, "You've got good asshole radar, Kid. Make sure you keep it."

I wished I could pass it on to her. Prissy's radar was shot to shit.

Our Redeemer

Prissy had a lot of boyfriends when I was growing up, I had a lot of crushes: Jack Lord from *Hawaii Five-O*, Hawkeye Pierce, Jerome the Giraffe and Jesus. Well, GOD actually. It was an on again off again sort of affair.

I took to wandering into churches when I was about seven. Soon as we settled into a new place, I'd walk around the neighborhood and find the nearest church — didn't matter what kind. I didn't care. It was about the feel of the place, what kind of hymns they sang and whether they actually answered my questions in Sunday School. I had a lot of questions.

Prissy never came with me, but she'd usually get up to see me off. She'd braid my hair and give me a quarter for the collection plate. She drank coffee, smoked, and listened to the radio while I was at church. Sundays made Prissy sad. Sundays and twilight.

My church-going started one Sunday when Prissy was sleeping one off. She'd been out to the Circle-J with Auntie the night before. She tried to dump me over at GT's, but I convinced her to let me stay home alone. We'd just moved into a new place and I had to get my room set up.

I didn't have much: a few clothes, my books, and this old radio Ritter gave me. I set it up beside my books, on top of my Samsonite — made a nice night table beside my mattress on the floor. I sang along with "Delta Dawn" while I did my circle ritual, then I had a bath and went to bed.

Prissy didn't bring anyone home with her that night, which was good, but she didn't want to get out of bed on Sunday morning. "Lemme sleep."

"What about our French toast?" We always had French toast for our first breakfast in a new place. Helped us start things off right. Just like every first-night Prissy was supposed to tuck me in and say, "Bean, are you happy?" She'd missed that little ritual as well.

Her face was puffy. "Later, Hon. I just need to sleep awhile more."

"Got a headache?"

"Body ache."

"Wild Turkey ache."

"What?"

"Nothing. Fine. I'm having Honeycombs."

Prissy pulled the pillow over her head. "Fine."

There were no Honeycombs. The empty box was on the table. Prissy must've eaten them after the bar. I pulled open the fridge. *Jesus!* I yelled at Prissy, "No milk!"

Prissy groaned. "Powdered in the cupboard. Beside the Puffed Wheat."

I hate powdered milk. And I'm gonna kill that Puffed Wheat. Only way Puffed Wheat is any good at all is covered in brown sugar, syrup and cocoa and shoved in a pan. Puffed Wheat Cake is fine, but powdered milk and Puffed Wheat plain are disgusting. I opened the cupboard and stared at the Puffed Wheat. *Fricken Welfare food.* I'd packed that damned sack of sawdust in our cooler at least five times. We'd been lugging it around for a year — like Prissy thought that as long as we had that stupid bag of Puffed Wheat nobody could say we didn't have food in the house. Prissy could be such a retard. I grabbed the bag and ripped it open. I whispered, "Puffed Wheat is not food!" I ground it into the linoleum. I clenched my teeth. I felt like my head was gonna explode. I wanted to scream and stamp my feet, but there was no point. She'd just kick the crap out of me for making a racket. I swept up the puffed wheat and threw it in the garbage. I cracked open a root beer.

Sundays made me sad too. All the stores were closed and there wasn't much to do. Other kids disappeared on Sundays. They went to visit grandparents or had to *spend time with their family*. My family was screwed. Ritter was gone and Prissy and Auntie were usually hung-over on Sundays. Best I could hope for was a dinner at Grandpa Tom's place and something good on Walt Disney. But that wasn't for hours. Sundays are long.

I went and looked at Prissy. She was frowning in her sleep. I put a glass of water and the bottle of aspirins beside her bed. I tucked the blanket up around her throat and kissed her on the head. She tasted like salt and cigarettes.

I decided to go for a walk and take a look around. There was a convenience store at the end of the block. Closed. *Stupid Sundays.* I walked up the next block looking for signs of kids. Another crappy neighborhood. No tire swings or Big Wheels in the driveways, just a lot of broken plastic crap lying around. I kicked a chunk of mud along the gutter.

Then I heard the singing. It was coming from a white building on the corner. I went in. It was one room, filled with benches — a church. I'd never seen a tiny church like that before. Only church I'd ever been in was the Knox Metropolitan when Goose's mom took us to hear the Christmas Carol Contest. The Knox is huge.

Goose and his family went to church every Sunday. He'd invited me along a few times, but I never went. He had to wear a suit. I thought if I went to church, I'd have to wear a dress. I hate dresses, so I figured I'd hate church too.

Nobody I knew talked about God much. I hadn't really thought about him — aside from Christmas carols about the baby Jesus and saying the Lord's Prayer at school. I liked the Lord's Prayer. In one school I was at, there was two kids who weren't allowed to say the prayer. They were Jehovah's Witnesses. They said that when we all stood up and recited the Lord's Prayer it wasn't really a prayer. They said we should only pray to God alone, in private. They also told me they couldn't have blood transfusions. I didn't know what that had to do with God, but it made me curious.

I asked Goose what he thought about God. He said, "He's our creator." Goose said that God created us in His image and that He sent His son, Jesus, to die for our sins. I asked him what sins we'd done, but he didn't know.

Our creator. I liked that.

I decided to believe in God. I liked the idea that someone was in charge.

I'd been praying for as long as I could remember, but I didn't call it praying until after Goose told me about God being our creator. Before that, I was just talking to the person I thought was writing us. I thanked her every morning for another day, and tried to convince her to let us have a good one. To keep us all safe. I'd been reading since I was three and a half. I read a lot. I was positive that someone was writing us. We were heroines, like Nancy Drew. I could hear our *author* writing us in my dreams.

> *Bean E. Fallwell was asleep — or seemed to be. The bruise on her face was almost healed. She was dreaming of horses. Dreaming that she was in a boarding school in England, that she had her own horse, and that her glamorous mother came to visit four times a year.*
>
> *Bean was in a competition. She was jumping. She was winning a jumping competition on her horse named Cheyenne and she knew her mother was in the stands. She ran to meet her mother after accepting her medal and there was a man with her.*
>
> *That man.*
>
> *That man Prissy brought home from the Circle J last week.*
>
> *That man who came into Bean's room.*
>
> *Bean sat straight up in bed. Eyes wide, she kneeled, and with all the fervour in her six-year-old frame she whispered, "Write better. Write better!"*

Maybe not quite like Nancy Drew.

The little white church smelled like lemons. The ladies all had hats on. They looked happy to be dressed up. Most of the men looked itchy in their suits — like they couldn't wait to get them off. They were all singing really loud. I stood at the back and listened. A lady in a purple dress came over and said hello. She smelled like lilies.

I shuffled. I wasn't dressed up. I had on ugly old Salvation Army clothes. My pants were too short. I hadn't even combed my hair. Auntie called it my *'scraggly ol' witch hair'*. It hung to the middle of my back, but I wouldn't let Prissy cut it. "Is it OK if I just stand here and listen?"

"Sure it is. Or you could go down to Sunday School. That's in the basement." Her voice was soft and quiet. She had white gloves on. I'd never seen a person wear gloves like that in real life. Only in movies.

"Are they singing down there?"

"Not right now, but it's where the kids are. They'll be up soon."

"I'd just like to listen to the singing, please. It sounds really nice."

"Would you like to come in and sit?"

"No thank you."

"Well, you're welcome to come any time." She handed me a piece of paper. It had a picture of Jesus on it and the name of the church, Our Redeemer.

"That's Jesus."

"Yes it is. Do you Know Jesus?" She asked.

"Not personally."

The lady nodded with a funny smile on her face.

I recognized Jesus because Spuddy painted a lot of religious pictures with her Tri-Chem. Pictures of Jesus with a bunch of kids or at his *Last Supper* or that one with the angel and the two kids on the bridge. The angel one was my favourite. You could only see the angel in the dark. In normal light, it looked like the two kids were alone but when you turned the lights off the branches of the tree turned into a glowing angel. That was done with 0258 Chartreuse Glow-in-the-Dark paint. I drove Spuddy nuts flicking the lights on and off to see that angel.

The lady patted my shoulder. "Maybe I'll see you next week," she said, and went back to her seat.

I stood at the back of Our Redeemer 'til the singing was over, then I slipped out the door and headed home.

Prissy was up, sitting at the table having a coffee and a smoke. "Hey, Hon," she said. "You still want French toast?"

I plunked onto a chair. "Nah. Can I have a coffee?"

Prissy put a bit of coffee in a mug with a lot of evaporated milk and stirred in two spoons of sugar. She handed it to me. "Stunt your growth," she said. Then she swatted at me, "Stop that. Jesus!"

I was tipping my chair back on two legs and tapping the front on the floor. Forgot about Prissy's headache. "Sorry." I leaned into the table, took a swig of coffee, and smacked my lips. "Ahh that's good."

Prissy sat back down.

"Hey, Priss?"

"Yeah, Bean?"

"How come we don't go to church?"

"Church?"

"Yeah. Church."

"I dunno."

"What if I went to church next Sunday?"

She shrugged. "What for?"

I shrugged back. "I dunno. Listen to the singing I guess." I slid the piece of paper across the table. "It's just around the corner."

Prissy looked at the paper. "Go if you want."

"He's pretty cute, eh?"

"What?"

I sipped my coffee. "Jesus. He's pretty cute. Maybe you should come too."

"Very funny," she said. "I don't think he'll be there — in the flesh."

"The preacher guy's cute, too."

Prissy rolled her eyes. "I'm sure. If you don't want French toast, what do you want for lunch?"

"Grill cheese."

She slid off her chair. "Grab the slices."

I got the cheese out of the fridge while Prissy put the pan on the stove. We buttered the bread — four slices, both sides — and then Prissy put two in the pan. She laid a Kraft Single on each.

"Extra cheesy pleasy," I said.

Prissy laid another slice on each. "Anything else?" Sometimes I liked to try *unusual* things on my grill cheese — carrots, pickles, ketchup potato chips.

"Nope. Lids please."

Prissy put the top on the sandwiches.

I pushed a stacking stool up to the stove. Leaning over the stove, with the egg flipper in hand, tongue between my teeth, I waited for the perfect moment. "There you go, ya bugger." I squished the melty cheese.

"Don't swear."

"Bugger's a swear?"

"Yep."

"Jesus."

Prissy laughed. "That's a swear too." Prissy was so pretty when she laughed. "Watch your sandwich."

The grill cheese was on high. Prissy cooked everything on high. I waved the flipper at her. "Help me flip. Do it like a pancake!" Prissy took the pan and flipped the sandwiches like a pro. I waited a minute and then squished them again. "Perfecto!" Prissy slid the sandwiches on to plates and cut them into triangles. I refilled our coffees.

We sat. Bean and Prissy Fallwell in our new house — a yellow kitchen table, grill cheese on Wonder Bread, and Sunday morning coming down.

WEDDING ANNOUNCEMENT:
RITTER EBERTS AND JACQUELINE GILES

From then on, I took to wandering into churches. I eventually stuck to churches that used the real Bible, not the Good News modern version. First of all, I preferred the King James version, for the poetry. And second of all, *The Good News for Modern Man* wasn't even the whole Bible — just the New Testament. There's no way you can understand God with only half a story. He's pretty complicated.

I went to a Catholic church with Ritter, a few times. It was confusing. I didn't know the rules about when to stand up and when to sit down and what to answer back to the priest. Ritter never went to church when he was with me and Prissy. He started going when he hooked up with a Catholic girl.

Her name was Jacqueline.

I met her one day when I was off school and me and Ritter were hanging out in his cab.

"She's still in school for Chrissake," I told Prissy. "We stopped off to see her at lunchtime. She goes to Miller. How the hell old is Ritter anyhow?"

"Not that old."

"Older than you?"

"A bit."

"So, what, he's like . . . twenty-six? Twenty-seven?"

"Thirty."

"Yeah. Well, she's sixteen — and she's gross. She's got zits, fer fucksake."

"Don't swear."

I'll show you some goddamned swearing, I thought. *God doesn't give two shits about swearing. Well, maybe the name in vain stuff. Christ's sake, God damned, Holy thunderin' Jesus on a jack pine.* "I use the word for *emphasis.*"

Prissy shook her head. "Christ, you got a smart mouth."

I smiled and pointed at her, "Swearing!"

"Emphasis," Prissy snorted. "You're eight years old fer shitsake. By the time you're ten I won't be able to understand a friggin' word."

I shrugged and gave her a grin.

She shook her head. "Get the cheese slices." Prissy liked it when I made fun of Ritter's new girlfriends. It cheered her up.

I handed her the Kraft slices. "The cheese Milady. Can I squish 'em?"

"Grab a stool."

"I'm tall enough," I said. I was, too.

Ritter married Jacqueline in the Cathedral. Their daughter Kyla was born seven months later.

"Randy Ritter strikes again," said Prissy.

I watched Prissy for a while after the wedding. I thought maybe she would be sad. Even though her and Ritter weren't married anymore, he still stayed over sometimes. Mostly when Prissy didn't have a boyfriend, but once in a while I saw his cab pull away from the house real early even when she was seeing someone else.

One night, just after Keith left and before Ritter met stupid Jacqueline, Ritter said maybe he should, *come back to us*. I held my breath. I was under the table in my usual position.

Prissy clicked her teeth. "You didn't leave us," she said.

I waited.

They just sat there quietly for a long time. Then Ritter got up. "I gotta go," he said.

Prissy poured another drink. Rye. "You don't want to stay the night?"

I peeked out from under the table. Ritter was just standing there, looking at Prissy. He was pressing his lips together real tight. He didn't say anything else. He just left. I didn't see him for a few weeks after that.

Me and Ritter had an on again off again sort of thing too. When him and Prissy split up, I didn't see him for a long time. When the dust settled, he started picking me up on Saturday nights for a while. I'd sleep over at his place, we'd spend most of Sunday together, and he'd get me home in time to watch Walt Disney. Sometimes he said he wished we could spend Saturday days together too, but he had to work.

That was fine by me. Satur*days* were for movies and hanging out with Goose. Even when me and Prissy lived across town, I always spent Saturdays with Goose. Then I'd have supper at GT's, or go out for food with Ritter.

Ritter didn't cook. Mostly he lived in tiny rooms that didn't even have a kitchen. In one of his places, I had to go all the way down the hall to use the bathroom. I made Ritter come with me and stand guard at the door.

For a while, we had the perfect set-up. I'd be over at Ritter's when Prissy and Auntie went out, and by the time I got home, Prissy would be alone and her hangover would be mostly gone. Then Ritter screwed it up. He'd be fine for a while, then he'd start drinking again and disappear for weeks at a time. GT said he couldn't help himself. Goose said Ritter was an alcoholic and that it was a disease. I just learned not to bet on Ritter showing up when he said he would.

Ritter only drank a little bit when I was over for a visit. He only got really drunk one time. He did a bad thing that night. Not the worst thing. I told myself that it was no big deal. He was drunk. But when he took me home the next day, I scrubbed myself raw in the bathtub and then I took Christina, the walking doll he'd given me, out to the backyard. I lit her on fire and I watched her melt. I was getting used to the bad things that men did, but I never thought Ritter would do it. Not to anyone. I told myself that he couldn't help it. That it was part of his disease.

It was no big deal. I just went away while it happened — like I always did. Going away is easy. You just blink and you're up and out of your body — watching from the ceiling. You don't feel what's happening to the body when you go away. You can even watch, it doesn't hurt. When I went away, I started up music inside my head to cover the sounds of what was happening. Jangly steel guitar. Sometimes, I'd ride that guitar right out onto the prairie, into the tall grass where no one could find me. I didn't do that very often, though. It's dangerous. Mostly, you have to watch; just in case.

I don't remember when I discovered going away. Seems I could always do it — since I was a tiny baby. I thought everyone did it.

I never told Prissy about what Ritter did. I just told her I'd rather stay over at Goose's or GT's on Saturday nights. She didn't ask me why.

Elvis Scarf

One Saturday, Prissy wouldn't let me go to Goose's or GT's. "Nope," she said. "Tonight you are coming out with the girls!"

"We going to bingo?"

"Nope."

"Bowling?"

"Nope."

"McDonald's?"

"We're going to the Paddock," Auntie yelled. She was in the bathroom, putting on her face. "It's your mother's birthday."

I felt horrible. Prissy always made a big deal out of my birthdays and I always made her something for hers. I grabbed Prissy's hand. "How could I forget? I'm so sorry."

"No sweat, Kiddo." She handed me a sparkly shirt. "Put this on."

"It's your favourite."

"Sure is. Put it on."

"I can't go to the bar. I'm too little."

"We're sneaking you in." Prissy'd already had a few shots of Wild Turkey.

I thought they'd take me over to the Paddock and I'd end up sitting in the restaurant part sipping cokes while they were in the bar. I'd already done that a few times. But they had it all planned. Prissy's friend, Larry, was the owner. All he said was,

"You see a cop, or anyone who looks official, split." Then he pointed at the back door.

There was an Elvis impersonator playing. He looked just like Prissy's pictures of The King; the young handsome King, not the pudgy guy in the white jumpsuit. I drank cokes with cherries floating in them and we danced all night. It was the best night ever.

When the singer asked the audience for requests, I screamed out, "'Polk Salad Annie'!"

He started laughing. "Well, ladies and gentleman, looks to me like we have ourselves a bona fide fan in the house. What's your name, little sister?"

I just about died. I wanted to crawl under the table.

"Bean E. Fallwell!" Auntie yelled.

"Well, Bean, this one's for you." Auntie dragged me and Prissy right up to the front of the dance floor. When the song was ending, Elvis reached down and draped a purple scarf around my neck. Everyone was screaming and screaming. I almost fainted.

Then they kicked into "Suspicious Minds" and we went and sat down. I thought maybe I sipped the wrong coke. I was dizzy.

"You're just star struck," Prissy said. She ordered me a water though, just in case.

We stayed right until the end. Elvis sang "Happy Birthday" to Prissy and gave her a hug.

I fell asleep in the cab, and let Prissy carry me into the house. I could've walked, but Prissy hardly ever picked me up anymore and it felt good to be carried. She tucked me in. When she tried to pull the scarf from around my neck, I opened one eye and said, "No way, Sister!"

She put her hand on my face. "You happy?"

"Yep. You?"

"Yep."

"Happy Birthday, Mom. I love you."

"I love you too, Kid. You have no idea how much."

"I do. A bizillion times a million."

"Good. Now go the hell to sleep. It's the middle of the night."

I sat up. "Hey, wait a minute!"

"What?"

"Where's the cake?" We always had confetti angel food cake with lemon icing on our birthdays.

"Ta-DA!" Auntie was in the doorway with a cake filled with candles. "Make a wish, Miss."

"It's a raging inferno," Prissy said. "I'm ancient."

"Wish for youth. Wish for beauty." Auntie crooned.

I kneeled on the bed. "Wish wish wish!"

Prissy closed her eyes and blew the candles out.

I asked her what she wished for.

She smiled. "I'll never tell."

We ate the cake on my bed. It was sweet and sour all at the same time and made spit gather in my mouth.

Three days later, we moved. Prissy started work at the Car Wash over on North Albert and we met Jack Vara.

Two

fabulous *adj* immense, amazing; excellent (*inf*); feigned or false; spoken or written about in fable; celebrated in story [L *fabula*, from *fari* to speak; see also **fable**]

fable *n* a narrative in which things irrational and sometimes inanimate are, for the purpose of moral instruction, made to act and speak with human interests and passions; any tale in literary form, not necessarily probable in its incidents, intended to instruct or amuse; the plot or series of events in an epic or dramatic poem (*archaic*); a fiction or myth; a ridiculous story, an old wives' tale; a falsehood; subject of common talk. *vi* to tell fictitious tales; to tell lies (*obs*). *vt* to feign; to invent; to relate as if true. [Fr *fable*, from L *fari* to speak].

— *The Chambers Dictionary* (Standard)

SHAZAM #14

Jack Vara was a hotgun cowboy with a crooked grin, a scorpion tattoo and a talent for weaving tales.

Me and Prissy called Jack "Guitar Man". He had a beat up old Gibson that he brought into work everyday. He started singing us Elvis songs over lunch. The gang who ate lunch with us made him do *Guitar Man* over and over — they loved the bit about quitting his job down at the Car Wash. Jack flirted with Prissy, taught me how to handle the hotguns, and he told us stories about his life. He'd had all kinds of adventures.

One day, he told me a story about the blue sapphire ring he always wore. We were sitting out back of the Car Wash on the picnic table. He was squinting at me though the smoke from his cigarette. Jack rolled his own smokes with Drum tobacco. I liked the way they smelled.

I was looking at the scorpion tattoo on his arm. "Did you know that if you place a drop of liquor on a scorpion, it will instantly go mad and sting itself to death?"

He smiled. "I did not know that."

"It's true."

"I'm sure it is." Jack took another drag from his smoke. "You ever seen a scorpion?"

"Course not. We don't have scorpions in Saskatchewan."

"You never been outta Saskatchewan?"

"Just once. We went camping — all the way to BC and back."

"You've been on some adventures then."

"Not really," I said. "I'm just a kid."

"You're lying,"

"Am not."

"I'd say you've been on quite a few adventures." He closed his eyes. "You have gone alone and you have gone with someone named . . . Gus? No Goose. Am I right?"

"How'd you know about Goose? He's the one that told me about the scorpion. He knows all sorts of cool stuff. He's my best friend."

"You and Goose like watching people, don't you?" I pretended I didn't know what he was talking about. He smiled. "How 'bout the adventures you've been having with those Kabos kids who live over by your grandfather?"

I squinted at him. Prissy could've told him stuff about me and Goose, but she had no idea what I was up to with the Kabos. It was bad. Candy Kabos was my age. Her brother, Sal, was three years older and I had a wicked crush on him. Sal was an excellent shop-lifter and he was training me. I was really scared, at first. I started with small stuff — candy mostly, mojos and nigger babies, and worked my way up to bigger things. One night, Sal dared me to grab a comic book from the corner store. I slipped Shazam #14 up my sleeve, went to the counter, bought a Fudgesicle, said hello to The Chink, and left. Sal said I was a *natural.*

I checked out the hole in the bottom of my sneaker, wondering if Jack knew about the comic or the other stuff I'd stolen. Nobody knew about that but me and the Kabos.

Jack laughed. "Don't worry kid, I ain't gonna squeal on you. I'm a bit of an adventurer myself." He held out his hand. "See this ring?"

"Nice," I said. It looked expensive. The thick band was silver, and the sapphire was a perfect square of blue blue stone. I wondered if he stole it.

"It's special." He twirled the ring. "It's why I know things. Like what you and little Sal get up to down at The Chink's."

I looked at him, innocently. "I have no idea what you are talking about."

Jack threw back his head and laughed. "Cool customer, aren't ya?" He tossed his cigarette butt and stood up.

I opened my eyes wider. "Pardon?"

He laughed again, "Pardon? You take the cake." He hunkered down so that we were eye to eye and gave me the gaze. Guitar Man had this look that he gave people. It made my stomach flip-flop sometimes. He looked right at you — right into you. "You don't trust me much, do you?"

"Just met you."

"Fair enough, Kid, fair enough." He leaned forward a bit. "I'm going to tell you a secret."

"OK."

"I trust you then you'll trust me. Right?"

"I guess."

"You can never tell anyone what I am about to tell you."

"OK."

"Nobody. Not Prissy; not even Goose."

"Cross my heart and hope to die," I said and spit.

"Alright." He held my arms, leaned closer. "This ring is magic." He was whispering right into my ear. I could see the ring flashing in the sunlight. It gave me a chill. "It lets me know things."

I shifted back from him a little. "Like what?"

"Like where people go and what they do."

"No way."

"How else I know about you and Sal and Mr. Mind?"

I just looked at him.

"*The Evil Return of the Monster Society*? Shazam #14? That worm and I have a little bit in common — wouldn't you say?"

"Mr. Mind is a telepath. He just reads thoughts, he doesn't — "

"Gotcha. I saw you take that comic. I saw Sal dare you and I saw you take it."

I believed him. He had a magic ring. "Where'd you get it?"

"Stole it off a dead Indian."

"Shud-dup!" I said. "That's stupid."

He didn't even blink.

"You really steal it? Off a dead guy?"

"Can I trust you?"

"Yeah."

"Really really trust you?"

"Yes. I already spit. What do you want — a blood-swear?"

"Good idea." He pulled out the knife he carried in a sheath on his hip. It was way bigger than the one me and Goose had used when we cut our thumbs up on his garage roof.

"Blood-swears are serious." I whispered.

"I know."

"Blood-swears are forever."

"I know. I need you to swear that you will never tell anyone what I'm about to tell you."

"You already told me. The ring is magic. I believe you."

"I didn't tell you how I got the ring."

"Maybe I don't care."

"But you want to know."

I did want to know.

"Swear and I'll tell you."

I gave him my hand. He nicked my thumb, nicked his own and we pressed them together. I looked him straight in his blue black eyes and said, "I swear never to tell." We were bound.

Jack sucked on his thumb. "I killed him."

"For a ring?"

"No. Because he asked me to."

"What?"

"He was all beat up. He grabbed on to me and said, 'Do it, bro — and take the ring. Don't let them get it."

"Let who get it?"

"No idea," Jack said. "He was beat so bad he couldn't really talk. He had blood running from his ear."

"He was dying. Blood from your ear means you're dying."

Jack nodded. "I did it quick and clean." He made a twisting motion with his hands, like he'd snapped the guy's neckbone. "I did what he asked and I took the ring."

I could hardly breathe. *He killed a guy.*

Jack looked around. "Nobody can ever find out where this ring is, right? I don't know who Buddy-guy's enemies are but they messed him up pretty bad, and I don't want any trouble — especially now."

"Now?"

"Now that I've found you and your mom. I don't want no trouble, now."

"Right."

Jack looked at me, hard. "You scared?"

"No." My hand was shaking.

We were bound.

A few days later, Jack came over to our place for dinner. He helped me peel potatoes, and cleared up the table after we were done. He even helped Prissy with the dishes.

I sat at the table with a Coke and watched them. They looked nice together. Prissy was wearing jeans. She said she didn't want to look too fancy, but she'd done her hair up in curls — all soft and sexy. She had her favourite salmon-coloured sweater on and green eye shadow. Jack was wearing a white shirt and black jeans that looked new. He'd shined up his cowboy boots, and he brought his guitar.

They smiled a lot while they were doing the dishes. Prissy looked pink. I couldn't tell if she was blushing or if it was just the reflection off her sweater. They didn't say anything, they just kept smiling at each other. Jack had a dimple in his right cheek.

When all the dishes were dried and put away, Jack sang for us. He sang "Dock of the Bay", "Raindrops Keep Falling on My Head" and "The First Time Ever I Saw Your Face". I watched Prissy. Her face went soft. She looked happy.

Jack looked at the floor. "You don't remember the first time I saw you."

Prissy smiled. "I guess not."

"First day at the Car Wash?" I asked.

He shook his head. He gave Prissy the gaze. "I saw your mom long before she started working there."

Prissy tilted her head — curious.

"When?" I asked.

He kept looking at Prissy. "Long time ago. Long-long ago and far-far away." He smiled. "I better get going."

When he was gone, I asked Prissy what the hell he was talking about. She said she had no idea, but she had a funny little smile on her face.

It was a long time before Jack stayed the night — at least two weeks after that first date. By then, we'd heard a few stories about him knowing Prissy from way back: before I was born, before she'd met Ritter, back when she was a teenager, even. Jack was in the stands watching her play softball the day she got hit with that bat and lost her teeth. He knew where we'd lived in Moose Jaw. He knew about Ritter hurting himself and our accident. He even used to come into the Husky when Prissy was working there. I didn't remember seeing him there, but he said that was because I didn't know him yet and he'd kept quiet. He said he'd known us forever, but that he was shy and, before the Car Wash, he'd only spoken to Prissy once. "It was a few months after Bean was born. Down by the creek. Remember?"

Prissy's forehead wrinkled. "Where?" Prissy usually just smiled when Jack told stories about having a crush on her when she was a girl. She didn't believe him. She said he was just *tellin' tales.*

Jack smiled. A tiny smile. "Down by the creek."

"Wascana Creek?"

He nodded. "Near the end of July. You were with Lip, and you were crying." Prissy's forehead crinkled more. She was trying to remember. I held my breath. Jack went on. "I was bummed out. Just heard about Dylan being booed at Newport for going electric. I thought the world had ended. I thought he'd never write a good song again." He laughed. "Fuck I was a dumbass."

Prissy scrunched her mouth in disbelief, "You're that freaky little kid?"

Jack held his hand up like he was swearing on a bible. "Guilty as charged. Not so little. I was thirteen."

I couldn't believe it. Prissy remembered him. He really had known us all along.

Prissy's eyes were big, like she couldn't believe it either. "You gave me a white linen hanky and said — "

"Don't cry Pretty Priss — Bob ain't dead yet."

Prissy was shaking her head and laughing. "Me and Lip had no freaking idea what you were talking about."

"Told you I was a dumbass." Jack was smiling from ear to ear. "You remember that?"

"Of course I do."

They held hands.

It was a dream come true — or maybe the answer to Prissy's birthday wish. A few days later, the Guitar Man moved in. Prissy had her Prince.

Picture of Lola

I was glad Jack moved in. That way, Prissy wouldn't be alone while I was away on my big adventure.

I hadn't seen Ritter since him and Jacqueline moved to Hamilton Ontario, just after Kyla was born. He called one night, out of the blue, and asked Prissy if I could come out for a visit. Jacqueline was in town, visiting her parents, and Ritter said he'd buy me a ticket to ride back with her on the bus. I didn't really want to go. I'd never left Prissy alone before. Jack said I should take advantage of the chance to travel a little. He promised to take care of Prissy.

It was my first adventure on a Greyhound. I took my big red Samsonite and a smaller bag with some books and apples for on the bus. It was fun. We stopped every couple of hours and got out for a stretch or a snack. I bought a postcard for Goose every time we stopped.

Me and Jacqueline sat in the back of the bus on the big bench seat. A cute guy with a guitar got on in Winnipeg, and came and sat with us. Jacqueline flirted with him. I saw them kiss when they thought I was asleep

Ritter and Kyla met us at the Bus Depot in Hamilton. Kyla was shy and hid behind Ritter's leg.

They lived in a big white house with a tent set up in the backyard. We slept out there a lot. It was hot in Hamilton — even at night. Ritter said it was the *humidity.*

Luckily, there was pool a few blocks away. Me and Jacqueline took Kyla there almost every day. They never stayed very long, but I made friends with a girl named Lola who only had one eye. Jacqueline let me stay at the pool as long as I wanted.

Lola didn't have a glass eye — just a puckered hole. She let me put my finger in the hole. I asked her if the empty socket hurt.

"Nah," she said. "Just tickles sometimes." Her and her mom were saving up for a new eye. Lola told me that she had a glass eye when she was little, but she grew out of it. I wrote Goose to tell him about it. Who knew that eye sockets grew?

Lola and I spent hours perfecting our dives. I liked diving and I loved being in the water, even though I couldn't really swim. Lola was an excellent swimmer. She taught me how to dog paddle and do the sidestroke. Our favourite thing was to let all our air out and sink to the bottom of the pool. We'd lie on the bottom, open our eyes, and watch the bodies swimming above us. I liked it best when the pool was mostly empty and I could just lie there and watch the light play on the water. I liked the sound — muffled and odd.

At home, I would lie in the tub with my ears below the water, thinking. I stayed in the tub for hours; drove Prissy crazy. Sometimes, I had my soakers at night after she was asleep so she wouldn't crank at me.

Hamilton was OK. Jacqueline said it was too damned hot to cook, so we ate a lot of pizzas. I played *flusher* with Kyla and read her stories. When Ritter was off work, we drove around looking at *the sights*. Sleeping in the tent was neat. It was all OK, but I missed home. I called Prissy every Sunday, and sent Goose a postcard every couple of days.

Near the end of August, Jacqueline's best friend, Andie, came out from Regina for a visit. Andie had long blonde hair and smoked Marlboros. She drank red wine, and threw back her head when she laughed. Her and Jacqueline had gone to school together. Andie was always saying, "I can't believe you have a husband and a two-year-old kid already — It's crazy!"

Jacqueline seemed a lot older than Andie. I thought about Prissy. She was sixteen when she got pregnant with me. Just like Jacqueline and Kyla. Prissy never seemed young to me. She never seemed old either. She was just my mom. I'd never really thought about it.

One night at supper, Jacqueline said, "Tomorrow we'll go over to the school and get you registered."

I just about choked on my pizza. "What?"

She smiled. "Well, you have to go to school."

I looked at Ritter. "What?"

He took a sip of rye. "We want you to stay with us, Bean."

"I can't stay here," I said. "What about Prissy?" They all just looked at me. "What the hell are you talking about?"

Jacqueline reached out to touch my arm. "Don't swear."

I shook her off and glared at Ritter. "You can't do this."

"I'm your father."

"So fucking what?"

Ritter had a big gut, but he sure could move when he wanted to. He grabbed me up, gave me a shake, laid me over his knee and slapped me on the ass like I was some kind of little kid. I started screaming my head off so he'd think he was killing me. Worked like a charm. *Adults are so retarded.* It didn't hurt. I was just embarrassed. I felt bad for Andie. She looked so shocked. I almost said, "It didn't even hurt. He used his bare hand — like some kind of *amateur*." I'd been whaled on with a hairbrush, a ruler, a flyswatter and a million times with the god-damned wooden spoon. Prissy grabbed whatever was handy. She didn't stick to the ass either. Ritter's little swats were a joke.

After he apologized and laid on the *that hurt me more than it hurt you* bullshit, I went to the tent.

I didn't know what to do.

I thought about trying to run for it. Ritter's wallet was always in his pant's pocket, and they all slept like rocks. *Just grab the cash and go. Find the bus depot and hop the bus home.*

They'd catch me. First place they'd look.

Hitchhike?

It's far. And who's gonna give a kid a ride and not call the cops? Weirdos, that's who. Probably get picked up by some god-damned pervert or something.

Just call Prissy.

Right. What the fuck can she do from so far away? She'll just freak out.

Call the cops.

And tell them what? That your father is trying to kidnap you. They won't care.

I didn't know what to do, so I went to sleep.

In the middle of the night, I woke up. Someone was outside, coming towards the tent. *Crap*, I thought. *I hope it's not Ritter trying to make up. He's probably shit-faced.* The door flap opened. I was trapped in there. I didn't know whether to pretend I was asleep or what. Not that that ever worked. I'd tried with Prissy's pick-ups when they wandered into my room at night. I stayed all tucked in, my whole self under the covers and pretended to be asleep. It worked for vampires and monsters, when I was little, but it never worked on mortals. I could hear somebody breathing.

"Ritter?"

"No. It's me." Andie. "You OK?"

"Yeah."

"You sure?"

"Yeah."

"I'm sorry I . . . " She didn't know how to finish.

I uncovered my head and sat up. "Don't worry about it." We sat in silence for a while.

"Bean?"

"Yeah?"

"You want to go home?"

"Yes."

"OK," she said. She reached out and smoothed my hair. "Get some sleep. We'll work it out." She started crawling out of the tent.

"Hey, Andie," I said.

"Yeah?"

"Thanks."

A few days later, we left. We said we were going to the store to get popsicles for everyone. We'd taken our stuff over to Lola's the night before. Her and her mom were in on the plan. It was all very cloak and daggery: slipping away in the night with all our stuff, making sure Ritter and Jacqueline didn't notice our things were missing, spending the next day with them just waiting for the right time to make a run for it.

Lola threw her arms around me and cried. She said she'd miss me; that I was her best friend. She said she'd never really had a friend before because people got freaked out by her missing eye. I thought that was crazy. I told her that she was beautiful; that she was funny and smart and if people couldn't see past one missing eyeball then it was their loss. She gave me a picture of herself. "So you never forget me." Like I ever would.

Prissy was surprised to see me. Ritter hadn't called to say I was on the way home.

"I bet he didn't," I said and went to my room.

Prissy followed. "You OK?"

I tossed my Samsonite on the bed. "I'm just glad to be home, Mom. I missed you." Prissy winced when I hugged her. "You OK?"

"Yeah," she said. "I tripped and bashed into the kitchen table. I'm OK, just bruised a little. I missed you too, Honey." She hugged me, tight. "I have news."

"What?"

"We're gonna have a baby!"

"No way."

"Way."

I jumped on her. We started squealing and she swung me around. When she put me down, I asked where Jack was.

"Out. He'll be back soon. Oh, he'll be so glad you're back. We were waiting to tell you before we let anyone else know. Now you're home — we can have a party."

"Can I call Goose?"

"Absolutely. Call everybody. But don't tell. Tell them we're having a welcome home party for you. It'll be a baby surprise."

I laughed. "Congratulations, Mom."

She put her hand on my head. "You happy?"

I took her hand and kissed it. "Absolutely."

We had a shaker that lasted all night long. Jack must've sang "Having my Baby" about thirty times.

MATCHBOOK: PRISSY AND JACK 4-EVER

Prissy married the Guitar Man in April. She was nine months pregnant on her wedding day. Prissy didn't really want to get married. She was happy just the way things were, but Jack convinced her that we should be a real family now that there was a baby on the way. She agreed to get hitched, but she made it clear that her and I were keeping our names Fallwell. Jack didn't like it much. "Them's my terms, Guitar Man," she said. "Take it or leave it."

He took it.

Prissy and Jack tied the knot down at the courthouse. Jack wore a baby-blue leisure suit and Prissy wore her favourite bright yellow mini-dress. Spuddy and Slim were the witnesses.

Auntie and I set up the party. We hung streamers everywhere and blew up a whole package of balloons. We had trays of sandwiches, chips and dip and lots of beer. GT found me two cases of matches with plain white covers. I used markers to personalize them — *Prissy and Jack 4-ever* in a big red heart. I scattered them around the livingroom for people to take home.

By the time Prissy and Jack got back from the courthouse, the place was rocking. Almost everyone brought a gift. Jack said he ought to get hitched more often.

Goose came, but he had to leave at nine. His mom didn't want him to sleep over when there was a party on — even if it was a wedding party. Before he left, Goose gave Prissy a kiss on the cheek. "You look beautiful, Prissy," he said. "I wish you every happiness." Prissy giggled and blushed. She always did that when Goose played *the little gentleman* with her. Jack walked up and Goose shook his hand. "Congratulations, Mr. Vara."

Jack slapped him on the back, "Call me Jack, ya crazy little bugger! And don't you worry about these two. I'm gonna take real good care of them for ya."

Goose looked him right in the eye, with a look I'd never seen on his face before, a hard look. "I trust you will, Jack."

That cracked Jack up. He slapped Goose on the back again and wandered off in search of another beer. He crossed Auntie's path on the way to the kitchen and spun her into a crazy polka. Everyone cheered. Prissy threw back her head and laughed, clapping along. She was glowing.

"Isn't he great?" I said to Goose.

"Sure," Goose said. "He's great." I could tell he didn't mean it.

Everybody else loved Jack. Auntie used to say, "Only problem with Jack Vara is that he's generous to a fault." Jack was always buying presents for people. "Money's for spending," he'd say. One time, he bought me and Goose a set of walkie-talkies. Not the baby kind, real ones with different channels and everything. He just brought them home one day — no special occasion or anything.

It was my fault Goose didn't like Jack. I told him about the ring. I shouldn't have, but I couldn't resist. I didn't tell him about the guy who had the ring before Jack — I just told him about how the ring let Jack know stuff.

Goose didn't buy it. "He is such a liar."

"He is not."

"There's no way you really believe all that crap he tells you."

"He knew about the comic."

"Yeah, well, he knows the Kabos. They probably blabbed."

"They wouldn't tell."

"They might."

"Why?"

"To brag, maybe. How would I know? They aren't exactly trustworthy."

"That's dumb."

"Yeah? Well, so is stealing." Goose didn't approve of my shoplifting. Easy for him to get all high and mighty about it, he didn't need to shoplift, his stupid parents bought him whatever he wanted.

"Yeah? Well, you're just too chickenshit to do it."

Goose shook his head. "You have got to be kidding. You call me chicken and that's going to make me march on down to the store and rip off Mr. Yee?"

"Who's Mr. Yee?"

"The man who owns the store. The guy you're ripping off."

I'd never thought of shoplifting as stealing from a person. I thought of it as stealing from a store. A store with lots of stuff. I'd never heard Mr. Yee's name before. Until that very minute, I thought his name was The Chink. That's what everyone in my family called the store — The Chink's. I didn't tell Goose that; I just closed my eyes and thought, *my family is fucked*. I felt like a retard — a racist fricking retard. "Guess I never really thought about it," I mumbled. "Hey, Goose?"

"Yeah?"

"What do you call those little black candies that look like babies? The chewy ones."

Goose's eyes softened. "I call them licorice."

We let it drop.

Goose never said anything when Jack was telling one of his stories, but I knew he had his doubts. He didn't believe that Jack knew me and Prissy from a long time ago. He didn't believe Jack at all. Goose was my best friend, but he could be a real stick-in-the-mud.

The wedding party went on all night. I crawled into bed around 4:30.

Prissy tucked me in. She sat beside me on the bed, and handed me a matchbook. "Thanks for these."

"No problem."

"Keep one for me?" I took the matchbook and tucked it under my pillow. She brushed the hair out of my eyes. "I love you, Kid."

I took her hand. "I love you too, Mom. We'll be happy now."

She kissed my head. "Sleep."

When she went out, I could hear Jack's friend, Frank, and Pearl laughing. Pearl was Jack's ex-girlfriend. She had a daughter named Darla who was a few years older than me. Jack still hung out with them. He took me over to their place sometimes. Pearl was always at work. Him and Darla would disappear while I sat around listening to records.

Jack called Darla Babycakes. He called me that, once. I told him not to. He asked me why not. I told him that I didn't like nicknames. He laughed.

Prissy told me to be friendly to Darla and Pearl, so I was, but they made me feel weird. I hoped they wouldn't be around much more, now that Prissy and Jack were married.

We were a family, and we had a baby due any day.

DEE'S BABY PICTURE

My little sister, Deirdre Anne Vara, was born six days after the nuptials. Elton John's "Pinball Wizard" was number one. I was ten years old and madly in love with Vinnie Barbarino.

Jack took me down to the hospital. We snuck into Prissy's room real quiet, in case she was sleeping. She was wide-awake, holding the baby. Dee was blotchy and bald and her eyes were as blue as Jack's sapphire ring. She was the most beautiful thing I'd ever seen. I moved the blanket down a bit and she grabbed onto my finger. "Hey there, little sister. I'm Bean." She smiled. "Look! She's smiling."

"It's gas," Jack said. Prissy shushed him. "Well, that's what the nurse said."

I didn't care what anybody said. She smiled. My sister held tight to my finger and smiled at me.

"You gonna help us take care of this little gal?" Jack asked.

I beamed at him and Prissy, "Absofriggin'lutely!"

I tucked Dee's scrunch-faced baby picture in the Samsonite, right along with the wedding matchbook.

Our first year with Jack was good. Prissy quit her job at the Car Wash to stay home with Dee. Jack said we could get by on his salary; that a baby needed her mother at home, and besides, getting a sitter was stupid when Prissy could just stay home and take care of the kid. It worked OK, for a while. Prissy liked staying at home. She kept the place spic and span, wore dresses a lot and, if we had food in the house, she had supper on the table when Jack got home from work.

Prissy liked having someone else in charge of things and Jack loved being the man of the house. He'd go out on payday, buy groceries and swagger home like he was returning from the hunt. He'd buy lots of meat — like steaks and roast beef and hamburger, a bag of frozen vegetables, a sack of potatoes, eggs, bread and milk. He'd buy pop and chips and he'd stop for a forty of rye and a case of beer on the way home.

The potatoes lasted the longest.

The rest of the food always ran out before Jack's next payday. Drove me crazy. It isn't exactly rocket-science to buy food for a month: Mac and cheese, lots of pasta, big cans of tomatoes and a bag of onions to make your own sauce, hamburger and pork chops (if they're on sale), baloney (sliced thin), a sack of spuds, a bag of apples and a big thing of Kraft slices, maybe some carrots or cans of veggies that are on sale. You get the bread from the MacGavin's Day-Old Store and keep it in the freezer. You don't buy freaking steak — that's for sure. Maybe a chicken, if you're celebrating something. We had roast beef over at GT's. We didn't buy it. I hated running out of food.

I started shoplifting baby food for Dee. I kept it stashed in our bedroom for emergencies. I made her eat a lot of vegetables.

We ran out of food *and* money every month. There were always diapers to buy, and formula, and smokes and booze. Jack was still *generous to a fault*; bringing home presents for everyone for no reason. Nice idea, but his cheques disappeared fast and they only came once a month. It wasn't quite as bad as the times me and Prissy had been on Welfare, but it made things tense. Prissy borrowed money from Auntie or Spuddy and then tried to get it off Jack on payday to pay them back. They started fighting.

The money Prissy borrowed was always for baby stuff, or food or smokes, but Jack said she was using the money to play bingo. Prissy still went to bingo once in a while, but it was always Spuddy's treat. Bingo with Spuddy was the only time Prissy got to go out. She needed it. She was going stir-crazy trapped in the house all the time.

When Prissy went out, I stayed out of Jack's way, and watched my sister. I was a good sitter.

Hospital bracelet: Deirdre Vara

Dee was sick a lot. When she was about seven months old, she got the Whooping Cough. One night, Prissy went to bingo. Jack was supposed to stay home with us, but he took off to his pal Frank's place. They had some deal in the works. I gave Dee her medicine, put her to bed, and called up the Kabos. I didn't hang out with them much anymore, but I felt like company and Goose couldn't come over on a school night.

We were watching TV. Sal was bored. He said that Jack and Frank were running dope. I said they were not. He said I didn't even know what dope was. I said I did too. He said, "Prove it." I was digging around looking for Jack's pot stash, when Dee started having a coughing fit.

I picked her up and walked her around the kitchen, bouncing her a little and patting her back. Her cough sounded bad. I rubbed her head with my cheek. She went silent. She wasn't breathing.

Before I could even think, Sal grabbed her and said, "Call the ambulance." I was on the phone when he slid Dee across the floor. She slid slow — a curling rock in a blue sleeper. When she hit the wall, she gasped and started to cry. She was breathing again.

Prissy pulled up in a cab just as they were putting Dee in the ambulance. I went mental. I started screaming at her that Dee had almost died and that she would have too if Sal hadn't been there. I kept screaming, "I'm ten for fuck sakes! She's sick! She coulda died!" I'd never screamed at Prissy before. I'd never said that I was afraid to watch Dee when she was sick. I wasn't afraid. I just did it, like I did every thing else. Until that night, I thought ten was old enough to do just about anything.

We went to the hospital, and Dee got put in an oxygen tent.

A social worker came. The ambulance guys heard me screaming at Prissy and filed a report. Stupid bastards.

The worker wanted to talk to me alone, so she took me down to the chapel. "How are you feeling?" she asked. She was young and shiny and out to save the world.

"I'm fine."

"That must have been pretty scary."

I nodded and kept eye contact. People think you're telling the truth if you look them in the eye while you lie. "It was scary, but Sal is a really good babysitter. He's smart. He knows just what to do in an emergency."

"Sal?"

"He's our babysitter. My mother and father are usually at home with us but if we need a sitter, we get Sal. We had him tonight because my father had to out to help a friend whose car broke down, and Mom wasn't home yet."

"I see. I understood that your parents had left you in charge of watching your sister."

"No Ma'am. I'm only ten. My mother says I can't stay home alone with the baby until I'm at least thirteen."

"And how old is this Sal?"

"Oh, he's almost fourteen. He's in grade eight. Next year he goes to high school. He's very responsible."

"And what time did your father go out?"

"Around quarter to nine, I think. His friend Frank called just after eight. Me and dad were watching *Barney Miller*. I told him I could watch Dee — she was asleep and Mom would be home soon — but he said *no way*. He called Sal. His sister Candy came too. Me and Candy are friends from school. We're in the same class. We did a science project together last year on the life cycle of mice. We had — "

She interrupted me, "What happened after your father left?"

"He wasn't gone very long at all when Dee started coughing. Sal picked her up right away. He said it sounded bad and that I should call an ambulance."

"You told the paramedics that your sister stopped breathing."

"She did." *Never get caught in a lie.* "But just for a second."

"And then this . . . Sal," she checked her stupid notes, "threw her across the floor?"

"Oh no. No no." *Stupid cow.* "He slid her. Softly. And when she bumped the wall, she started to breathe again. The doctor said that Sal's quick thinking saved Dee's life."

She closed her book. "I'll need to talk to your mother and father."

"Of course." I took her hand to walk back to the room. I could tell she wasn't quite buying it.

"You call your mother Prissy."

"What?"

"The paramedics said they thought you were just a neighbour kid at first because you were calling your mother Prissy."

I shrugged. "Must've been the shock."

When we got back to Dee's room, Jack was there. Luckily, he didn't reek too much of booze or dope or whatever the hell him and Frank had been up to. The worker went straight for him with her hand out. "Hello Mr. Vara. I'm Sylvie Draper from the Department of Social Services."

I whipped past her and threw myself around Jack's neck. "Oh Daddy, Daddy, I'm so glad you're here! It was awful. I was scared but Sal did real good. You're right, he is the best babysitter. He saved Dee's life."

Jack held on to me and played along. "It's OK, Baby. It's OK now. Dee is going to be fine."

I smiled up at him like he was my knight in shining armor. "Did you get Uncle Frank's car fixed?"

He chuckled and wiped my tears away with his thumb. "Sure did, Honey." He gave me a big hug. "There's my brave girl. Your mom says you phoned the ambulance."

"I did. Sal was holding Dee and she was coughing and coughing and he said — "

Draper cut in, "I'd like to ask you a few questions, Mr. Vara."

He stood up. "Sure thing." I tucked right in beside him, and he kept his arm around me.

"What time did you leave the house?"

"Around nine, I think. I don't remember exactly."

"And who was in charge of taking care of the children?"

"Sal Kabos."

"You often get this Sal Kabos to watch your girls?"

"Sure. He's a good kid. Responsible. Bean here is tight with his little sister."

Draper turned on Prissy. "And where were you, Mrs. Vara?"

"I was at bingo." Prissy was sitting beside the bed, watching Dee and wringing her hands. Her eyes were red from crying.

Jack cut in, "Why all the questions?"

Draper turned back to him. "I need to know who was taking care of your daughter."

"And we've told you." Jack said.

"She's a very sick little girl."

"I know," Prissy said. "I took her to the doctor. He said she'll be fine. Kids get sick. It's not my fault. It's like when Bean got — "

"Anyways," I jumped in. "We had a babysitter and Dee was doing real good today. We all thought she was getting better."

Jack backed me up. "I never would've left if I knew she was so sick."

Draper decided to give it up. She didn't believe us, but she couldn't prove anything. "All right then," she said. "I guess this was a misunderstanding."

Shit, I thought. *If she tells him I freaked on Prissy in public, I'm dead.* Jack wasn't a spanker like Ritter. He was a beater. I'd already had to stay home from school twice to avoid questions about bruises. Prissy said I just had to watch my P's and Q's. I tried, but I never really knew what was going to set him off. Finding out I'd gotten the Welfare on our asses would piss him off sure-as-hell.

Jack tensed up. "A misunderstanding by who?"

Draper glanced over at me to let me know that she was onto me, but she didn't tell Jack about me yelling at Prissy in the street, thank God. "You take care." She gave Jack a tight little smile and left. We listened to her heels click off down the hallway.

Jack looked at me. *Here it comes,* I thought. My stomach tightened. *He knows it's my fault. He knows everything.* "Good save, Kid."

I nodded, relieved. I looked at Prissy. She was staring at Dee and wringing her hands again. I wanted to say that I was sorry for what I'd said earlier. I hoped she wouldn't tell Jack. "She'll be OK, Prissy."

She nodded without looking at me.

That night, I couldn't sleep. *They almost got us,* I kept thinking. Ever since we'd left Ritter, I'd been terrified that the Welfare would come and take me away from Prissy.

It was all Mrs. Quint's fault. Mrs. Q hated my guts. She hated all the Fallwells. Prissy said it was because Mr. Quint spent so much time down at GT's. Auntie said Mrs. Q was a twisted old bitch who should mind her own business. GT just said, "Ignore her."

Goose heard Mrs. Q tell his mom that she didn't approve of Prissy raising me on her own. She said divorce was wrong and that Prissy and I should've stayed with Ritter, even if he was *nuttier than a pecan pie.* She said that Prissy had affairs with Alden and Gerard and who knew how many other men. She said, "Those Fallwell girls are all loose, no account hussies, including that mother of theirs that ran off with a traveling man."

I asked Goose what a traveling man was.

"A man who travels, I guess."

"Yeah, but what's it mean? Like a traveling salesman or something? Like the jokes?"

"I guess. Must've been a long time ago. Maybe your grandmother opened the door one day and fell in love."

"Yeah, right."

"Maybe he was like a gypsy man or a pirate and he *seduced* her — like in a movie. Maybe he just took her hand and she followed. Just up and left everything for his flashing gypsy eyes." Goose waggled his eyebrows.

"That's stupid."

Goose shrugged. "I think it's romantic."

"I think it's . . . rude. What kind of person just up and leaves her own kids."

"Yeah. That is rude," he said. "You'd have to have a real good reason."

"No such thing." I said. "You don't leave your family. Prissy left Ritter, but she didn't leave me. She wouldn't. Ever. Stupid old Q-bag is just jealous, that's all. She's stuck kissing stupid old stinkass Q-ball with the halitosis!" That was mean. I liked Mr. Quint. His breath was pretty rank, though. "I hate that woman."

"She told my mom that you're going to drag me down the *path to perdition*."

"What the hell is that?"

"Dunno, but it sounds fun." Goose could always make me smile.

Mrs. Quint caught me once, hiding out in her corn patch, waiting for the Petersons to get home from church. The Quints had the best garden on the block. They had a whole empty lot between their place and the tracks. I liked to sit out in the corn, where I could see out but nobody could see in. I'd lie on my back, between the rows, watch the sky and listen to the wind.

That crazy old lady must've been watching me all morning from her upstairs bedroom window. I fell asleep, and she snuck up on me. Scared the bejezus out of me. She stuck her face right up to mine and talked low, like a snake, all sss's and spit. "You should leave Gussstave alone. You're a bad influencccce, you are. I sssee you. I ssssee what you do. You're a little trashy trouble maker and you'll end up the ssssame way your tramp of a mother did. Slutsss is whatssss." She was a horror, like Gollum in the *Lord of the Rings*.

I twisted hard, broke away from her, and ran like hell.

"I should call the Welfare on you! Don't think I won't. They'll take you away Brat Ebertssss — and you'll never ssssseeee Prissssssy again."

I turned at the end of the row, "My name is Bean E. Fallwell you old cow — and if the Welfare should come and take anyone away it's you, ya crazy broad! You ever call my mother a tramp again and I'll — "

"You'll what — you little trashy trash?" She was heading down the row as fast as her wrinkled legs could carry her.

"I'll snatch your wig off and let you run bald-headed through the streets!" Her hand went to her hair. She did wear a wig, but she wasn't completely bald under it. She had these freaky little hair tufts all over her head. Goose and I saw her once, through the Quint's upstairs window, dusting off all these glass figurines without her wig on. It was creepy. We never looked in the Quint's windows again.

She stood in the corn patch holding her hair on.

I hightailed it home.

Later that day, I asked GT if the Welfare could come and take me away. He asked where I'd gotten such a *blamefool* idea. I told him, and he marched right over to the Quint's and rang the bell. He took off his hat when she came to the door. I watched from behind the Peterson's fence. I rubbed my arms where her claws had cut into me.

Mrs. Quint was surprised to see him. "Why Thomas Fallwell!" she said.

"Afternoon, Gert."

She glared at him with a squinchy look on her face — like he was polluting her steps by just standing on them.

GT held his hat in his hands. "I came here to say a simple thing. Leave my grand-daughter alone."

Her hands fluttered up to her chicken neck. "Why I never . . . "

"You and I have had our differences in the past, Gert, but it has nothin' to do with that little girl, and if I hear that you're tellin' her any more horror stories about the Goddamn Welfare coming to get her . . . Well, Gert, I am just liable to come over here and put my boot right up your arse." He put on his hat and walked down the steps. She just stared after him, speechless, for once. At the bottom of the steps, he turned and tipped his hat to her. "Have a nice afternoon, Mrs. Quint." Then he winked right at her. I thought she'd die where she stood.

GT was the best.

I didn't have much trouble with Mrs. Q after that, but I never forgot her threats about calling the Welfare on us. I'd heard stories from kids at school. Kids got taken away by the Welfare all the time. They had to go and live in *foster homes*, where they got beat all the time, and had to wear ugly clothes, and hardly even got fed. There was no way I was going get taken away by a Social Worker — no matter what. I didn't want go to any foster home, and nobody was separating me from Prissy — or from my sister. They needed me.

Yelling at Prissy in the street was stupid. I'd interrupted her later, in the hospital, because I thought she was going to start blabbing to Draper about how I was sick a lot too when I was a kid. That's all we needed. They'd think it was her fault. It wasn't. I had Pneumonia a bunch of times when I was a kid, and now my sister had the Whooping Cough — so what? It wasn't Prissy's fault, but the stupid Welfare would think it was. Prissy was a great mom, the best, and nobody was taking me or Dee anywhere long as I had anything to say about it.

That night in bed, I prayed. I hadn't been going to church much, but I still talked with God a lot. I said *Thanks* every morning. Our lives were pretty good. We had a place to live, enough food most of the time, and we were together — which was the most important thing. I didn't ask God for stuff. I knew he wasn't a shopping centre. But that night, I needed a favour.

I flooped on to my stomach and pulled my knees up. "Hey, God — Bean here. Thanks for today, even if it was a tough one. I guess you know that Dee is in the hospital. Please watch over her. Keep her safe and bring her back to us."

I crunched up into a tighter ball. "I guess you also know I threw a hissy at Prissy tonight. I'm sorry. Please don't let them take us. I promise I'll try harder to control my temper — just please, please, don't let them take us away.

Thanks. And thanks for making sure Sal knew what to do tonight. I know you're always there, watching out for us.

Bless Dee-dee and Prissy and Jack, Goose and his mom and dad, Auntie, GT, Spuddy and Slim. And especially bless the Kabos. Help us all to sleep well tonight and wake up to a glorious day tomorrow. Amen."

I flipped onto my back and stared at the ceiling. I hoped Dee wasn't afraid, all alone in the hospital. "We'll be OK, Little Dee," I whispered. "I won't let anyone separate us. Ever. I promise."

I covered up my head and tried to sleep.

Ouija Instruction

After the Welfare scare, Jack moved us out of the city. He said we'd be better on our own. Away from everyone.

We moved to a little town in the valley. It had a gas station, a café and a lot of empty houses. There was a potter living in the old school house, and a bunch of hippies camped out in the church. We lived in a little purple house, kitty-corner from the café. I took the bus to school in another town.

I had two friends in that town: Sawyer, a black lab that I met my first day in town, and Star, a hippy chick who worked at the café. Sawyer could jump about six feet straight up into the air to fetch a stick. Star was a waitress and worked the potato peeler machine out back of the Homestead Café.

The potato machine looked like a little cement mixer. Star filled the barrel shaped tumbler with red-skinned potatoes and flipped a switch. It started rolling. She ran water through it and it drained out the bottom with bits of potato skin. When she was done, she tilted the tumbler and the naked white potatoes rolled out into an enamel basin that she carried back inside.

I snuck over one day, and stuck my hand in to feel the inside of the tumbler wall. It was rough, like sandpaper.

"Take your hand right off if you're not careful." Star was leaning against the doorframe. She had thick red braids and freckles. She wore a flowered dress and big brown boots. "Wanna try it?"

"Sure."

· "Hold the hose." She flipped the switch. The tumbler rolled and I washed away all the peelings.

"Cool."

Star had a pretty smile. She taught me how to use the peeler machine and the fry cutter and gave me my first waitressing job. I worked Saturdays. I was an excellent waitress. Star let me carry out the food and I hardly ever spilled. We had a great time working together. "Take your fun where you find it," she always said.

Prissy wasn't having much fun. She mostly stayed at home with the baby. When Jack went into the city, we played crib, like in the old days. I won a lot. Prissy seemed distracted. She was sad. She missed Auntie and GT and Spuddy and Slim. I invited Star over once, for tea, but her and Prissy didn't really hit it off. Prissy didn't even want me around. She kept telling me to *go the hell outside and play*.

I spent a lot of time running around the hills with Sawyer. Our favourite thing to do was climb the cut hill over by the old highway. It was hard. They'd cut a hill in half to put in the highway. It was steep — all loose dirt and cacti. Some days, it took us an hour to climb up. You could walk up the side, easy, but that wasn't any fun.

Once we got to the top of the hill, we'd hike over to the graveyard. It was old and abandoned. I tended the graves. I swept the snow off, pulled up the dead weeds, and imagined the lives of the people buried there. I figured most of them had spent their whole lives living in and around that little town. I couldn't imagine that. We still moved every few months. I wondered what it would be like to hold still — to be born and raised and buried on the same patch of earth.

I liked graveyards, but I didn't want to get buried. I wanted to be burnt. I told Prissy it was because I had a deadly fear of being buried alive –- even though Goose said that was impossible nowadays, because of *embalming*. The real reason was that I just couldn't imagine staying in one place forever. Burnt and scattered. That's more my style. And if someone wants to visit my place of rest, or tend my grave — let them tend the wind. Let them stand on the prairie and let the wind tend them.

There were lots of children's graves on the hill: babies who didn't make it, or kids who weren't here very long. One day, I found a grave for a two-month old baby that had died right on my birthday. There was a little lamb on her headstone.

I told Prissy. She said, "People die every day. There's probably a million people who died on your birthday."

"Yeah. But I never found their graves."

She wouldn't even walk up to the graveyard with me to look. "The baby's sick," she said. "I can't take her traipsing through the hills. It's cold out there." Dee didn't have the Whooping Cough anymore, but Prissy fussed over her every time she got a sniffle.

I went over to the café and told Star about the grave. She patted me and made me a vanilla shake. "What was her name?"

"Gloria," I said. "Gloria Arella."

There was an old guy sitting down at the end of the counter. He snorted.

Star winked at me and poured the guy a refill. "You know the Arellas, Hank?"

"Sure as hell did. That little gal just went on home."

I slid onto the stool beside him. "Went home? What's that mean?"

"That little girl just refused to be part of that fambly if you're askin' me," he said and spit into his tin. The old timers who came into the café had little tins they carried around to spit their snuff in. Made me gag. "She got herself born, took a look around and decided to head back to where she came from. Good thing too. Ain't one of those Arellas ever came to any good."

"But . . . "

"But what?"

"You can't just decide to die."

"Why not?" He spit in his tin again.

"Well, you can *suicide*, but you can't just die."

"Why not?"

"That's crazy. You can't just die if you don't like your family. Nobody gets to pick their family."

"Course y'pick your fambly," the old guy snorted. "We all know that!"

I looked at Star. She shrugged. He spit one more time and then tucked in to his liver and onions. That was the end of the conversation.

I sipped my milkshake. Most kids think they're adopted at some point, or that a roving band of Gypsies switched them at birth into a family where they don't quite belong. I sure as hell thought that about my family sometimes. Only trouble is,

I look exactly like Prissy Fallwell. There's no mistaking that my family is my own.

Prissy didn't like me hanging out with Star. It was OK for me to help out at the café on Saturdays, but I wasn't supposed to hang around at the church. There were six people living there, and a whole bunch that came and went from the city. Star and her boyfriend Mick were the friendliest. The others were either cranky or stoned.

I figured they were just bored. They never did anything. Star worked at the café and sewed clothes for everyone. Mick was always banging around the church, fixing something. The other hippies just laid around all day, listening to music.

"They smell," Prissy said.

I defended them. "Their water's broke. Mick's fixing it."

"I just don't want you hanging out over there."

Jack was bouncing Dee on his knee. "Them hippy chicks don't wear no underwear." He was always saying stuff like that. Dirty stuff.

"You'd know," Prissy said. She said it real low, so he wouldn't hear her.

Jack hung out at the church sometimes. He sold the hippies dope. I saw him do it once. He didn't know I was there. He swung in the front door shouting, "Special delivery!" and plopped a bag of weed and something wrapped in tinfoil on the table. One of the girls started kissing him.

"You better split," Star said.

I climbed out the back window and went home.

I saw Jack try to kiss Star once. She laughed — not mean, but like he was only joking. Jack didn't like Star much after that.

Prissy said I should find a friend my own age — someone from school.

"What's the point?" I said. "We'll just move again." I was sick of making friends. I was sick of changing schools so much. "I miss Goose."

"I know," Prissy said.

"Can he come out for the weekend?"

"If his mom will let him." Goose hadn't stayed over since Prissy married Jack.

Jack grunted. He was sitting at the kitchen table, with Dee on his knee, dividing a big bag of pot up into little bags. "That kid is weird."

"Jack."

"Well, he is."

"He's her best friend."

"Boyfriend."

I hated it when he said that. "He's not my — "

Prissy jumped in, "He's not her boyfriend. They're ten."

"Exactly. He's a guy. She's a girl. Why can't she find a friend here?"

"I'm sick of finding friends."

"Bean." Prissy warned me to cool it. Wouldn't do me any good to piss off Jack.

A few weeks later, Goose came for the weekend. I'd lobbied Prissy and Jack, cleaned the house, stayed away from the church, played with Dee and gotten all A's on my January report card. Goose promised his mother that he would call her twice a day, collect.

I took Goose over to the church to meet Star. Sawyer came with us. Star shook Goose's hand. "Great to meet you, Goose. Bean's told me a lot about you."

"Is Star your real name?" he asked.

"No." She scratched Sawyer's head. "Sarah, actually."

"That's a pretty name."

"It is."

"Nice to meet you, Sarah Star."

"You guys headed into the hills?"

"Bean's taking me up to the graveyard. We're going to commune with the spirits." Goose had found a Ouija Board at a garage sale.

"And we'll have a picnic," I said. "I made sandwiches."

Star reached into her skirt pocket and pulled out a square wrapped in waxed paper. "A treat."

I smelled it. "Halvah."

"What's that?" Goose asked.

"Tasty," said Star. "Have fun. And stay cozy." We had a lot of snow, but the day was warm.

We climbed up Cut Hill and headed for the graveyard. I showed Gloria Arella's grave to Goose, and told him what the old man had said about her deciding to die. "You think that's true? That we choose our families?"

He thought a bit. "I don't know." He pushed his glasses up. "If we did, why would anyone ever choose a crappy one?"

Made sense to me. "Star says the church gang is her family now."

"What's wrong with her real family?"

I shrugged. Star never talked about her family.

We spread out our tarp beside Gloria's grave, and pulled out the Ouija Board. Goose tossed me the lid with the instructions on it. I always like to read the instructions for things. He cleaned off the board with a silk handkerchief while I read.

"You think we qualify as a lady and a gentleman?" I asked.

"Close enough." He checked the legs on the little table. "Think you can avoid frivolity?"

"Cross my heart and hope to die."

"Funny. Let's do it." Goose lit a candle, and we sat cross-legged with the board on our knees. We stared into each other's eyes, took our mittens off, took four deep breaths and laid our fingertips on the table. Sawyer lay beside the blanket with his head on his paws.

The table started moving around right away. Then it stopped.

I thought Goose was moving it, but I played along. "Is there anyone there?" The table slid in a circle. It landed on YES. I gave Goose a smirk.

1st — Place the board upon the knees of two persons, lady and gentleman preferred, with the small table upon the board. Place the fingers lightly but firmly, without pressure, upon the table so as to allow it to move easily and freely. In from one to five minutes the tablet will commence to move, at first slowly, then faster, and will be then able to talk or answer questions, which it will do rapidly by touching the printed words or the letters necessary to form words and sentences with the foreleg or pointer.

2nd — Care should be taken that one person only should ask questions at a time, so as to avoid confusion, and the questions should be put plainly and accurately.

3rd — To obtain the best results it is important that the persons present should concentrate their minds upon the matter in question and avoid other topics. Have no one at the table who will not sit seriously and respectfully. If you use it in a frivolous spirit, asking ridiculous questions, laughing over it, you naturally get undeveloped influences around you.

4th — The Ouija is a great mystery, and we do not claim to give exact directions for its management, neither do we claim that at all times and under all circumstances it will work equally well. But we do claim and guarantee that with reasonable patience and judgment it will more than satisfy your greatest expectation.

5th — In putting the table together wet the tops of the legs, and drive them firmly into the table. Care should be taken that they are firm and tight.

6th — The board should be kept smooth and free from dust and moisture, as all depends upon the ease with which the feet of the table can glide over the surface of the board. Rubbing with a dry silk handkerchief just before use is advised.

WM. FULD
INVENTOR AND MANUFACTURER
GAMES — PARLOR POOL TABLES — COLLAPSIBLE KITES
THE MYSTIFYING "ORACLE" TALKING BOARD, Etc
Factory and Show Rooms, 1226-1228-1306 N. Central Avenue
BALTIMORE, MD., U.S.A.

He shook his head and mouthed, "Not me." Sawyer started to whine.

"Who are you?" I asked. The table slid to NO.

Goose tried, "Are you Evil or Good?"

The table slid to G. It paused and then kept moving. O – O – D.

I whispered, "Well, of course it would say that. It's not about to tell us that it's some evil spirit."

Sawyer barked. He started wagging his tail.

Goose looked at the dog and then at me.

"Go ahead," I said. "Ask it something."

"Will you talk with us?"

YES.

"Do you know us?"

The table moved in small circles and then stopped.

"What's that?" Goose whispered.

I shrugged. "Maybe?" The table slid straight to YES. "Who am I?" I asked.

B – F

"Hey, I'm the asker," Goose whispered. "How old is B.F.?"

1 – 0

I stuck out my tongue and waggled my head. "Bor-ring" I mouthed.

"How old will B.F. be when she dies?"

1 – 6

"Nice!" I made a face at Goose and intoned, "And how will I die?" The table started to spin.

"How will B.F. die?" Goose said.

B – L – U – E

"Blue?" I whispered. "I'm gonna die by blue? What? I'm gonna get struck by a serious case of the blues? The sky is gonna fall on me?"

Goose hissed at me. The pointer was still moving.

S – T – O – N – E

Goose looked really serious. "Blue stone?"

The table slid. YES.

"What the hell does that mean?" I whispered at Goose.

He closed his eyes. "Ouija, we do not understand. Can you tell us more?" The table moved in small circles. "Ouija, we must know. How will Bean E. Fallwell die?"

G – M

"Helpful," I whispered. "My turn. Ouija board Ouija board, let me know — when will Goosey go man go?" The table just sat there. I tried to push it. I was going to make it say that Goose would die even sooner than me — at fourteen or something — but the table wouldn't move.

"Stop it Bean. This isn't funny." He stared hard at the board. The pointer moved to YES and then to NO.

Sawyer jumped up and started barking.

Goose ripped his hands off of the Ouija and flipped it over. He was shaking.

"Chill, man," I said. "It's just a dumb game."

He held out his hand. "Matches."

I passed him my Zippo.

"Where'd you get this? Never mind." I used to carry matches around, but I'd lifted the lighter from the Bay a few months earlier. Goose looked around and then he went to the path leading out of the graveyard and started to dig a hole.

"What the hell are you doing?" He didn't answer so I started packing up the Ouija.

"Hey, Mutt," he called, "C'mere." Sawyer went to him and started digging too.

"What are you doing? The ground is frozen."

Goose kept digging. "Not totally." They dug a bit of a dimple. "Gimme that," he said. "And get some sticks."

"What are you doing?"

"We're burning the damned thing — that's what."

"Don't be crazy. It's just a dumb game."

He looked at me. "It isn't."

I gave him the Ouija. He ripped the board in half while I gathered twigs. I built a fire with strips of cardboard from the box and the twigs. I pocketed instruction number four:

> The Ouija is a great mystery, and we do not claim to give exact directions for its management, neither do we claim that at all times and under all circumstances it will work equally well. But we do claim and guarantee that with reasonable patience and judgment it will more than satisfy your greatest expectation.

Goose lit the cardboard. Once the kindling caught, he laid the board on top of the flame. It burned purple. He threw the little table on. It melted and burned black.

"That's toxic," I said.

He nodded and watched it melt. He poked at it until it smouldered. We buried it all under a mound of snow.

Goose was pale and his mouth was a tight little scrunch.

"Hey, kid," I said, "Wanna sammich?"

He looked at me and laughed. "Sure."

We ate bologna sandwiches and the halvah Star had given us. I gave Sawyer a drink of Tang in the thermos lid. He lapped it up.

"Hey, Bean," Goose said.

"Yeah?"

"I love you, y'know."

I screwed the lid back on the thermos, and stood up. I leaned down to him. "I love you too," I said and pushed him over. "Ya crazy fuck!" I ran like hell and he came slip sliding after me. Goose never could catch me. I'm fast.

SAWYER'S DOGTAG AND STAR'S EARRING

Sawyer died on Ground Hog day. I found him out near Cut Hill. He'd been hit by a car. He wasn't all messed up — just cold and dead. He had a bit of dried blood coming out of one ear and some pink foam around his muzzle.

I sat with him awhile.

I heard boots crunching through the snow. "Shit."

I looked up. It was Mick, Star's boyfriend.

"He's dead," I said.

Mick crouched down, took off his glove and put his hand on Sawyer's side. "Poor old bugger."

We sat awhile and then Mick went and got Star and Gary, the potter. Sawyer was Gary's dog. I never really thought of Sawyer belonging to anyone. We wrapped him in a red blanket and carried him home.

We buried him that night, in Gary's garden. Gary thawed the ground with a blowtorch and dug a grave. Mick built a coffin. Me and Star gathered wood and lit a big bonfire. The hippies all came — decked out in their finery. Prissy, Dee and Jack came. I called Goose, but his mom wouldn't drive him out. There was a storm warning.

We stood in a circle around the grave and everyone told stories about Sawyer. Gary told about how he found Sawyer when he was just a scrawny little pup. Someone abandoned him up at the gas station. He followed Gary home and stayed. Mick told about how Sawyer would carry tools to him — even up on the church roof. "Never knew a dog that could climb a ladder." We laughed. Sawyer did love to help out.

"I just met Sawyer," I said. "He was the best stick catcher I ever knew. He was my friend."

Star stared into the fire. "Tonight is Imbolc, the Festival of St. Brighid, a cross-quarter day in the wheel of the year. We light fires on this night to call back the light. We call on Brighid to guide our friend, Sawyer, to the Summerland." She tossed something on the fire and it flamed up — sparks dancing against the night.

Gary gave me Sawyer's tag to keep. He said Sawyer had perked up a lot since I came to town. Sawyer was a lot older than I'd thought. He'd been with Gary for over ten years.

I went over the school steps to sit by myself for a while. Star followed me. Her hair was out of the braids. It was long and curly and clean. She smelled like incense. She sat beside me. I was rubbing Sawyer's name on the tag. "Will you put that in your suitcase?"

I'd told her about my Samsonite and some of the things I kept in there. I told Star lots of stuff. I didn't tell her about what the Ouija said that day in the graveyard, though. I didn't tell anybody. I had just tucked the strip of cardboard in the side pocket of my suitcase. Number four. It was a warning. "Yeah." I tucked Sawyers dogtag in my pocket. "I'll keep this."

"To remember what?"

"Today, I guess."

"Know what I think?"

"No."

"I think you should remember Sawyer's life instead. We carry our hurts with us in our bodies, whether we want to or not. Mark the bright things, Bean." She took out one of her turquoise earrings and gave it to me. "Remember me too."

"You're leaving."

"Yeah. Mick and I are heading out to the coast."

"We're leaving too." *Like always.*

"I heard. Jack got a new job, right?"

"Yeah." We stared out across the yard.

Gary was sitting with Jack, Prissy and Dee near the fire. Gary and Jack were sharing a bottle of rye. Prissy and Dee were staring at the fire. Dee could almost walk already. She was growing fast. Mick played guitar and sang "Mr. Bojangles". The hippy girls danced. Swirling. Shining like magpies against the snow.

It was my first funeral.

PICTURE: JACK AND THE KILLER PICKEREL

When we left the valley, we made the rounds of small town Saskatchewan. We lived in: Wakaw, Makwa, Melville and Ogema, Woodrow, Lockwood, Rocanville and Yarbo, Preeceville, Holdfast, Saltcoats and Kelvington. And so on. We never stayed anywhere too long. I tried to follow Star's advice and gathered the bright things.

Moving was OK. I kept my Samsonite packed and pretended we were a roving band of gypsies. I still liked moving into new houses. New town, new start, new stories to tell. You can be whatever you want in a new town — especially if you know you aren't staying too long. I slipped into whatever void there was in a new school. I didn't do it consciously or anything; it just happened.

Sometimes, I was a Jock. If the school had a weak team, I'd become the star player — didn't matter what game: softball in Melville, volleyball in Pense, soccer in Nokomis. Whatever.

In Ogema, I was the long-jump and triple queen. We went to a tri-town Sports Day, down the road, and I told my coach that they had to move the boards back. "I'm gonna jump the pit."

He talked to the officials, but they just laughed. Said there was no way some scrawny kid in grade six was going to jump the pit.

I cleared the pit on my first jump. Landed on the grass, slid like gooseshit, and bashed the hell out of my head when I landed. They moved the board back.

If the new school was athletic, I became an Artsy. I could dance, sing a song, play a flute — do anything I tried.

Mostly, I lied. Stupid little lies to back up my newest persona, or big crazy stories about where we came from and why we'd moved to town. Usually something tragic. I kept Prissy posted. "Your father was a Russian Count and he died in a plane crash and we lost all the money to your evil mother who ran away with a German basket salesman."

"Uh huh. Is that a German man who sells baskets or a man who sells German baskets?" Prissy always played along. My silly stories never hurt anybody.

Jack just laughed. He was the King of Liars. My personal favourite being, *It'll be different here. It'll be better. We'll stay.* Never was and we never did. He found some new job: fixing cars, driving truck, selling Watkins, selling watches, selling Kirby Christly vacuum cleaners, and we were off to a new town.

The towns blurred together. A main street with a hotel, a Post Office and a Co-op, some shit-assed house with an ugly plastic bathtub. Jack wasn't the best house picker.

I wrote to Goose a lot. I'd always find someone to hang out with in new towns, but I never got very attached. Goose was my only real friend. I wrote him about the towns, what my new school was like, and the kids I was hanging out with. He wrote me about what he was doing, movies he'd seen and books he'd read. He always included some new fascinating fact he'd found. *Coca-Cola was originally green. Many years ago in Scotland, a new game was invented. It was ruled "Gentlemen Only. Ladies Forbidden" and thus the word GOLF entered into the English language.* His letters made me smile.

One night, when we were unpacking in a new place, Jack asked me what was in the Samsonite. He came into the room as I was sliding it under the bed. He poked the suitcase with his foot. "How come you never unpack that thing?"

"Don't need to."

"Why not?"

"I just don't need to."

"If there's nothing in there you need, what do you lug it around for?"

Dee was setting up her stuffed animals. "It's her treasures," she said.

He sat on the bed. "Lemme see."

I hefted the case up beside him and snapped it open.

Dee crawled into his lap. She was always trying to get into the suitcase. I kept it locked. I wore the key around my neck. She reached in and pulled up a stack of pictures. "That's me!" Her baby picture.

"We should frame that," Jack said.

"Sure. I just didn't want it to get lost in the shuffle."

"Pickerel!" Dee squealed. She was holding a picture of Jack with a huge fish.

Prissy was in the doorway. "That the Nosoy-Nopoy Killer?" We all laughed.

Nosoy-Nopoy Beach had been one of my favourite places. We lived out in the middle of nowhere in an Airstream Trailer. It was cool, as trailers went. I didn't even mind that there was no bathtub. It was nice living by ourselves, out at the Beach. Jack was calmer out there. He said there was less stress. Prissy and Dee went swimming sometimes. I watched. I hadn't swum in a lake since me and Goose went to see *Jaws*. I knew there couldn't be sharks in a Saskatchewan lake, but I wasn't taking any chances.

We lived at Nosoy-Nopoy because Jack was in charge of a fish farm. There was a big fish corral where the fish grew fat on the stuff we fed to them. Jack said they went to Chinese restaurants and fish and chip joints. Wasn't any cod or halibut in there; mostly carp and buffalo fish. We ate the Jackfish that snuck in.

On round-up day, Jack gave me pair of hip waders. I was supposed to walk slowly through the water in the big corral and help him herd the fish towards this gate thing that led to a smaller corral. The next day, the fish would be scooped up in a big net when the guys came for the slaughter. I wasn't looking forward to the slaughter, but the herding was actually sort of fun. Prissy was helping too. We were doing great, until this fish turned on me. A pickerel. It came at me with its mouth wide open and I could see all its pointy little teeth. I ran for it.

Jack started yelling, "What the hell are you doing? What the hell's going on?"

It's hard to run in hip waders. I fell over and the waders filled up with freezing cold water.

Dee was on the beach, laughing and clapping.

Prissy came slopping over to see if I was OK.

I coughed lake water. "It was after me!"

"What?"

"A huge pickerel was after me." As soon as I said it, I knew I was in trouble. *Who runs from a pickerel?*

I turned to look at Jack — expecting an explosion.

"A pickerel?" He says, and he starts to laugh. He starts to laugh — not the fake, punch you anyway, laugh — but a real honest to God belly laugh. "A fucking pickerel!" Then he gets a wild look in his eye. "Let's get him!" He starts wading through the corral, looking for the fish. He looks up at us and smiles. He smiles the sweet storytelling, fun lovin', Guitar Man smile that we hardly ever see anymore. "C'mon kid!" He waves Dee into the water and the chase is on.

The four of us laugh and splash and flounder around in the water, searching for that pickerel.

I find it over in the northeast corner. "Over here. I got him! I got him!"

Jack runs over in slow motion. "Hold 'im, Bean!"

"I got him cornered."

Dee laughs and claps.

Jack dives in and comes up with that girl-eating pickerel right in his hands.

We barbequed him. I brought Jack a beer while he was basting the fish with butter. I asked him how his hand was.

"Just a nick." The pickerel's fin sliced his hand open when he grabbed it.

"Bled a lot."

"Blood's good. Cleans the wound." He reached into the air and caught a shimmery blue dragonfly.

"Don't hurt him," I said.

"I won't." He held the dragonfly cupped in his hands. "They eat mosquitoes, y'know."

"Yeah?"

"Yeah. You can tie a thread to a dragonfly's leg and loop it around your ear and he'll be your own private mosquito catcher."

"No way."

"Way. I seen my old man do it a million times." He smiled, and let the dragonfly go.

That was the only good story I ever heard about Jack's dad. Mostly we heard about how tough he was — how he never took shit from no one. Sometimes, when Jack was drunk and sad instead of drunk and mad, he told us awful stories about how his dad used to beat him.

I wrote Goose about the Dragonfly, and my near death experience with the Nosoy-Nopoy Killer.

The pickerel day was a good day.

The bad days mostly had to do with Jack's temper. We never really knew when trouble was coming. Even the worst days could start out good. We'd be laughing and happy and, suddenly, Jack's eyes would go cold and my stomach would tighten up.

We also had a little trouble with teenaged girls. We always had a lot of people hanging around our place — especially teenagers. They all thought Prissy and Jack were the coolest parents ever. Jack pulled beer for them and sold them pot. All the girls had crushes on him. We made jokes about it. I thought it was cool that all the teenagers liked us. 'Til Nokomis.

Jack had two little "girlfriends" there. One Saturday, we were having a water fight. Everyone was running around soaking everyone else, and Becky Simpson ran upstairs and locked herself in the bathroom. Becky was cute and blonde and giggly and madly in love with Guitar Man.

Jack climbed up onto the roof with the garden hose and soaked Becky through the window. Then he climbed in and tied her to the toilet. I was outside the door picking the lock. I got it open just in time to see them kissing.

Becky was fourteen.

"Uh oh, Babycakes," Jack said. "Someone's jealous."

Becky screeched like a hyena.

I left.

His other girlfriend, in Nokomis, was a stupid doper named Dianna. She was sixteen.

It was Prissy's idea to get out of Nokomis.

It was around then, that our moves started to change. They got even faster. They turned into sudden, middle of the night, sneaks. I didn't notice the change, at first. Prissy and I had been moving since we left Ritter. We were always running toward something — some new job for Prissy, some new man — searching for something. Each place held possibility. Jack was like that too, at first. But then it shifted, and we were running away — from bad jobs and stupid towns. Jack was just one step ahead of trouble, and it became clearer and clearer that nothing ever really changed, no matter where we went.

Jack was mean. He'd always been mean, but it was like we had some kind of amnesia. Like the crazy violent things never happened. In the beginning, it was easier to believe that. The violence was sudden and horrific, but then there were long long periods of fun and laughter and . . . we forgot.

As time went on, we just got used to it. It was gradual. Started with the fights about money, which were mostly yelling. Then it was fights about Prissy going to bingo, Jack thinking she was out gallivanting with Auntie. The yelling turns into a slap, the slap turns into a punch, I get in the way trying to make him stop and *blammo* — Prissy and I are getting knocked around so often we think it's normal. The honeymoon periods of apologies and presents get shorter and shorter, and the, *I will kill you if you ever try to leave me* threats start. We walk on eggshells, trying not to set him off. Doesn't work, of course, because anything can set him off. We settle into a life lived with an ache in the belly, and a tension around the shoulders.

I started blaming Prissy — wishing she would just shut up, stay quiet. She couldn't. She'd set him off and then, after he hit her the first time, instead of just shutting the hell up, she'd say something retarded like, *Does it make you feel like a big man — hitting me?*

It does, I wanted to scream. *It does exactly that, so stop saying it!* I never said that to her, of course. I just stepped in and tried to draw his fire.

Prissy was the lippy bitch, who made his life hell. I was the little fucker who got in his way when he tried to teach Prissy a lesson. And Dee? Dee was silent — just like I taught her.

From the time she was a baby, every time a fight broke out, I tucked Dee away in our bedroom. "Stay here. Stay quiet. Be good. Be quiet and you won't get hurt." No matter how crazy a fight got, Dee never made a sound. She just watched. She watched Prissy get called down and hit. She watched me wade into the middle of it, making noise, a red flag flapping in Jack's face, drawing him away from Prissy. She watched us both get the shit kicked out of us and she never made a peep.

The violence was bad, but sometimes I think the heartbreak was worse for Prissy. She loved Jack. He was breaking her heart with all his little sweeties. She made jokes about it and laughed along with him when he told stories about *his girls*. She got lines around her eyes and smoked more.

I didn't think much about the girls, other than to be embarrassed if they were too close to my age. I stood guard against the fist, but the rest slipped by me. Jack broke Prissy's heart, and I didn't even notice.

Jack was holding the picture, smiling. "That was a good day."

I smiled back at him. "That's why I kept the picture."

Like Star said, I didn't need to mark the bad days.

Rumble Fish

When we moved to a town called Biensol, Jack swore he was going straight. He got a job at the elevator shoveling grain. He wasn't going to sell any drugs. He wasn't going to hit us ever again.

Biensol. The name bodes well, doesn't it? It was officially named by the French wife of the first man to settle there — Samuel Stigmann. Bien sol — *good soil* — a nice place to put down roots. Too bad we didn't have any.

It started out OK. Like a lot of things.

The house was the best one we ever lived in. It was big and old and clean and had a white picket fence. There was a clawfoot bathtub and Dee and I each got a room of our own.

When we first saw the tub, Prissy, Dee and I climbed right in. Jack walked by as we were all giggling in there. "Christ," he said, but he smiled. "I'm going to the Elevator."

We pulled into Biensol just after Christmas.

Once the Maverick was unloaded, and I'd stashed the Samsonite, I was ready for a recon. I checked on Dee. She was asleep in the bathtub. I covered her up with her sleeping bag. Prissy was crouched in a sunbeam unloading the kitchen box.

We still travelled light: a bag of clothes each, the velvet Elvis, a big pot, a small pot, a roaster and the electric frying pan, stuff to eat on, eat with and drink out of, the coffee pot, the chipped brown teapot, the #1 MOM mug that I gave Prissy for her twenty-first birthday, and my Samsonite, of course.

"Hey, Priss. Need help?"

"Nah. Go on."

I pulled on my parka and my red toque. I gave Prissy a kiss on the head. "Need anything?"

"Grab some hamburg for supper?"

"Sure."

"You know where the store is?"

"Gotta be on Main Street, right?"

Prissy stood up. She swayed a little and put her hand on the fridge door to steady herself. She rubbed the bruise on her side. She looked around the kitchen and smiled. "It'll be better here." She pulled over the cooler we always tossed the ketchup in, and opened the fridge. "We still got some eggs. Grab us some cokes too." She pulled the cash out of her jeans pocket.

"Y'betcha."

I stood in the yard and looked around. After dark, I would sneak out and lay my circle around the yard. Prissy used to help lay out my circle of protection. Now I did it in secret — in the dark when everyone was asleep. I had tucked my original stick, stone, feather and bone into the Samsonite during the Small Town Tour. We were moving too fast. I was afraid that I'd lose them. Now I just used whatever I could find. Maybe that's why it wasn't working so good.

I used to set up my circle inside, to keep bad people out. By Biensol, it was about keeping something in. If I could keep all the madness hidden within, if no one knew, we'd be OK. I could hold the centre, somehow, and keep Prissy, Dee and me together.

We were living a weird half-life — half real, half not — but I was losing track of which half was which. In the night, there were drugs and fists, and Jack's little girlfriends. In the daytime, we all pretended the other world didn't exist. I'd get up, wash, make my lunch and go to school — like no one knew.

They all knew. We weren't exactly touching down in New York City. This was Strasbourg, Tisdale, Armpit Scratchmybum. I heard teachers talking in the halls. "So sad, isn't it? She's so smart." *Fuck you.* I'd smile and hand in my test for another A+.

I stood outside our new place and took a look around. South to mainstreet. North to the school. I crossed the street and headed West. I stood at the edge of town and inhaled. Flatland. It felt good.

I went to check on Snapper. Jack had her boarded at a farm on the edge of town — MacGregor's place. He'd dropped her off the week before we moved. We'd had Snapper for about six months. She was the biggest thing we owned. Jack won her in a poker game. She was mostly Shetland — an old, cranky, piebald, mongrel runt of a pony — but she smelled of hay and warmth and Dee loved to ride her. It was my job to exercise Snap everyday. I loved it. She was small, but feisty. I couldn't believe I actually had a horse of my own.

I crossed the highway and trudged out to MacGregor's. The old man waved. He was working on an old John Deere combine. "No rest for the wicked!" he said as he climbed down. "You must be Bean. You're father said you'd be out."

I stuck out my hand. "Yes Sir."

We shook. "Call me Mac." He took me to the barn and showed me around. "You not in school yet?"

School. Wonder what it'll be like this time. I smiled. "Tomorrow's soon enough. We just got here. I like to take a day to look around before I . . . " *Before I what?*

He laughed. "Before you take up the yoke, eh?".

"Yeah."

"Smart." We headed over to the stall Snap was in. "Letting her get used to the place before I put her out in the pasture with the others. She's a good pony." He patted her rump. "Pleasure to meet you, Bean. You plan to come out every day?"

"Yes sir. After school, most likely."

"All righty then. You need to know where anything is, just ask."

"I will. Thank you, sir."

"Mac."

I grinned. "Thanks Mac."

He nodded and left.

Snap snorted steam at me. "Sorry, no treats today, Sugar." I scratched her between the eyes. "Not enough time for a work-out, but how about a brush, eh?" I found my pouch of horse tools on the shelf and gave Snapper a brisk brush, combed her mane and tail, and then wrapped my arms around her neck and inhaled her. "You're a beauty, you are. I'll be back tomorrow and we'll go for a run." I put my tools away, tossed some hay in the manger, smacked Snap on the butt, and headed out.

Mac was still working on his tired combine. I waved.

The way back into town took me past the school. I skirted the edge of the schoolyard. *Tomorrow's soon enough.* There was an outdoor rink at the bottom of the schoolyard. It had a warm up shed and speakers, which meant they played music. *Nice.*

Prissy got me new skates for Christmas — red figure skates, with picks and everything. They had black blade guards. They were the first new skates I ever had. I was trying to learn to spin. I wished I could take lessons, like my cousins. Dora's kids, Cassie and Jen, took all kinds of lessons: skating, dance, baton twirling. I was determined to learn how to spin — maybe even jump — by the end of winter.

I hung over the boards thinking about Christmas. It hadn't been too bad that year. We went to GT's and I got to stay up all night with the adults, putting together toys for the kids. The adults all drank, but nobody got into a fight — not even the next day when the kids were screaming and the grown ups all had hang-overs. I'd lobbied and connived and cleaned the whole house twice in order to convince Prissy and Jack to buy Dee a Barbie Camper Van. Dee squealed and squealed and Jen didn't even say, "I got one of those last year." Jen was Dora's youngest. Her and Cassie always got the best, latest, thing and usually lorded it over us. They were the rich ones in the family. Dora and Shoog both worked. They owned their own house.

I looked up at the school. A kid was looking out. *Better blow.*

The railroad tracks ran past the school. I could walk them up town, but that'd take me past the elevator and I didn't feel like seeing Jack. I *ambled* across the school ground, and took the inside route downtown.

Main Street was two blocks long — a hotel at one end and a farm implement store at the other. There was a Co-op food store, a Chinese/Canadian restaurant, a Credit Union, and a Post Office.

I grabbed a pack of buns, a pound of burger and three cokes at the Co-op. The old lady at the till smiled at me. "Shouldn't you be in school?"

"Just got here."

"Where you from?"

I flashed her my gap toothed grin. "Regina."

The lady packed the groceries into a paper sack. "You'll like it here. It's quiet."

"Thank you. I like it already, Ma'am."

The lady smiled again. Ma'am always made them smile.

I slid along the street and into the Post Office / Dry Cleaning Depot. "Afternoon, Sir." The postmaster was a grizzled old guy in a curling sweater. "I'd like one stamp please."

"Certainly."

I stood on tip-toe to look at him over the counter. "I got a little packet." I pulled a wax paper envelope out of my pocket. It had five stamps in it. I snuck money for stamps to write Goose everytime Prissy sent me to the store. She didn't notice if I bought one at a time.

He smiled. "Getting a little old isn't it?"

"Still works," I said, and slipped the stamp in. I slid the change across the counter. "Thank you. See you next time."

"Absolutely," said the postmaster as he watched me swing out the door.

I kicked my way home through the freshly fallen snow. *Nice town. Maybe it will be OK.*

Our new house looked pretty in the snow. I went in the back door and kicked the snow off my boots. Prissy was at the table, drinking tea and having a smoke. "So?"

"Pretty nice. They got a rink down by the school. I checked on Snapper. Want help with supper?"

"Sure. You can help me make the patties."

"Excellent!" The house was warm and Prissy smelled of smoke and lemons. I plunged my hands into the bowl, squeezing bread crumbs and egg goo into the burger.

Prissy smiled. "It's gonna be better here, Bean. I know it."

It wasn't better. It was worse.

Belinda Stigmann, the great great granddaughter of the town founder, had blonde rich-girl hair, wore t-shirts over top of turtlenecks, and ran the elementary school with an iron fist.

I tried the t-shirt over turtleneck thing. Felt hideous. Usually, I didn't care much about what I wore, but my overwhelming instinct, in Biensol, was to blend in. To, somehow, keep myself off of Belinda Stigmann's radar. Disappearing isn't easy when you're the new kid in small town Saskatchewan.

Belinda's best friend, Jacy, was the most beautiful girl I'd ever seen. She was Finnish and looked like a Barbie doll. She had long, straight, clover honey hair, and skin like a Cover Girl. Her eyes were grey. She was super smart. We might've been friends, if things had worked out differently.

My best friend in Biensol was Dave Stigmann, Belinda's third cousin. He was five foot nine, had lanky black, Joey Ramone, hair, and he was always in trouble. Dave and I were science partners, for a day, and our experiment blew up. We were working away, mixing chemicals in a beaker, and suddenly there was a *smack!* and the whole thing erupted in a beautiful green and purple flame. I watched the flame for a minute and then put a lid on it. It reeked. We became friends in detention.

I brought a book.

Dave was restless. He slouched in his desk, flicking an elastic. "Whatcha reading?"

"*The Crystal Cave.*"

"Boring."

"Nope."

"All books are boring."

"Not to me."

Dave clicked his teeth. "What's it about?"

"Magic."

"Like sawing people in half?"

"No." I kept reading.

"Like what?"

"Like seeing the future."

"Who'd want to?" I looked over at him. He was kind of cute.

"There's sword fights."

He flipped his hair out of his eyes. They were green. "Huh?"

"It's about the olden days in England, when people could see the future and do magic. There's this kid and he's a bastard and he — "

Dave started laughing.

I sighed. "A bastard — like he has no dad."

"That's no reason to call him a bastard."

"That's what it really means."

"Bastard?"

"Yeah. You can look it up if you don't believe me."

He leaned in. "So, what about the little bastard?"

"He meets this old hermit guy who teaches him stuff and shows him this crystal cave where he learns to see the future."

"Why?"

"I dunno yet. Hey, you like horses?"

"I guess."

"I've got a horse."

"I thought you were from the city."

"I'm from a lot of places. I have to exercise her when I get out of here. You wanna come?"

"OK."

Dave laughed when he first saw Snap. "That's a horse?"

I saddled her up and told him to get on.

"I've never ridden a *pony*."

I smiled. "Dare ya."

He climbed on. Snap ran straight for the trees and knocked him off. He looked stunned.

"It's a test," I said. "Get back on."

"You nuts?"

"C'mon."

"She's loco."

I started to laugh. "You been reading westerns? C'mon. She just does that because she's tired and lazy."

"So why ride her? Maybe she should retire — to the glue factory."

"You chicken?"

"No."

"Then get back on. And stop insulting her."

Dave got to like old Snap — even stayed on her most of the time. We started hanging out after school. We'd walk down the tracks out to Mac's place. I'd saddle up Snapper, and we'd take turns riding. We brought Dee with us sometimes. She was a good rider, hung on to Snap like a bur as we ran beside.

After we took care of Snap, Dave and I usually walked along the tracks away from town and I updated him on whatever book I was reading. He never read the books I suggested, but he liked hearing the stories. Then we'd head home for supper. After supper, I went skating.

One night, at the rink, Belinda came over while I was lacing up my skates. "So is Dave your boyfriend?"

"No."

"Right."

I kept lacing my skates. *Go away.*

"He's a punk."

"Is not."

"My dad says he's useless as tits on a bull and he's going to end up in jail like his brother." Dave's brother, Grant, was in prison for punching out an RCMP.

"He's your cousin."

"So?"

"So why's your dad saying bad stuff about your own family?"

"They're bad. That whole patch is bad."

She's the bad patch.

She reached out and touched my hair. "Why is your hair like that?" I'd been using Prissy's curlers to curl my hair at night — those black prickly ones that you held in with plastic pokers. I hated sleeping on the curlers, but I hated my hair more. I thought the curls looked nice. I liked to wear my red toque that matched my skates and have the curls fluffing out below. "You're supposed to brush it out y'know." She tugged on a curl. "You don't just take the curlers out and leave big ugly sausages all over your head."

My face got hot. I knew she was right. *Why didn't Prissy say anything? Why didn't the damned teacher say anything yesterday when I showed up for school pictures looking like a wiener head? Christ.* I smiled up at Belinda. "I like it this way."

"You do not."

"I do. It's my style." *Never flinch.* I skated off. *Stupid bitch.* Now I was going to have to keep being Sausage Head so she wouldn't know she was right. *Crap.* I tugged my toque down and did a nonchalant figure eight.

"Tell Laura I Love Her" came on over the loudspeaker. I forgot all about Belinda and slipped into my routine. I made up skating routines. Story songs were best. I imagined the whole thing — skating faster and faster and trying for a spin as I envisioned Tommy dying in the twisted wreck. I didn't usually get too into my routines when there were people around, but that night I got carried away. I hit the boards.

"What are you doing?" Belinda again.

I decided on the direct approach. "Why are you talking to me?"

"Free country."

"Where's Jacy?"

"Who cares? C'mon, I'll show you how to do a Sow Cow"

Salchow — invented by Ulrich Salchow in 1909. I could learn a jump. I followed her.

The next day, Belinda showed up at Mac's just as me and Dave were finishing up with Snapper. "Hey, Bean — wanna come over?"

I looked at Dave. He shrugged. "I gotta head'er anyhow." He walked off down the tracks.

The Stigmann's house was huge, clean, and smelled like a forest. Belinda's room was pink and white, with carpet and a canopy bed. I'd never seen a canopy bed in real life. Belinda asked if I wanted some juice.

"Sure." I plopped on the bed trying not to look impressed. The bedspread was purple and pink chenille. It felt new. I smelled like horse.

She came in and handed me a big glass full of juice.

The juice was so cold it made my head ache and it tasted like sun. "Wow, that's good." *Sure as heck ain't Tang.*

Belinda was watching me. "It's from concentrate."

"I know." *Concentrate. Concentrated Orange — that's exactly what it tastes like.* I took another sip and then set it on the dresser. "Nice room." *What am I doing here?*

She shrugged. "What should we do?"

"I dunno." She had a record player and a stack of 45's. "We could listen to music."

"You ever Put Out?"

"What?" *the hell?*

"Put Out."

I stared at her blankly.

"You take ten deep breaths and then someone squeezes you, hard as they can, and you faint." She flipped her hair. "It's cool."

"Why?"

"You ever passed out?"

"No." *Not on purpose, anyhow.*

"It's cool. C'mon. Stand over here."

I stood in front of her white dresser. *I'd rather drink the juice.*

Belinda stood behind me. "Put your arms up in the air." I did as I was told. She peeked her head around and looked at me in the mirror. I could smell her hair. VO5. *Gee, your hair smells terrific!* I did not giggle. "Trust me?"

"Sure." *Not for a second.*

She wrapped her arms around my ribs and pressed in close behind me. "Ten breaths, deep and fast as you can, and then try to hold your breath. I'm gonna squeeze you hard as I can. Hold the air 'til I squeeze it out. Don't worry about falling. I gotcha."

What am I doing this for? I started taking deep breaths. At nine, I closed my eyes. At ten, my head filled up with black and my arms flopped down. I felt a tingle all over and I slumped to the floor. I kept my eyes closed for a bit and then opened them.

"You go?"

"Don't think so. Feel weird though."

"Well, you gotta practice. Neat eh?"

"Yeah. Neat." *Neat?* "Super."

"Do me."

"OK."

She placed my arms. "Right here, so you can squeeze all the air out. And hard hard hard, OK?" She stared straight at the mirror. At ten, I squeezed her hard as I could and she slumped. When she opened her eyes she said, "Cool. High. You smoke?"

"I have."

"Wanna?"

"No."

"Why not."

Bile rose in my throat. *Because Jack caught me sneaking one of Prissy's cigarettes last year and he sat me down in front of everyone and made me smoke a cigar. I puked 'til blood came out and shat myself in the bargain.* I shrugged. "I don't really like it."

"OK."

My head ached. I drank the rest of the juice. It wasn't cold anymore, but it still had a taste that went straight to my blood and cleared my head. "I better get home."

Belinda was digging through her underwear drawer. She pulled out a pack of smokes. "Going to the rink tonight?"

"Yeah."

"I'll pick you up."

"OK." I went home.

Prissy was cooking pork chops. "Almost ready, Hon. Set the table?" Jack was home for supper, so it was quiet. Things weren't going too well at the Elevator. He probably wouldn't have the job long.

I was finishing up the dishes when the doorbell rang. "I got it." *Crap.* I wasn't ready and Belinda Stigmann sure as heck wasn't getting in our house. I never had people over. Except for Goose, of course.

She was standing on the front step. Prissy was behind me. "C'mon in. I'm Prissy — Bean's mom."

Belinda beamed her perfect tooth smile. "Hello Mrs. Fallwell."

I grabbed my coat and skates. "Let's go."

Jack growled from the couch. "Put your damned coat on."

Belinda widened her smile. "Hello Mr. — Vara." Kids always asked me why Prissy and I had a different last name than Jack. I said it was because we were liberated.

Jack was sizing up Belinda. She was blushing under his gaze. That's all I needed — for Jack to take up with the twelve-year-old town Princess. I zipped my coat. "C'mon."

"Great house," she said, as I dragged her down the steps. "Your stepdad's cute."

Jacy was at the rink when we got there. She started skating over to us and then stopped. Belinda dragged me around by the hand the whole night, laughing really loud, like we were having the best time ever. Jacy looked miserable, but she stayed. She played with the little kids — tightening their skates and playing Crack the Whip.

"Walk me home," Belinda said when we'd taken off our skates. She lit a smoke on the way. It started to snow. "Jacy's a cow."

I didn't say anything.

"Well?"

"She seems nice to me."

"Well, that's because you don't know her. Trust me — she's a grade A slant-eyed cow. I know. We used to be best friends."

Used to be. There was someone standing up near Belinda's place. I squinted. "Hey, it's Dave."

Belinda huffed.

I ignored her. "Hey, Dave."

"Hey." He had his hands tucked into his jean pockets. Dave never wore mitts. "Belinda."

"Dave." A sneer. They stared at each other a minute. Belinda blinked first. She tossed her smoke. "See ya, Bean."

"Yeah." She went in. I looked at Dave. "Whatcha doin'?"

"Hangin' out. What are you doing?"

"We were at the rink." He was looking at me funny. "What?"

"Nothin'. C'mon I'll walk you." We shuffled across town in silence, watching the snow. It was dark. The only streetlights were downtown.

"C'mon!" I yelled, and took off at a run. We slid halfway down Main Street. "C'mere. Look." We stood under the street lamp in front of the Post Office and watched the snow swirl down.

Dave's mouth was open. Snowflakes on his cheeks. "Feels like I'm moving."

"Like we're in a fast fast tunnel heading for the light. Cool, eh?"

Dave looked at me and laughed.

"What."

"You do weird stuff, Bean."

"But isn't it beautiful?"

"Yes. It is." He walked me home. At my gate he said, "Bean? Be careful."

"Belinda?"

"Yeah."

"I know."

A few days later, Belinda pulled me aside at recess. "C'mon."

"What?"

"Come on!" She dragged me to the basement of the school. To this room where there was a big concrete tank full of water. "Here." She handed me Jacy's mitts. Beautiful hand-knit mitts. *So soft.* Jacy had a hat and scarf to match. "Chuck 'em in."

"Her grandmother made these."

"Who gives a rat's ass?"

"Her Grandmother's dead."

"Chuck them in."

Why on earth would I do that? Jacy'd never done anything to me. I liked Jacy. I watched myself throw the mitts into the cistern.

Belinda smiled and led me back outside. "C'mon, let's smoke."

"I don't smoke."

"I do." She was trying to be so tough. I just followed.

The fight was three days later.

Out on the playground.

After school.

Me and Jacy in a circle of kids. "I'm not going to fight you, Jacy."

Belinda at the edge. Smoking. Smug. Acting cool, like she didn't care, but I could see a weird triumph in her eyes. *She's excited.* She'd maneuvered the whole thing and I was a dupe. By the time I figured it out, there was no way to stop it. I could walk away — we'd move soon and it wouldn't matter two shits what this gang of drooling yee-haws thought of me — but Jacy was fighting for her life. She was from here. She had to fight me or she'd be a loser for the rest of her life.

"I'm not gonna fight you, Jacy."

She kept swatting at me. Ineffectual. Like a fly buzzing. I wondered if she'd ever been in a fight before. *Probably not. She's too perfect: straight little Chicklet teeth, perfect line of a nose with an irresistible upturn, ash and honey hair, poreless skin. Perfect.* I lowered my hands, refusing to even fend off the flapping. "I'm not going to fight you."

Jacy landed a smack. On my cheek.

"Don't."

She hesitated.

I kept my hands at my sides, willing her to stop. *Don't do it, Jace.*

"Hit her." Belinda. Eyes pressed into slits. Almost foaming at the mouth.

What is that? I thought. *How can she hate me so much?*

Jacy's next punch landed on my other cheek. It wasn't a hard punch, but there was a rule — *no hitting the face. Marks on the face show.* "Don't touch my face."

I was pretty scrawny, but I knew things in my body that none of them knew. I knew what hurt the most and what brought blackness quick. A punch in the gut — no wind. You bend to suck air and there's a smash right into that spot — the jaw in front of the ear. The white light blazes, the knees fold, and you're out.

I don't remember the fight.

I remember red.

Red and a roar. Then red red red and something hot and sticky on my hands and Dave yelling, "Bean. Bean! Stop."

And at the end of my arms — Jacy's head. *Sticky.* Cement red from the bashing. I take my hands off her. *Hair on my hands. Ash red honey.* I back away. Roar fading and Dave, "C'mon. C'mon!" Pulling me away from the silent circle. *My hands are red.* I see her lying there. *I should help her.* "Why isn't anyone helping her?" Red everywhere and the eyes — all staring at me. *They're scared. Of me.* And I see Belinda's eyes. She isn't scared — she's excited. *She's stupid. She should be scared.* She meets my eye — and she goes white. *She is white and I am red.* I almost puke, because I like it. I like that I make Belinda stop breathing. I like that for the first time in her spoiled fucking rich-girl life she's afraid of something. *She is afraid of me.* Belinda runs.

I shake my head. I say, "Help her."

The circle of kids stare at me.

"Somebody fucking help her!"

They move towards Jacy.

I turn away and start walking — to the tracks and South. *Windigo. I've been bitten by the Windigo. That rage. That rage is in me. Blood rage. Raging for blood. Jacy's blood. Blood of an innocent on my hands.*

Two miles out of town, I sit down. Shake. Breathe. *Breathe. Stop shaking.* I stop shaking.

Dave sits next to me. "Where you going?"

"Away."

"You can't"

"I have to."

"You can't." His hand is on mine. *Blood. Jesusgod. My hands are covered in blood. Her blood. My blood. It's in my blood.*

I stand up. "I gotta go."

"Bean. It's OK."

"It isn't."

"She'll be OK."

"I wanted to kill Belinda." *Eat her heart like a Windigo. Blood, it's from the blood. Jack's blood cut into me. Jesusgod what have I done?*

"Bean. Look at me." His hand on my face. "Bean. It'll be OK." *He thinks so. He doesn't know. He doesn't know what I am.* "It will be OK."

"I smashed Jacy's head in."

"Heads bleed a lot. She'll be OK."

Heads do bleed a lot. Never hit in the face. Never bash in the head. I close my eyes. "Shit. Oh Shit. I smashed her head in."

"It's OK." Touching my hair.

"It isn't." *It isn't it isn't it isn't.* "I didn't mean to . . . I . . . "

"You went nuts."

He says it so earnestly that I start to laugh. *Nuts nuts nuts I'm a big bag of nuts.* Dave smiles. I can't stop laughing. "It's not funny." I start to shake again.

Dave laughing too. "Not funny." But we can't stop. Rocking back and forth.

I push at him. "Stop or I'll pee my pants."

Dave wraps his arms around himself, "I'm freezing my nuts off." He gets up and stamps his feet.

"Me too." I snort. "I'm losing my nuts!"

Dave pulled me up into a hug until I was done shaking. Then he asked me what a Windigo was. He said I was muttering something about a Windigo when he was chasing me down the tracks.

"It's nothing."

"Didn't sound like nothing."

"It's an old Cree legend. A beast with a heart of ice that wanders the world until its feet fall off. Sort of cannibal."

"It eats people?"

"So they say. Maybe it just eats their souls." I was thinking of Jack. Of Jack's blood cut into me. He was eating my soul. "Never mind."

Dave shook his head. "You read too many stories."

"Yeah." It was all that blood. There was blood all over my hands. Blood on Dave's hands — from my face.

We cleaned our hands off in the snow. Red on white.

"Here." He took some snow and cleaned my face.

"Jesus."

"Shhh." He wiped my face with the bottom of his Black Sabbath t-shirt.

"Thanks."

"Yeah."

We walked back into town through purple light. Hands in our pockets, heads down, watching our boots kick through the snow. My boots. His hightops. He walked me right to my door. "You OK?"

"Yeah." He started to walk away. "Hey, Dave." He stopped. He looked so small, like a kid. The left knee of his jeans was ripped. "Thanks."

"No problem." He smiled and I felt a strange ache in my middle.

I went inside. The TV was on. Potatoes boiling on the stove. Prissy sat at the table. Coffee and a smoke. "Hiya, Hon."

I pulled my parka off. Blood on the cuffs. "Hey." I poured myself a coffee.

Prissy smiled. "How's Snap?"

"Uh. Good. Fine." *Crap. Poor Snap.* I'd have to sneak out later to feed her.

"Supper's almost ready."

"OK." I wrapped my hands around the coffee mug. They ached. *They'll call soon. Someone will call or the cops will come and it'll be for me this time.* I sipped the coffee. "Ahhh, that's good."

"Rough day in the trenches?"

"Not bad." *Can she see it?*

"You like it here?"

I almost laughed. "It's OK."

"School good?"

"Long as I don't blow anything up."

Prissy hardly ever asked about school anymore. She used to ask all the time, when it was just the two of us. "You OK, Honey?"

I smiled. Prissy looked tired. "Sure, Mom. I'm good. I'm going to wash up." I escaped to the bathroom. I leaned against the door, dizzy. I took a deep breath. I ran the water as hot as I could and plunged my hands into the scald. I looked at myself in the mirror. Dave missed a spot — a brown spray of specks on my cheek. I scrubbed it off.

"Supper!" Prissy called.

I gathered Dee up from in front of the TV, "C'mon, Kid." She was warm and smelled so good I almost cried. Crayons and Play Doh.

"Sammy's seeping."

"Sure she is." Sammy was a gerbil I brought home to keep Dee and Prissy company during the day. I bought her off a kid at school.

"She seep my room. She was cold."

I detoured into Dee's room to take a look." I set her down when I saw what she'd done. *Jesus.*

Dee stood in the doorway. "Sammy cozy."

She'd put the gerbil's cage on the radiator. The metal was hot. I pulled my sweater down over my hands and lifted it to the floor. Sammy was dead. "C'mon, Kid. We'll let her sleep awhile."

We went to the table. There were only three plates. I breathed a sigh of relief. No Jack tonight.

"Yahooo!" yelled Dee. "Smashed 'toes!" We had mashed potatoes almost every night, but Dee never lost her joy in them. She liked them with ketchup swirled in. She gnawed on her meat, humming her happy food song.

"Jack's working late," Prissy said.

Right. I pushed my food around. I couldn't eat. "Looks good, Mom. I'm just not real hungry."

"You OK?"

"Yeah, just not very — " I ran to the bathroom and threw up. Hot liquid. Sour. I laid my head against the cool porcelain. *It's in me.*

Prissy gave me a glass of water and felt my head. "You're hot. You better lay down. Maybe it's the flu."

"Yeah, maybe." I crawled onto the couch.

Dee dragged her sleeping bag out of her room and covered me up. "You puked."

"Yep."

"You seep."

"Yeah. Thanks Kid."

The phone rang. *Here it comes.* Prissy answered it. "She's not feeling well."

I raised my head. "Who is it?"

"Dave."

I got up. "Gimme."

Prissy shook her head and smiled as she passed me the phone. She winked at Dee. Dee giggled. They sang, "Bean and Davey sitting in a tree. K-I-S-S-I-N-G."

I rolled my eyes and turned my back on them. "What's up?

"You sick?" He sounded worried.

"What do you think?"

"You OK?"

"Yeah. Prissy thinks I'm getting the flu." The phone felt heavy. I looked at Prissy and held out my empty water glass. "You mind?" While she got me more water, I talked fast and low. "Do me a favor?"

"Sure."

"Go feed Snap?"

"Already did."

"Thanks, man."

"No prob. She's OK, Bean."

"Good."

"Jacy," he said. "She's OK. She got stitches but she's OK."

"How do you know?"

"I called Belinda. She says that nobody will tell."

"What?" I didn't understand. I beat a girl's head in.

"Belinda says nobody'll say what happened."

"What, does she rule the world or something?"

Dave didn't laugh.

"Dave, that's insane."

"We'll see. You sure you're OK?"

"Yeah. I'm fine. Thanks for calling. I'll see you tomorrow."

"Not if you're sick you won't." Prissy handed me the water and held out her hand for the phone.

"I gotta go, Dave. Prissy has her Serious Mother voice on."

"OK. Bye."

"Bye." I handed the phone to Prissy. "I'm just gonna go to bed."

"Good idea. Who rules the world?"

"What?"

"You said someone ruled the world."

"Oh, just this chick at school. Thinks her shit don't stink." I headed for my room. I stopped and turned back. "Prissy?"

"Yeah?"

I waved her over and whispered, "I think the kid cooked Sammy — can you check?"

Prissy's eyebrows lifted and a laugh plopped out. "Oh, Jesus." She straightened her face. "Poor thing."

I shrugged with a *what can you do* face. "Poor, poor thing." I shuffled off to bed.

The next day, after Jack left for work, Dee helped me put Sammy in a shoe box. She was mad at herself. "Way to go Ex-lax," she mumbled.

"It's — Smooth move, Ex-Lax."

"Yeah."

"It wasn't your fault."

"I cook her." She'd heard me tell Prissy.

"But your heart was in the right place." She didn't understand what I meant. "You didn't mean to hurt Sammy, right?"

She nodded.

"You were trying to take care of her."

"Yeah."

"You just didn't know the best way to do it. C'mere." I pulled her into a hug. "It's not your fault, Honey."

We buried Sammy in the backyard. We sang.

"Good night Sammy
Good night Sammy
Good night Sammy — we're sorry to see you go."

I laid a flat rock over the grave. "Ashes to ashes, dust to dust."

Dee stuck in a Popsicle stick cross. "I Sorry, Sammy."

Prissy stood at the foot of the grave. "See ya later, Sam."

Then, we all went inside and ate funeral sandwiches. Peanut butter and jam — with the crusts cut off.

I stayed home for two days. No one called but Dave. He took care of Snapper and told me Jacy wasn't at school either. She got twenty-seven stitches. Her nose was broken and her eyes were black. Her parents tried to get her to tell them what happened. She wouldn't say. All the parents tried. Everyone in town thought it was a boy — *romance gone wrong.* Nobody ever told.

Jack found out. Like he found out about everything. One night, during *The Price is Right*, he said, "Heard Jacy's back at school." I looked over. He licked the thumb scar, from where we'd done our blood swear, and smiled. *We're bound.* I went in the bathroom and puked 'til blood came out.

I never talked to Belinda again. Or Jacy.

Me and Dave still hung out — a bit. I went to school, exercised Snap, and went home. The red skates gathered dust.

I wrote Goose about the fight. I didn't tell him how bad it really was. I couldn't.

That spring, Jack tried to off himself.

We were in the kitchen. Prissy was sitting at the table, smoking. I was teaching Dee to play Jacks on the kitchen floor.

There'd been a fight. Things weren't going well at the Elevator.

Instead of storming out and heading to the hotel, Jack went downstairs. That was weird, but I didn't really think about it at the time — I just stuck by Prissy. I figured Jack was drinking down there. I was waiting for round two.

The shot was really loud.

Prissy jumped straight up, and came down stiff — like Wiley Coyote falling off a cliff. I almost laughed, but then she went still — no breath even. We stared at each other until she said, "Go look."

Dee didn't move. She sat on the floor holding the jacks. Looking at me.

I hated that basement. It was all rickety stairs, dust, and dimness. Gave me the heebies.

He was lying on the floor, under the light. He wasn't dead; just nicked his head and bled.

His blood was purple. It was hot — steaming on the cement floor. I put my hand in it. I wanted to lick it. I could smell Rye really strong and I wondered if I could taste it in his blood. I didn't lick it. Dee was watching.

Prissy stood behind her. "He OK?"

"He's breathing." I looked at the gun. I picked it up, went upstairs, and called the ambulance. I put the gun on the table, washed the stinking blood off my hand, and got me and Dee a glass of milk.

The ambulance came and the cops came and I watched the lights on the trees outside. They were pretty; like fireworks. They bundled up Jack and took him away.

Prissy stood there, crying.

Dee and I drank our milk.

A cop came and stood by the table. A Rookie. I could tell. He was white as a sheet. Probably never saw a guy shoot himself before. I got him a glass of milk.

"Thanks." His hands were shaking.

"No problem."

"How old are you?"

"Twelve."

We drank our milk.

He asked if I was OK.

"No," I said. "He missed."

Prissy blamed herself for the shooting, of course. Jack worked all the angles.

A few weeks later, when Dave and I walked out to Mac's, Snap was gone. I started running. Dave belted after me. "Bean, wait! What's going on?"

I beat him to our place. The door was locked. I looked in the window. The Velvet Elvis was gone. Everything was gone. *Crap.*

There was no note.

Dave huffed up. "What's going on?"

"They're gone."

"What?"

"They're gone, man." *Shit.*

"What do mean they're gone?"

I sighed. "Looks like we're moving."

"Oh."

We'd been in Biensol for four months.

Dave and I sat on the bottom step and tried to read. Dave was finally reading *The Crystal Cave*. He read slow.

My stomach hurt. *They left without me.* We'd moved on the spur of the moment a bunch of times, but they'd never left me behind. *Prissy wouldn't leave without me. Would she? No, I just have to wait. Prissy will come and get me.* I sat there and read. What else could I do?

A car pulled up and a couple got out. "Bean?" The man spoke.

I looked up from my book, hair in my face. I'd stopped curling it. "Yeah."

"We're the Guteleutes." They were both very shiny. Clean. Pressed. *Church people.*

"Yeah?"

"Your mother sent us."

"Where is she?"

The woman moved forward. "She's at our place with your father and your sister. We came to pick you up." I could read her thoughts on her face. *Poor thing,* she thought. *Poor bedraggled thing.* The man moved forward with his wife. I watched them. The lady wore a dress. Her hair was round — curled and brushed out. She didn't have any makeup on. The man wore a suit. *Church people for sure.*

The man crouched in front of me. "You're moving." His voice was gentle. He had crinkly, smiling, eyes and he smelled like hay.

"Why are you wearing a suit?"

He laughed. "I always wear a suit when I come to town to meet a lady." He looked at Dave. "And who would you be?"

Dave stood and shook the man's hand. "Dave. Dave Stigmann."

The man smiled. "Good to meet you, Dave. Matthew Guteleute."

I tipped my head to the side. "Gotta dime?"

"For what?"

"So I can call Prissy." The lady twitched a bit at that. "My mother."

The man handed me a dime, and I headed off down the street.

The lady looked panicky. "Where are you going?"

I kept walking. "There's a payphone down at the hotel"

She came after me. "We'll drive you."

I turned and looked at her. "Lady, I ain't getting in your damned car 'til I talk to Prissy Fallwell. What's your number?"

Dave walked me to the hotel. The couple followed, in their car. I dialed the Guteleute's.

A girl answered. "Hello?"

"Can I talk to Prissy Fallwell?"

"Fallwell?"

"Yeah. Prissy Christly Fallwell. It's her daughter, Bean."

"Bean?"

Prissy must've heard my name and grabbed the phone. "Bean?"

"Hey, Pris. What's going on?"

"Where are you?"

"At the Hotel."

"With the Guteleutes?"

"Yeah. They're waiting in the car."

"Well, come here."

"Where's here?"

"Their place."

"We movin' in with the Guteleutes?" *Jesus. What next?*

"No."

"So where we movin' to?"

"A farm near here."

I heard Jack in the background. "Where is she? Tell her to get here."

"Bean," Prissy said. "Just get in the car."

"You got my Samsonite?"

"Of course I have your suitcase. I shoved all your other stuff in bags."

I can't believe you moved without even telling me. "Snap there?"

"She's at our new place. We'll go there tonight."

"I've got a library book. *Rumble Fish*."

"So drop it off."

"The school is closed." *You retard*.

"We'll mail it back then. Just get in the car, Bean."

I sat on the line in silence. *I don't want to move*.

"Bean?"

I didn't answer. There was nothing to say.

"Bean. Get in the damned car."

"Fine." I hung up. I turned to Dave and said, "Guess we moved."

He shuffled.

I leaned in and kissed him on the cheek. He blushed.

I got in the Guteleute's car. *Rumble Fish* went into the Samsonite. I never returned it to the Biensol library, and I never saw Dave again.

Torn Camp Mihkwaw T-shirt

That's how I met the Christians. No idea how the hell Jack met them, or why we moved.

The Christians lived on a farm in the northeast. They were Mennonite — the kindest, most generous people I ever met. When we arrived that day, the two youngest girls ran out to meet me. They took me by the hand and showed me around the place. They had the biggest garden I'd ever seen. A huge barn and a pen full of sheep. The quonset was full of machinery. We climbed up on the roof.

"Are you a Christian?" Rachael asked. She was a year older than me. Her sister, Elly, was a year younger.

"I guess so," I said. "I pray and shit."

Elly giggled. "We don't say that word."

"Pray?" I said it as a joke. I was mad about moving and I wanted someone to blame. I knew it wasn't their fault. Jack probably got in trouble down at the Elevator. The girls just stared at me. "Sorry. I meant *stuff* — I pray and stuff like that. I pray a lot."

"But have you accepted Christ into your heart?"

"What for?"

"To be your Lord and personal Saviour."

I knew that me and God were OK, but I never actually, formally, invited Jesus into my heart. I wondered if it would make a difference. "Is there a special prayer, like *Our Father* or something?"

We bowed our heads up there on the Quonset roof and prayed.

I didn't say anything to Prissy or Jack about *becoming a Christian*. It was between me and God. I tried to swear less, and be kinder to Dee. I wasn't mean to Dee, but sometimes I got mad when she wrecked my stuff or whatever. I tried to practice *forgiveness*.

We started going to church with the Guteleutes — all of us. That was a little weird. Prissy'd never come to church with me before. Far as I knew, Jack had never been inside a church — but he knew all the hymns, so he must've gone when he was a kid. Funny that he'd never told us any stories about that.

Sometimes, Dee and I stayed overnight at the Gute's. Their house was warm cozy, and there was always lots of food. They had six kids — three boys and three girls, all blonde — the Mennonite Brady Bunch. Before breakfast, Matthew read from *Our Daily Bread* — this book with Bible verses and something inspirational to think about during the day, and every night Amy, Mrs. Guteleute, read us a Bible Story before we went to bed.

Dee thought it was crazy that the Guteleutes didn't have a TV. I thought it was crazy that they couldn't go to movies or listen to regular music. They were only supposed to listen to Christian music, but Rachael had a Beach Boys tape we listened to a lot. "Be True to your School" was one of my favourites. Guess that was strange, since I was always going to different schools, but there it is. I wanted to be loyal — to be part of a group and to have something to *be true to* even if it was a dumb school. I didn't think about it much. I just liked the song.

That summer, I went to Bible camp with Rachael and Elly — Camp Mihkwaw. Other than my disastrous trip to Hamilton, I'd never been away from Prissy for more than a weekend. I was worried about leaving her and Dee for two weeks; but Prissy said I should go. I never wanted to admit it, but I loved being away from home — at GT's, Goose's or the Guteleute's, even with Ritter, except for that one time. I could relax. I knew that Camp Mikwah would be two weeks of breathing easy, having fun and, as the Gute's said, *growing closer to God.*

I took the Samsonite, just in case.

Kids at the camp were really friendly. It felt like a big happy family. We got to sing a lot and ride horses. We made crafts and did little skits. We all had a crush on a string-bean counselor named Danny.

One night, the counselors woke us all up and gathered us in the dining hall for a sort of game. It was like a play. We pretended that we were in Russia and we were sneaking out to a Bible meeting. If we got caught, we'd be thrown in prison, or maybe shot on the spot. The counselors told us that the church, in Russia, was super strong because Christians had to fight for their right to believe in God. They said, "If you have to fight for something, it becomes more precious." Like that was some big secret we couldn't comprehend.

We went through the woods, two by two. It was so dark, we could hardly see. A light swept over us and we all froze. We heard dogs barking, and footsteps, but they didn't find us. We kept moving. We twisted and turned so much that I couldn't tell where we were.

We came into a clearing. Danny, everyone's dreamboat, was there with a Bible. Since Bibles were illegal in Russia, none of us had ever seen a real one, only bits of scripture passed secretly from hand to hand. We all sat silently, and he began to read John Chapter 14.

He just got to the part where Jesus is saying, "I am the way, and the truth, and the life: no one cometh unto the Father, but by me," when a bright light snapped on. There were dogs barking and people shouting. A bunch of soldiers rushed into the clearing, grabbed Danny and started dragging him off. Everyone was screaming and running. I grabbed Elly and Rachel and shoved them down, behind me, and told them to shut the fuck up. I watched the soldiers. They didn't have guns. They didn't see us. I thought it was real until I recognized one of the soldiers. It was the camp cook.

I turned around and the girls were staring at me with big huge eyes. I'd pushed them into a patch of Poison Ivy. My shirt was torn.

"Sorry I swore."

Rachel finally spoke. "Why did you do that?"

"I was upset."

"No. Not the swearing. Why did you push us behind you."

"To protect you."

"But . . . I'm bigger than you."

I laughed.

Elly started crying like crazy. She'd peed her pants. She wasn't the only one.

I doubt Camp Mihkwaw ever pulled that stunt again.

Two days after I got home from camp, Elvis died. Prissy went into mourning. Jack didn't even make fun of her. He played her Elvis songs on his guitar. I made her cups of tea, held her hand, and we prayed for Lisa Marie and Priscilla and all the fans aching around the world.

It was around then that I started praying for Jack to become a real Christian. He came to church with us, but he was still mean sometimes. I thought if he really, truly, *let Jesus into his heart*, he wouldn't hurt us anymore. I prayed that the calm would last. That maybe we could just stay there, near the Guteleutes, and be normal. Maybe even be Christian, like them. Calm and shiny clean. Quiet and safe.

Instead, Jack got busted.

PURPLE BOTTLE

We'd started a little family tradition of visiting old, abandoned, farm-houses at night. We just looked around, at first. Then, we started taking stuff. I knew the houses weren't really abandoned like Jack said. I knew good Christians didn't steal. I did it anyway. It was family time.

We were on the way home the night the lights came flashing. The trunk was full. The cops pulled us over, and took everything. Dee had a plastic pumpkin. The kind you use for Halloween loot. She didn't want to give it up. I told the cop it was hers, from home. "Jesus, What do you think? She's gonna steal a plastic pumpkin?" They let her keep it.

They came to the house and rounded up all the stolen goods. Jack hadn't sold anything. We just kept it. They didn't get the little purple bottle I'd tucked into my Samsonite. I had found it outside of one of the houses. It was one of the first things I'd taken.

Jack got sent to P.A. The Pen. The Prince Albert Penitentiary. He got a three-year sentence for robbery.

I couldn't believe our luck. I tried to talk Prissy into leaving.

"What do you mean?"

"I mean escape. Flee. Go somewhere that he can't find us."

She laughed.

We had already tried to leave a few times. The first time, we just went over to Auntie's — a brilliant move. Jack came over, cried, and we went back. The second time, we borrowed money off Spuddy and caught a bus to Calgary. He found us. Jack always found us, and we always went back.

Jack knew everything we did. Even stupid stuff. He knew who I hung out with after school; who Prissy stopped to talk to on the street. If Prissy stepped out of line, he'd sit there and smile, and turn that bloody bluestone ring of his and shake his head. If I messed up, he'd spin the ring and lick the scar on his thumb from our blood-swear.

I hated Jack and I wanted to leave, but Prissy wouldn't. She said we'd move back to Regina and wait for him. I wrote Goose and told him we were moving back, but first we were going to visit Jack in the penitentiary. I said I'd be just like Holly Golightly, going to visit Sally Tomato in Sing-Sing. We packed up. I gave Snap to the Guteleutes.

The P.A. Pen was nothing like Sing-Sing.

There was a whole crowd of visitors. The kids were all scrubbed and spit-shined, dressed in clothes that still had store-bought creases in them. The women reeked of cheap perfume and Aqua Net. They all had coolers, like they were headed for a frigging family picnic. Everyone knew each other.

We filed into a big room filled with wooden tables. Prissy paced and smoked. The prisoners filed in and the women and kids jumped all over them. Couples started making out in the corners. Prissy hugged Jack and apologized for not bringing anything. "I didn't know I could."

"It's OK."

We bought ham sandwiches from a vending machine. They were stale. Prissy and Jack held hands and whispered to each other. Dee squished her sandwich into duck shapes and tried to get Jack to admire them. I just sat there, scratching at the new dress Prissy made me wear, wishing I'd waited in the car.

THE BULLET

A three-year sentence isn't really a three-year sentence. Jack was out in a few months. We were living over by GT, and I was back at Cawanas with Goose. We were in grade eight.

Prissy had a job. She was waitressing out at the Husky again. Jack couldn't find any work. He went on a bender and put Prissy's head through the wall.

I dragged Dee in to our room, shoved her under the bed and told her to stay there.

I ran to GT's. "You gotta call the cops. He's killing her this time." I didn't think GT knew what was going on with us. I thought if he knew what Jack did to us, he would stop him.

GT just sat there. He was on the couch. He looked at me strangely and then he looked back at the television. He just sat there, smoking.

I curled up in the corner, watching him. I didn't cry. I never cried, anymore. There was no point.

Jack came. He had a gun.

GT just sat there.

Jack told me to get in the car.

I went. GT just sat there.

Prissy and Dee were on the bed — on Prissy and Jack's bed.

He threw me into the room, and he sat in that doorway all night with a gun on us. Talking. I don't remember what he said. I went away. I slipped up to the ceiling and set the jangly steel guitars playing, drowning him out. I kept my face towards him, so he'd think I was listening. When he said, "Stop looking at me," I moved my eyes to the wall. I watched from the ceiling for a twitch of his finger on the trigger, for a muscle jump. I watched Prissy, willing her silent. I watched Dee, so still. *How can a three year old hold so still?* I watched us all.

I thought, *This is it. He will kill us now.* I tried not to think about GT. *How could he just sit there?*

Somewhere around dawn, Jack threw Prissy on the floor. He tossed the gun onto the bed and undid his belt. I didn't know if he was going to fuck her or beat her. Didn't matter. My eye followed the gun. He tossed it onto the bed. Right in front of me.

I watched myself from the ceiling. I watched myself pick up the gun and tell him to stop.

He laughed. Then he just stood there. Smiling at me. Like he was daring me to shoot him. Like he knew I could never do it. Like maybe he wished I would.

It felt like we stared at each other for a long time.

It was all very clear. *I'm a minor. I can kill him.* I was very calm. *If I kill him then it will be over.*

Then Dee started screaming and I snapped down, back into my body. I lowered the gun. I wish I could say that I was thinking *You're not worth it.* I wasn't thinking anything. I was looking at Dee. She never screamed, no matter what was happening. I thought she must be hurt.

Jack hit me. I fell down. My head was ringing.

I got up.

He hit me again. His blue sapphire ring split my left eyebrow.

I got up.

He broke my nose. I went down. He flailed at me with the belt. I tucked into a ball.

When he stopped, I got up.

I didn't cry. I just stared at him. I felt blood coming out of my left ear. I smiled and said, "She was beat so bad, she couldn't really talk. She had blood running from her ear." The story he'd told me about a dying man. A lie about how he'd killed a man. A lie about his stupid blue sapphire ring.

He left.

I cleaned up Prissy and Dee and put them to bed. I took a bullet out of the gun and tucked it in the Samsonite. I walked down the alley and threw the gun into a garbage can. I washed up and sat on the couch. I fell asleep.

Prissy woke me up later and gave me a grilled cheese sandwich. "He's back," she said. "He's asleep."

Goose called that night to see if I was sick. I'd missed school. I told him I had mono. I told him not to come over; that I was contagious. I stayed home for two weeks. None of us went to the hospital. I had a chipped tooth and my nose healed crooked. It's still crooked.

That was the last time Jack Vara hit me.

GT's TOPHAT

The next month, GT went into the hospital. He had cancer. He was dead in a week. Jack was a pallbearer. We had the wake at GT's place. The Petersons came. They had a sandwich, and then Mrs. P said they had to leave. People were drinking. She didn't like Goose around that sort of thing, even if it was for a funeral. She gave me a big hug and said if I ever needed anything, I should call.

Goose hugged me and whispered, "It's illegal to drink beer out of a bucket while you're sitting on a curb in St. Louis."

"A cockroach can live several weeks with its head cut off — it dies from starvation," I whispered back.

After the Petersons left, Jack came up to me and tried to put his arm around me. I told him to get the fuck away from me. It was the first time I ever swore at Jack — to his face. I said it low. I didn't want to make a scene.

Jack's eyebrows went up. He smirked, but he moved on.

Gerard, the old shiny-shoed friend of the family, heard me. "Was that necessary?" he asked.

"Absofuckinglutely," I said. "And it's none of your goddamned business."

Alden was there too. Another pallbearer. One who deserved to carry GT. He came over and asked how I was doing.

I hadn't cried yet. "Did you know he was sick?"

Alden's eyes teared up. "He seemed tired. I just thought he was getting old." He wiped his eyes. "He knew. I think he'd known for a long time. He just didn't tell anyone. When I took him to the hospital, he told me to bring his pills. He had them hidden in the dresser in his room. There were so many pills. It was . . . I think it was pretty bad these last few months. He was on some pretty heavy shit." He tried to smile. "Guess he's OK, now."

"Yeah." It was hard to breathe. "I didn't know what was wrong with him." I was thinking about the night I'd come over. I was thinking about him sitting on the couch while Jack pointed a gun at me and took me away. GT had always stood up for me. I couldn't understand why he didn't do anything, that night. He'd looked at me so strangely. Maybe he was stoned and thought it was all some crazy nightmare. I'd never know.

"None of us knew, Bean. That's how he wanted it."

"Yeah." I smiled a little. "Crazy old crapsuckin' coot!"

Alden's laughter cleared some of the hurt from his eyes. "Ratlikkin' rapscallion!"

"Sneaky son of a sorry-assed . . . spit-likker."

Alden raised his glass and his voice, "Here's to the sweetest, most creative sonofabitch to ever string together a chain of cusswords. To Thomas E. Fallwell! May he be half an eon in heaven before the devil knows he's dead. To Tom!"

I raised my Coke. "To GT!"

Everyone raised a glass. "To Thomas E!"

I looked over at Prissy. She was smiling through tears. She'd always told me the E in my name was for Elvis, and here it was for GT. I gave Alden a big hug. "I'm glad you're here. I'm glad you carried him. I'm glad you were here to take him to the hospital. I'm glad —"

He hugged me close. "Hey, hey. It's OK, Bean. It'll be OK."

"I know. I'll just miss him, that's all."

"Me too, Sweety. Me too." His eyes were tearing up again.

I kissed him on the cheek. "Thanks, Mister."

He smiled a little. "No problem, Lady. And hey, if you ever need anything, I'm in the book, OK?"

"Sure. Thanks. I better go check on the kids."

He nodded, "I'll see you, Bean."

"Yeah." I went around to the backyard. Dee and the rest of the rugrats were playing around with the dogs, ol' Floke and Tate. *God, those dogs must be ancient,* I thought. Tate was running around like a pup, but Ol' Floke wasn't playing much. He just lay in the dirt with his big sad eyes fixed on Mr. Quint who was sitting, alone, on the back step.

Q-Ball sat there, in his rumpled suit, with his hands hung between his legs and tears streaming down his face. I went and sat beside him. We watched the kids 'til they got bored with Tate and ran into the front yard looking for more ice cream. We sat awhile longer, watching Tate tear the stuffing out of an old Chevy seat.

Mr. Quint took out a hanky and wiped his face. "I'll miss him, Bean."

"Me too."

"He was my Best Friend."

Old Floke hadn't taken his eyes off of Mr. Quint. I went and unhooked his chain, "C'mon, Boy." He looked at me once and got up. I took him over to Mr. Quint. "I think Floke should stay at your place now, if that'd be OK with Mrs. Quint."

His eyes started running again and he didn't even bother to wipe them. "It'd be an honour. The old cow can have as many conniptions as she wants." We smiled. Conniption had been one of my favourite words as a kid. I found it in GT's dictionary — *a fit of hysteria, rage, etc.* Mr. Quint hung his head. "I wish he'd told me, Bean. I wish I could've done something."

"You did do something. You were his best friend. You loved him."

"Well, we go back a ways."

"He'll be glad you and Floke are together."

"Yes. I do believe he would be."

When we were cleaning up, my aunt Dora asked where Floke was. I said I gave him to Mr. Q. and she threw a hissy — like she did every time somebody did something without her permission.

"How's that old man supposed to take care of that dog?" she snarked at me — like Q-ball was some old feeb who couldn't open a can of Dr. Ballard's and fill a bowl with water.

"Same way GT did, fer Crissakes!"

She took a step towards me. "Don't you swear at me Bean E. Fallwell."

"Then shut the fuck up," said Auntie Lip.

Dora stopped in her tracks. "Don't encourage her."

Lip just kept washing the dishes. "What do you care, anyhow?"

Dora sputtered a bit.

Lip turned from the sink and wiped her hands on a tea towel. "Way I see it, Bean did you a favour."

Dora sputtered some more. "But that dog — "

Auntie Lip kept wiping her hands. "Tell them."

Dora's lips disappeared. "It doesn't matter. Done is done. Take these," she said, and shoved some tablecloths at her daughter, Cassie.

Lip wouldn't let it go. "What were you going to do with the dogs, Dora?"

"Just leave it," Dora snapped.

"We're taking Tate home," Jen piped up. "Right, Mom?"

"Yes, Dear." Dora wiped her sweaty hands on her slacks. "Looks like we're about done here. I'll lock up and we can all meet here tomorrow to start packing things up."

"Taking Tate home," I said. "Just Tate? I thought you were taking both dogs". Then, I got it. I turned on Dora. "You vicious cunt."

Prissy whirled around. "Bean!"

"You were gonna put Floke down, weren't you? What the hell is the matter with you?"

She took a step back. "This has nothing to do with you."

"There's nothing wrong with Floke. What were you gonna do — slip him some poison and toss his body at the bloody Nuisance Grounds?"

"We were taking him to the vet," Cassie said.

"You knew?"

"He's a mangy old mutt and he smells."

"Oh. So you just kill him? He was GT's Friend!"

"There is no need for hysterics," Dora sniffed.

"He's my fucking friend!" I could feel my heart beating.

Auntie Lip was saying something about how everything was OK now because Mr. Q had Floke but that Dora had no right to decide to put him down without asking us and how it was just like Dora to always think she was in charge of everything.

"I am in charge!" Dora screeched. "I'm always in charge. I have to be. I'm the only sane person in this whole entire family! I'm the only one with a frigging ounce of brains in my head!"

I cold-cocked her.

She went down and I was on her before anyone else could move. I smashed her and smashed her. "I hate you! I hate you!" I screamed. "You think you're so smart! You think you can do whatever you want! I hate you!"

Lip and Prissy pulled me off. "Jesus, Bean. Stop!"

Dee was crying. I went to her. "It's OK, Honey, it's OK. I'm sorry. Shhhh." I sat there, panting, holding on to Dee while they helped Dora up.

Dora gave Prissy the keys to the house and told her to lock up when we left. She didn't look at me on her way out. Cassie and Jen did though. They stared at me with big saucer eyes, like I was some kind of nutcase. I stuck my tongue out at them, and they scurried off behind their mother.

"Anybody want tea?" Auntie said.

"No, we should get home," said Prissy.

I looked at her. "Don't tell Jack."

Auntie laughed, "No love lost between Jack and Miz Molly, Bean. I wouldn't sweat that." Dora hated that nickname. She'd never let us call her that. We did it anyhow.

"Promise me you won't tell him." I looked at Dee. She was just a kid, but she could already keep a secret if she promised.

They all promised.

I didn't want Jack to know. Just like I hadn't wanted him to know about the fight in Biensol. He'd turn it into one of his stories. He'd tell people about it like it was some funny story. He'd tell people that I was just like him.

I am nothing like Jack Vara. Nothing.

Auntie gave me a hand up. "Where the hell did that come from?"

I shrugged. It had felt good to hit Dora. I never liked her. She never liked me. She was always making fun of me when I was kid for using big words. She was always bossing Prissy and Auntie Lip and even GT around. She had her big fancy house and her kids had all those stupid lessons and she went around pretending to be all nice and normal, but I'd gone over to their place one time and found Cassie beat to shit in her bed. She told me it was Dora who hit her. She'd spilled her Kool-Aid on the new couch. Dora was a big Fake. *I'm glad I hit her.*

We finished up putting away the dishes, and locked up. Before we closed the door, Auntie asked if there was anything of GT's that I wanted. I said, "Yeah, but I'll get it tomorrow. Wouldn't want Dora to think I stole anything." I wanted his tophat.

On the way home from the wake, me and Prissy and Dee held hands. Prissy looked tired and sad. I squeezed her hand. "Thomas E. eh?"

"Yep," she said.

"Does it stand for anything?"

"He'd never tell," she said. "Not even when you were born and we gave it to you."

"What's his birth certificate say?"

"He lost it. Never got it replaced."

"Hmm. Maybe it does stand for Elvis."

"Could be."

Dee tugged on my arm. "My belly hurts."

"Teach you to eat five ice creams," I said, and gave her a tickle.

"Dohn!" She giggled and squirmed away. "I'll puke for sure!"

"C'mon. I'll piggy-back ya."

I got GT's tophat, but Dora wasn't pleased. She had a look on her face like I was going to sell it as soon as her back was turned. It went into my Samsonite along with the funeral announcement. I was still trying to mark the bright things in life, but darkness slipped in as well. Life's like that.

Ticket Stub: Beachboys Concert

When high school started, we were still living in the same place so I started school at North Central Collegiate, with Goose. When I registered, I gave them GT's address. Auntie was living there.

Sure enough, we moved — again and again and again. For a while, we kept moving to houses in the same neighborhood. Then, Jack went to work out on a ranch near Moose Jaw.

He was out there for a few months before Prissy said, "We're moving to Moose Jaw." We were shopping at the Safeway over at Rosemont. We were taking the cart to the car.

I'd been waiting for it. "I'm not going."

She laughed, and kept loading groceries into the car. "We're all going."

"I'm not changing schools again."

"What the hell are you talking about?"

"I'm not going, Prissy." I didn't want to move and I sure as hell didn't want to move out of Regina with Jack Vara again. It had gotten to the point where I couldn't even stand to eat at the same table as him. I could always hear him chewing, even if it was soft food like Kraft Dinner. Jack made me sick.

Prissy went ballistic. She grabbed me and started screaming in my face. "You're getting a little too big for your britches, Missy." People were watching, but Prissy didn't care. "You'll do what I goddamned tell you, you little bitch."

"I'm not going."

She slapped me.

I shook the hair out of my eyes. "I mean it."

She cried.

In the end, nobody moved to Moose Jaw. Jack got fired for something or other. We moved again, out of the neighborhood but still in Regina. I hopped a city bus to school.

Goose and I celebrated my revolt by attending a Beachboys concert. They rocked out *Be True to Your School.*

I stayed at North Central until we graduated.

PROGRAM: GUYS AND DOLLS

I was almost finished grade ten by the time my school records caught up with me. I got called into the office. Mrs. Willard, the vice principal, sat me down. "Bean, how many schools have you gone to?"

"I have no idea."

"We have records from eighteen elementary schools."

I nodded.

"That's quite a few schools." She flipped through the file. "There are still some gaps."

"We moved a lot. I missed school sometimes."

"Yet you managed to keep your marks up. That's extraordinary."

I shrugged. I knew what was coming.

"And you haven't moved since you came to North Central?"

I liked Mrs. Willard. I didn't like lying, though I'd started doing it almost compulsively. I lied about everything. For no reason. I'd lie about going to the 7-11 for a Slurpee when really I'd just sat in the park staring. Didn't make sense, but there it is. "We've moved."

"I see."

"I don't want to change schools anymore."

"Whose address is this?" she asked, holding up my file.

"My grandfather's. Well, my aunt's, now."

"I see. But you don't live there?"

"No."

"Is this phone number current — for your aunt?"

"Yes."

She nodded. "All right, Bean. Thanks for coming down." She closed the file.

I stood up. "Do you need my new address?"

"No," she said. "We've got an address on file for you and that's good enough for me."

"Thanks."

"You're welcome. I'll see you at the show next week." She smiled. "Break a leg."

We were doing *Guys and Dolls*. I was Adelaide.

That was the year I gave up on sports and become a full-time Artsy. I'd run Track in grade nine but the first time we ran the Cooper Test, in grade ten, I fell down. After a few laps, I couldn't get my breath. Coach Matigan kept yelling at me to run through it. I'd been running Long Distance, Cross Country just two months earlier. Back then, I could run the entire twelve minute Cooper almost flat out. I kept running, but I couldn't find my old rhythm. I couldn't catch my breath. I couldn't feel my tongue. I passed out and woke up on the bench.

Matigan was leaning over me. I pushed her back a little so I could breathe. She smelled like *Love's Baby Soft*. Seemed like a weird smell for a gym teacher. I sat up. I held onto the bench until the gym stopped spinning. She told me I'd hyperventilated.

I tried to run a few more times, in class and on my own. I couldn't get my breath. It felt like something was wrong.

I told Prissy. She said it was probably nothing.

Goose said I should get it checked out.

I went to the first appointment alone. The Doctor examined my ribs. I hated sitting there without a shirt on while he tapped and prodded. "They've always been like that, " I said.

"Like what?"

"Stickey-outy." I hated my ribs. Hated my whole scrawny body, but especially my ribs, which stuck out farther than my mostly non-existent breasts.

He hemmed and hawed and decided to take x-rays.

I asked Prissy to come to the next appointment with me.

The doctor asked Prissy if I'd ever been in a car accident. She said I wasn't. Prissy forgot things.

"We were in a wreck when I was about five," I said. "But I wasn't injured."

"Have you been hit? Struck somehow, in the upper abdomen or the ribs?"

Only about a million times.

Prissy looked at the floor.

I kept looking at the doctor. "Pardon me?"

"Your ribs aren't, as you said 'poking out'. They are actually caved in. They're pressing on your lungs. Your spleen has been damaged. From the looks of it, it's an old injury."

Prissy looked up. "Her spleen?"

"Yes. Still seems to be functioning, so it's not much of a cause for concern. I'm just wondering how this could have happened. Injuries of this sort often stem from a sharp blow when the patient is young."

"Umm. She fell a lot when she was a kid."

I did not.

The doctor shook his head. "It would have to be a very serious fall."

I looked over at Prissy. She was looking at the floor again. "The swag lamp." She looked up.

I told the doctor about tripping over the lamp cord, when I was a kid, and doing a face plant on the hardwood floor.

"We took her to the hospital," Prissy said. "They fixed her nose. It was broken. They didn't say anything about her ribs."

"They must have missed it," I said.

"It's possible." He looked at the x-ray again. "But it would've hurt like hell."

I smiled. "My nose hurt like hell. They probably gave me pain killers."

He let it go at that. "Your bones are hardening. That's why you can't run like you used to. You can't get enough oxygen"

"Can you do anything?"

"We could operate, but it would be major surgery. We'd have to go in and lift out your ribs. Basically split you open and pull them up. Might work."

He sounded like a lunatic. I asked if there were any other options.

"Sure," he said. "Stop running."

So I did. Gave me more time for other stuff.

Goose and I still hung out. We didn't have sleepovers anymore, but we were together all the time, working on the school paper, sitting on the student council, singing in the choir and acting in shows. People kept thinking we were going out, which was hilarious. Neither of us dated — at all.

I don't know why Goose never asked anyone out. Guess he felt as uncomfortable in his body as I did in mine. He'd had a growth spurt in grade nine. Went from five-six to six foot two in about a month. He was tall and gangly and bumped into things a lot. He was cute though — six foot two, eyes of blue, shaggy blonde hair that curled around his ears. There were lots of girls, especially in the Drama club, who would've gone out with him. He usually scored the lead role in our shows.

I scored lead roles too, but not because of my looks. I was actually more of a quirky side-kick, physically, but I could fake it. It was weird. Whenever we did a show, guys would start talking to me for a while. One time a guy actually said, "You should wear makeup more often." Sans makeup, I was not the belle of the ball.

On stage, I could be a sharp tongued beauty, a witty cute girl, an icy cold villain, and in the case of Adelaide, a bleached blonde bimbo with a heart of gold. Off stage, I was awkward and shy and increasingly *moody*. At least that's what Prissy called it. Goose and I called it the Mean Reds — as in, *"Suddenly, you're afraid and you don't know what you're afraid of."* Like Holly says in *Breakfast at Tiffany's*. It was a strange, empty feeling. Like there was an enormous hole in the centre of my chest. It seemed to come over me out of the blue, preceded by the curious smell of warm dish-soap.

I first noticed the Mean Reds after Prissy and I left Ritter. Originally, I thought the emptiness, the sadness, was from missing him. It was more than that.

I still caught Prissy smoking in the dark, sometimes. She'd call me over to sit with her. When Jack showed up, I'd go to my room. He didn't like us sitting together in the dark. He had nothing to worry about. We never talked about leaving anymore. We didn't really talk about anything anymore.

Some nights, I lay in bed and thought about the time before Jack — back when Prissy worked at the Husky, and threw me birthday parties with confetti cake, and asked me if I was happy. It seemed forever ago. I guess that ache, that sadness, came from missing Prissy when she was right there at the kitchen table.

GT was gone. Auntie wasn't around much. She'd met a guy. We only saw Spuddy and Slim on holidays. Big fake happy holidays when Prissy baked cabbage rolls and cooked a turkey and Jack bought his stupid presents for everyone. All I had was Goose and little Dee.

Dee was five. A chubby little bundle of blonde who worshipped me. She made Prissy bring her to all of my shows and she told her friends I was a famous actress. I was her hero — which was cool, until she started getting me in trouble.

Dee got in trouble a lot. She got picked on at school. When I asked her why, she just shrugged.

The day Willard called me into her office, there was a gang of native girls waiting for me outside the school, after rehearsal. One of them stepped forward. The biggest one. "You Bean?"

"Yeah."

"What kinda name is that?"

"A foolish one?"

"You got a smart mouth. Guess it runs in the family."

Goose came out the door. He came over and asked me what was going on. I said I had no idea. I didn't recognize the girls. All I could think was that it had something to do with Jack. Like always. The girl talking to me looked about my age. "Do I know you?" I asked.

"No. But I hear you're going to kick my ass."

Goose laughed. "Sorry. Bean's not much of an ass-kicker."

The girl stepped towards me. "Not what your sister says."

"My sister."

"Yeah."

"My sister is in kindergarten." *Damn it Dee. What the hell have you got me into now?*

"Yeah. So's mine"

Great. "And. They're fighting?"

"Yeah."

"So, we're supposed to fight."

"Yeah."

I almost laughed. "I don't think so."

"What?"

"I'm not gonna fight you. I don't even know you."

She took another step towards me. "Chicken-shit."

I didn't step back. *Whatever you say.* "Yes. I am. I am a chicken-shit."

"Tell your sister to shut her hole, then."

I looked at the girl a while. She kept clenching and unclenching her fists. She looked nervous. Talking tough — but scared underneath. I smiled. "Okay."

The girl looked confused. Her posse looked disappointed. She took another step in. "I mean it."

I nodded. "I hear ya. I'll talk to Dee tonight." I turned and walked away. Goose followed. We didn't look back until we were out of the schoolyard.

"Jesus," he said. "I thought they were going to jump us."

I blew out the breath I'd been holding. "Me too." Regina is a mean town, racially. Goose and I had never run into any trouble. We were from the neighbourhood, so we didn't get hassled much. I didn't want to start now.

That night, when I tucked Dee into bed, I told her what happened after rehearsal.

She held the covers up to her neck. "You didn't fight her?"

"No."

"Why?"

"Dee, I don't fight people."

"Why?"

Because if I start, I can't stop. I sighed. "What's your problem with this girl in your class?"

"She's a dirty nitch."

"Don't say that."

"Why not?"

"It's a bad word for Indians."

"Oh." She looked away.

Nitch. Nitchee. Goose said it came from an old Indian word, *NiiJii*, meaning friend. "So, what's your problem with this girl?"

Dee scrunched up her face. "She picks on me."

"Why?"

"I dunno." I waited. Dee pulled at her covers. "I didn't do anything!"

"OK. Just stop telling her that I'm going to beat her up, or fight with her sister."

Dee looked at me. "You're supposed to protect me."

"Yeah. Well, sometimes you're going to have to work things out for yourself."

"How?"

I shrugged. "Make friends with her."

"Yeah, right."

"Make her laugh."

"What?"

I smiled. "Always works for me. They can't hit you if they're laughing."

Dee sighed and turned to the wall. "Never mind."

I didn't know what else to say. I patted her. "Sorry, Kid. Sometimes you gotta fight your own battles."

I went to my room. I sat on the bed. I listened. Prissy and Jack and Charlotte the Harlot were upstairs watching TV. Charlotte was Jack's newest girlfriend. We all pretended she was a boarder, but I knew Jack was sleeping with her. Didn't even seem weird. That's how screwed up we were.

I missed the Guteluetes. I missed their lemony clean house and chores on Saturdays and praying together. Our house was a sty. It smelled of grease and diesel and dope. Jack was dealing again.

I climbed out the window and headed over to Cawanas school. I went there a lot, at night. There was a spot, over by the Kindergarten room, where you could climb up onto the roof. It was quiet up there. I lay down, and stared at the moon. When I was a kid, the moon was a magic companion that I could talk to. *The Lady on the Moon*. That night, the moon was just a stupid rock circling another stupid rock that I was stuck on.

I was tired. Of everything. Tired of the constant stomachache of stress from wondering when Jack would go off on Prissy again. Tired as hell of her defending him when he was sleeping with a sixteen-year-old girl right under her nose. Tired of trying to figure out why the hell Dee was in trouble all the time. Well, I knew why she was in trouble, I just didn't know how to stop it. Dee was good as gold at home — scarily quiet and well behaved. At school, she was a holy terror. She was at Cawanas. She had my old Kindergarten teacher, who told me that Dee lipped off to everyone. Teachers, other students, didn't matter. I tried to talk to Dee about it, but she said the teacher was lying. Everyone was always lying. Nothing was ever Dee's fault.

I rolled to the edge of the roof and looked down. I thought, *If I jump here, I might die.* Might was no good. I needed a higher building — or a harder surface to land on. I was too tired to jump.

I went home. I didn't sneak back in. I went in the front door. Prissy and Jack were still up, watching TV. Charlotte had gone to bed.

"Where the hell you been?" Jack said.

"Walking." I kissed Prissy on the head. "Goodnight," I said, and headed to my room. They were both shocked. I hadn't kissed Prissy on the head in years. "Don't forget, we open *Guys and Dolls* next Friday. You gotta see Goose as Harry the Horse. He's great."

Three

freedom *n* liberty;frankness; outspokenness; unhampered boldness; separation; privileges connected with a city (often granted as a merely symbolic honour); improper familiarity; licence. [OE *freo*; Ger *frei*; ON *fri*]

fool's paradise *n* a state of happiness based on fictitious hopes or expectations. [OFr *fol* (Fr *fou)*, from L *follis* a windbag]

— *The Chambers Dictionary* (Standard)

JACK'S RING

I left home near the end of grade eleven.

Goose and I had jobs at the Pinder's Drug Store down on Broad Street. He came to pick me up for work one night and Jack broke the rules. Goose and I were in the kitchen with Prissy. We were all laughing. Goose was telling stories about having to work the cosmetics counter. He was actually better at working there than I was. He gave make-overs. Prissy asked what he could do for her and Goose said she was beautiful just the way she was. Jack came in and asked about dinner.

Prissy said, "I haven't started yet. I'm talking to my boyfriend."

Jack pushed her and she banged back into the cupboard. Goose looked down at the table.

Jack left.

Prissy laughed. "Oh he's just jealous."

I went downstairs and started to pack.

Goose came down. He watched me toss some books in the Samsonite. "What's going on, Bean?"

"Did you know Lorne Greene had one of his nipples bitten off by an alligator while he was host of Lorne Greene's *Wild Kingdom*?"

"I did not know that."

"Can I stay at your place?"

"Of course." He sat on the bed. "You OK?"

"Sure." I snapped the suitcase shut. *I will be.* "C'mon, we'll be late."

Two weeks later, I went back home to grab a few things — clothes mostly, my curling iron.

Dee was home alone. "Whatcha doin'?"

"Going."

"Where?" She was so little. *Take her,* I thought. *Take her take her TAKE HER!*

I can't take her — the Welfare'll get her — I'm not old enough.

Take her!

I can't take her — Prissy will die if I take her.

"I have to go, Dee. I'm leaving. I left two weeks ago. Didn't you notice?" *Christ.*

TAKE HER!

Dee's lip trembled. "I just thought you were busy at school and work. I just thought you were coming home real late. Jack says he's gonna skin you when he sees you. He says — "

I cut her off, "I'm staying with Goose.

She started to cry. "Don't go Bean."

Shit. You can't leave. He wins if you leave.

I pushed the hair out of her eyes.

One of us will die if I stay. I will kill him or he will kill me. He will kill Prissy. I can't stay. He broke the rule. Never touch us in front of others — Never ever never ever never ever . . .

But a push — not a hit. That's not so bad.

No. A broken rule a broken rule — house comes tumbling down.

I hugged Dee and left.

I saw a glint on the kitchen table. Jack's ring. I took it.

That night, after bingo, Prissy called. She wanted me to come home. I said I couldn't.

She said, "What about me and Dee?"

I said, "That's gotta be up to you."

She said, "What do you mean?"

I said, "You need to leave, Mom."

She said, "I can't."

Goose's mother stood across the table from me. She didn't say anything. She just stood there.

"I can't come home, Prissy. I can't. Ever. I won't." I hung up.

Mrs. P didn't say a word. She made tea. We sat at the table and drank it.

"I'm sorry she called so late," I said.

"Don't you worry," she said. She poured me another cup of tea. She stood for a moment with her hand on my shoulder and then she left.

My hands started to shake. My throat hurt. I wished I could cry. I couldn't remember the last time I cried. I wished I could slip out of the body — but I couldn't. No jangly guitars, no watching from above. Just tea and aching. I had left home.

My eyes watered, a little.

I stayed with the Petersons until the end of grade eleven. They wanted me to stay with them until graduation, but I needed to be on my own.

Goose was glad I had left home, but he was scared. I knew why. "I took it."

"Took what?"

I pulled out Jack's ring.

"Jesus, Bean." He took the ring. "How'd you get it?"

"It was just sitting on the table."

"I thought he never took it off."

I shrugged.

He held out the ring. "You have to give it back."

I took it. "No."

"What if this is why . . . "

"Why what?" He didn't answer. "It's OK."

He was pale. "What's OK?"

"I know what you asked the Ouija."

"What?"

"I know what you asked after it said, *B.F. will die at sixteen, by a bluestone, by G.M.*"

"Bean."

"You asked if G.M. was Guitar Man — and it said, *Yes.*"

He nodded.

"Then you asked if you could save me, didn't you?"

He nodded.

"And it said, *No.* That's why you got so mad. That's why you burned it."

"Bean, what are we going to do?"

"I've done it. I left."

"But . . ."

"It's between me and him."

"I know, but . . . What if he comes after you?"

"I don't know." I tucked the ring in my pocket. "I don't think he will. Why would he? He doesn't need me."

"I don't know. Maybe we should — "

"I know. Listen to me. He broke the rule. Even he has rules, and he broke the biggest one. He pushed her in front of you. Had you ever seen him do that before?"

"No."

"No. Because that's fucking *rule number one* — never hit any of us in front of a witness. He's losing it."

Goose opened his mouth, but no sound came out.

"What?"

"Nothing."

"What!"

He blinked a few times. "What about Prissy and Dee?"

"I don't know." It was all I could say.

Jack never showed up — at the Peterson's or at school. I never went back to the house. On my seventeenth birthday, Goose threw me the biggest party ever. He smiled and smiled. We thought it was all over.

TICKET STUB: JOHNNY CASH

When I was seventeen, I ran into Ritter in front of the Bus Depot. He was sitting in his cab. I walked by and then went back. I stopped beside his window. "Hey, Ritter."

He looked up and blinked at me. "Bean?"

Adda go, Dad. You don't even recognize me. "Yeah. It's me."

"How ya doin'?"

"Good. You?"

"Good." I watched him look me over. I had on my usual uniform, a shapeless burgundy sweater, a long loose black skirt over ripped up long-johns, and beat-up combat boots. My hair was dyed black with red tips, spiked on top, long in the back. Goose called it my *punk mullet*. Ritter's eyes were grey and tired looking. *I thought they were blue.* He smiled. "You're tall."

I smiled back. I hadn't grown since grade eight. "I'm old."

"How's your mom?"

"You probably see her more than I do." Prissy was working in the Bus Depot coffee shop.

"Yeah. She seems good. Says you left."

"Yeah."

"How ya doin'?"

"Good."

"You're in school, eh?"

"Yeah."

"Grade twelve, right?"

"Yeah."

"Where you livin'?"

"Out by the Golden Mile."

"Hey, you wanna go to a concert tomorrow night?"

Same old Ritter. I don't see him for years and he suddenly wants to hang out. "Sure." I wrote down my address and phone number on the back of a cab receipt.

"I'll pick you up around five. We'll grab some food first."

"Sounds good."

"Say hi to your mom."

I went in, and grabbed my usual spot at the counter — third stool from the end.

Prissy put a coffee in front of me. "Hi ya, Hon."

"Hey, Priss."

She swung away to take care of a customer. She looked good. She was back in her element, behind a counter slinging hash and coffee to the regulars. They loved her, like always. I wondered how long Jack would let her stay. She brought over a fresh creamer. "You see Ritter out there?"

"Yeah. He says *Hey*."

"So, you finally stopped and said hello."

"Yep." I sipped the coffee. Tasted like crap. *Hot water knocked stupid*. Didn't matter. I didn't come for the coffee. I came to see Prissy. "He's taking me to a concert tomorrow night."

"Johnny Cash."

"What?"

"It's Johnny Cash."

Should've known. "Guess I better polish my boots, eh?"

Prissy laughed. "You eating enough? You look thin." She brought me a grilled cheese.

Ritter showed up at 5:30. We went to Bonanza for dinner. I had the salad bar.

"Sure you don't want a steak? You used to love steak."

"Yeah. I just don't feel like one, tonight." I didn't feel like telling him I'd gone vegetarian. I didn't want to explain. It was more necessity than ideology, anyhow. I'd stopped buying meat when I left home. It cost too much. Now I couldn't stand the taste — the way the fat coated my mouth when I bit into a burger, or a steak. "I'm good with this."

"Suit yourself."

By the end of the concert, I was back in love with Johnny Cash. "That was great."

"'Course it was."

"No, really. He's fabulous. That was really really great!"

"You love Johnny Cash. We used to listen him to him all the time."

"Yeah. I just forgot how much I loved him." *How did I forget that?*

"You remembered the words, though."

"I did, didn't I?" We'd sung along with every tune. "A Boy Named Sue" was the best. Johnny's son-in-law played guitar with the band. During the song, they played a video where the kid played Sue and Johnny played the dad. The fight scene was vicious. "Thanks for taking me. I really enjoyed it."

"Sure." We drove in silence for a while. "You doin' OK, Bean?"

"I'm fine. Really."

"You need any money?"

"No. I'm good, Ritter. Don't worry." I knew he didn't have any. "I got a scholarship — for University next year."

"Yeah. Prissy told me." He suddenly looked shy. "I'm real proud of you, Bean. I don't know where the hell you got your brains, but Prissy says you're real smart. You really class valedictorian?"

"Yeah." I gnawed on my thumbnail. "It's no big deal." *Christ, now I sound like a snot.* "How are Jacqueline and the kids?"

"Good. I guess." He stopped for a red light. "We split up."

"Oh. Sorry."

"It's OK. She's young."

"Yeah." *Poor bugger. Guess that's what you get for marrying someone who's only eight years older that me.*

"Wanna get a coffee?"

"I better get home. I have homework. Algebra."

"OK."

Crap. That sounds like bull. "Maybe next week."

"Yeah. Sure. That'd be great."

We drove to my place. I got out. I stuck my head back in. "Thanks for the concert and dinner. It was great. I'll see ya next week OK?"

"Sure. You take care."

"You too." I turned to go. I turned back. "Hey, Dad?"

"Yeah?"

"If I ever have a kid, I think I'm gonna name her — "

He joined in, "Bill or George or anything but Bean!" Least we could still laugh together.

I turned to wave good-bye once I was in the building. He honked and drove away. *Bean. Who the hell names their kid Bean?*

I lived in a bachelor suite on the second floor. My building was smack dab in the middle of the student ghetto behind the Golden Mile Plaza. The hallways smelled of neglect — overcooked food, tobacco smoke and stinky feet — years of grime trapped in the rug. My place had no carpet. It was bright and tiny and clean. I had a rollaway cot, two orange stacking stools, and the red and black velvet hope chest Goose built for me in Shop. Mrs. P gave me a set of old dishes, some pots and cutlery. Prissy gave me a popcorn popper.

The first time she came over, Prissy was shy. "Nice tub," she said. I saw her take note of the stick above the door and then look for the other markers. I'd moved my circle ritual back inside. "Only one door, though."

"Yeah."

"You OK with that?"

"Yeah." *I'm the only one here. I don't have to escape myself.*

After the concert, I threw myself on the bed and looked at my walls. *Maybe I should get a Johnny Cash poster.* I had a lot of posters. The main room had James Dean, Marilyn, Bogey and Elvis. Che Guevara was in the bathroom with David Bowie. *Mostly dead people. All dead if you see Bowie as Ziggy Stardust.*

I got up, slipped on a Gordon Lightfoot cassette and made a package of Kraft Dinner. *Should've gone for the steak.* I smiled as I mixed the butter into the macaroni.

Prissy made KD with water. Just water.

I read the instructions one time, when I was around six. "Hey, Prissy, it says you're s'posed to put butter and milk in this."

Prissy was in the bathroom, getting ready to go out with Auntie. "In what?"

"Kraft Dinner."

"What for?"

"I dunno, but that's what it says." We didn't have any butter, of course. We used margarine. "Hey, Prissy?"

"What?"

"Is margarine the same as butter?"

"Margarine is butter."

"Oh. Should I put it in?"

"What for?"

"Cuz it says."

"Do what you want."

Directions

- Stir pasta into 6 cups of boiling salted water.

- Boil rapidly, stirring occasionally, 8-9 minutes, or to desired tenderness. Drain.

- Add 3 Tbsp butter or margarine, 1/4 cup milk and cheese sauce mix. Stir until pasta is well coated.

I got the margarine out of the fridge. We were out of milk, so I used a little can of evaporated. It tasted awful. "I definitely like your recipe better," I said as I helped Prissy zip up her red go-go boots. "You look pretty, Mom. Have fun tonight."

Prissy kissed me on the head and turned to go. "Keep the door locked," she said. "I'll be late."

Now, I made Kraft Dinner with milk and extra butter. Well, extra margarine. I still didn't buy butter — too expensive. I forced myself to buy fruit and fresh vegetables, like broccoli. I looked for what was on sale.

Prissy used frozen or canned vegetables and we only had fruit once in a while. When we learned about the Canada Food Guide in school, I told her we needed to eat fruit or we'd get *the scurvies*. She bought me some canned peaches.

It wasn't that Prissy was a bad mom or a bad cook, she just didn't think about food much. She cooked the way her mother had — on high. She boiled vegetables 'til they were soft and cooked meat 'til it was hard. She had a few specialties, though. Prissy Fallwell made the best cabbage rolls in the world. "Sour cabbage," she always said. "That's the trick. It's gotta be sour cabbage."

I made cabbage rolls with Prissy a million times. It's easy.

Get your biggest bowl. Mix up hamburger, eggs, salt and pepper, chopped up onions and some minute rice. Peel off the cabbage leaves and trim the thick bits at the bottom. Spread the best cabbage leaves out on the counter, and plop a scoop of the meat on them. Roll the leaf over the meat and fold the ends in. Finish rolling, and make sure the ends are tucked in tight. The rolling is the trickiest part, especially for a kid, but you get really fast, once you get the hang of it. When you've got all the rolls made, get the big roaster ready. First, lay some of the left-over sour cabbage leaves on the bottom. Then, lay the cabbage rolls in. Line them up nicely and tuck a few around the edges. You can fit a lot of cabbage rolls in a big roaster. Make two layers. Then, mix up a can of tomato soup with a can of water and pour it over the cabbage rolls. Cook them in the oven at 350 for a few hours and voila — the best cabbage rolls in the world!

On Thanksgiving, Prissy and Dee brought me some vegetarian cabbage rolls — made with rice, onions and celery — no meat. "I made them special," Prissy said. They also brought me an angel food confetti cake with lemon icing.

Dee said, "Can't you even come home for holidays?"

I ate my Kraft Dinner in my lemon-fresh bachelor apartment, and fell asleep listening to Gordon sing about loved ones, lying sleeping, in a place far away.

BOOK FROM GOOSE WITH REBEL PROGRAM

The day of graduation, Goose gave me a book. It was a hardcover blank journal, brown with a picture of the three fates on it. He had filled it with our favourite poems and song lyrics. It ended with "Up on Avenue A", and a note from Goose:

> *Here we go — off into the world.*
> *I'm scared Bean. Not of the world out there, but of something more. You and I have grown so close. Too close, I sometimes think. It's so hard to hide from someone who knows you better than you know yourself. I know there are things you need to hide. There are things I need to hide, too (believe it or not!). But, as I sit here tonight, all I can think is "Please God, don't let*

us lose each other. Don't let us get lost in the world."
We won't, right?
We won't.
See you on the other side.
All of my love, Goose

It had been a strange year. I was living on my own and something was eating at Goose. I didn't know what it was.

We did *Rebel Without a Cause*. I played Judy, the Natalie Wood part, and Goose was Plato. We went a little mad.

Plato is a weird weird kid. Playing him made Goose weird, too. He withdrew from everyone and started drinking. A lot. He'd grab a Slurpee or a Big Gulp at lunch, spike it with vodka and sip on it all afternoon. No one noticed.

I noticed, but I was too screwed up to do anything about it. I worried a lot about Prissy and Dee. I worried, but I didn't go home.

Goose became Plato and I became Judy. Judy whose father hates her and calls her a tramp. Who feels like the ugliest thing in the world. Judy whose mother is . . . ineffectual.

When the curtain came down on closing night, I blinked and woke up. *What now?* It was our final show of the year. My final show. Everyone was hugging and laughing. I left. Half an hour later, Goose found me under the makeup table. I was still in my costume. I was drinking Wild Turkey. I'd watched everyone change and leave for the cast party. Nobody noticed. Nobody ever noticed anything. Except Goose.

He hunkered down. "What's up?"

"I'm never gonna get to do that again."

Goose crawled under the table. It was a tight squeeze. "What are you talking about?"

"I'm never gonna act again."

"Who says?"

"You know this."

"Know what?" He took the Wild Turkey. "I don't know anything." He took a swig. "Well, one thing."

"What's that?"

"It is impossible to lick your own elbow."

"Yeah?"

"Try it."

"No thanks. I believe you." I took the bottle back. "What do bullet-proof vests, fire escapes and windshield wipers all have in common?"

He thought a minute. "They are all good ideas."

"Yeah. And, they were all invented by women."

"You want to be an inventor?"

"I want to do something important."

"Ahh, I see. And acting isn't important?"

"Not really."

"Oh." We sat awhile. "That's bullshit."

"What?"

"Bean, you can do whatever you want. I don't think you have to be a dumb lawyer or a social worker or go work with the lepers or whatever the hell it is you think you should do. I think you should go be an actress."

I took a big swig.

He took the bottle from me, clambered out from under the table, took the floor and sang me a lovely rendition of "Up on Avenue A", using the bottle as a mic.

I crawled out from under the table and gave him a standing ovation. "I love that song."

"I know."

"I love you, Gustave Peterson."

"Who wouldn't?" He capped the bottle and gave me a squeeze. "Life's a tightrope, baby. Don't look down."

My valedictory speech made everyone cry.

The speech was for Goose, mostly. It was about the power of friendship. We were eighteen years old and he'd already saved my life twice. Once by letting me move into his house, and once by telling me I didn't have to be a lawyer.

Who am I kidding?

Goose saved my life a million times.

The summer after graduation, we got a place together. We were still working six 'til midnight at the drugstore and I got a second job waiting tables at Vera's Café. I worked breakfasts, 6:00 AM to 10:00. Goose thought I was crazy to work so much, but I still couldn't sleep, so I figured I might as well be working.

I got by on about four hours of sleep. When I slept longer, I had nightmares. I never remembered them clearly. I just woke up afraid and more exhausted than when I went to bed.

Living with Goose seemed to ease the nightmares, somehow. They tapered off and by the fall, I could sleep eight hours straight.

When school started, I quit the drugstore job and kept my job at Vera's.

Goose studied Political Science and Philosophy. I studied Theatre. We read each other's books, and helped each other with our papers. Goose was an excellent researcher. I was a fast typer. It worked out.

I asked Goose if he thought we were cheating.

"Nah."

"You ever cheat?"

"No. You?"

"Once. Math. Grade four. I copied off Michelle Ostenchuk."

"Ostenchuk? She wasn't even good at math."

"I know. We barely passed."

Introduction to Acting was my favourite class. On the first day, the prof had us all walk around the room for a while. Then he asked us who we thought had the biggest personal space. The obvious choice was the big jock looking guy who was studying Education.

"Nope."

We named a few other guys.

"Nope. Nope. Nope." Then, he smiled. "It's Bean. Seriously. You all moved out of her way, every time. Why do you think that is, Bean?"

I was surprised, and embarrassed somehow. "I dunno."

"Hey," he said. "You didn't do anything wrong. It's just interesting."

When I told Goose about it, he nodded. "Obviously. It's your North End strut."

"My what?"

"When-oh-when will you embrace your heritage as Spam Suckin' Trailer Trash?"

I punched him.

"Kid-ding! But admit it, you're a tough little bird let loose amongst the soft underbellies of the upper-middle class. We're . . . different, Sweetie."

"You aren't."

He smiled. "I am."

I didn't want to be different.

That night, I went to Goose's room. "You awake?" He wasn't. I poked him. "Hey, Mister!"

"What?"

"You awake?"

"Am now. What's up?"

I sat on his bed. "You know me, right?"

"'Course I do." He looked at me. "What's the matter?"

"I change," I said.

"What do you mean?"

"I mean, everywhere I go, I change."

"We all change."

"Not like this."

He sat up. "What the hell are you talking about?"

"I think I become whatever people want me to be."

"Don't we all?"

"I dunno." I was scared.

"Hey, hey, c'mere." I crawled in beside him. He gave me a squeeze. "What's the matter?"

"I dunno."

"What are you thinking about?"

"About all those schools I went to, and how I was different in every one."

"Different how?"

"Like sometimes I was a jock."

He laughed. "I never believed that."

"I was."

"So?"

"So, I'm not a jock."

"That's for sure."

"But I was."

"Then they must've really sucked. What's the big deal?"

"Don't you think it's weird?"

"No. I think it's human. You wanted to fit in, that's all. You wanted to have a place."

"I guess."

"We all want to fit in."

"I guess."

"I know. You were always the new kid. You just wanted to blend in."

"Yeah, but then, who am I really?"

"Ruby Tuesday."

I elbowed him.

"You're my Bean. Mistress of disguise, but at heart, good ol' Bean E. Fallwell. OK?"

"OK." We were quiet for a while. "Goose?"

"Yeah?"

"You know who I hate?"

"Nope."

"Holden Caulfield."

"Who?"

"Holden Caulfield."

"I thought you loved Salinger."

"I do. I even love *Catcher in the Rye*. I just hate Holden. He's such a whiny little upperclass shit. I get what he means about everyone being phony, but he's the phoniest. Little poser shithead."

"Feel better?"

"Yeah."

"OK. Now sleep. And Bean?"

"Yeah?"

"Don't put your head under the covers. I might fart."

Goose drifted right off, like always. I watched him sleep.

I smelled dish-soap. I got the ache in my middle.

I missed Prissy and Dee. I hardly saw them anymore. I wouldn't go to the house, so we had to meet at my place, or downtown. Sometimes, we went to the Novia Cafe for grilled cheese. Prissy wasn't working at the bus depot anymore.

I curled into Goose and closed my eyes.

Another year slipped by.

Goose got a girlfriend.

I didn't really date anyone. I smooched a couple of guys, and even had a short-term fling with a fella. I was in Theatre after all.

I liked Goose's girlfriend, Natalie. She was nice. She was a little jealous of me at first, and didn't really settle down 'til she started spending the night. They had very loud sex.

Sometimes, I'd wander out of my room in the middle of the night and find Goose at the kitchen table, smoking in the dark. We'd head over to the park and hang out on the old bridge. We'd sit there, with our legs dangling over the edge, and stare at the moon's reflection in the water. We called her the *Lady in the Lake*.

One night, I asked if he remembered the Moon Landing.

"No," he said. "We were like . . . what? Four?"

"Do you remember meeting me?"

"Sort of. I remember the way my mom tells it, anyhow."

"How does she tell it?

"She says I was out in the front yard playing, minding my own business when this scraggly-haired little girl came along and started talking to me. She says she came to the window to listen. Up 'til then I'd been pretty shy around other kids. I got teased a lot because I had glasses."

"And a wimp-assed name," I cut in. "Who names their kid Gustav and then doesn't understand that he'll get the snot kicked out of him on a regular basis?"

"Am I telling the story or am I telling the story?"

"You're telling the story."

"Indeed Ms. Bean — speaking of atrocious things to name an *innocent* child."

"Fun-nee. Go on."

"So anyway — this scraggly bit of white trash is hanging over our fence and — "

"Your mother never called me white trash in her life. Did she?"

He thought. "No. But she does call you scraggly."

"Still."

"Oh yeah."

"Nice. On with the story."

"Where was I?" He took a breath to find his place. "Oh, right. There's a girl hanging over the fence and Mother is listening in, in case her little man is in trouble, but it turns out that her wee man and the lovely lass make friends. She stands in amazement as the two children walk to the alley and her son scratches something in the dirt. The little hoyden appears to read it."

"Your name."

"My name," he assents. "Though dear old Mother couldn't see that far. A while later, her son comes inside with a shiny face and says, *I have a new friend and her name is Bean E. Fallwell and she's three and half and she can read and she's been to the drive-in and from now on my name is going to be Goose.*"

"And so it was."

"And so it is."

"You used a rock."

"What?"

"You used my chalk rock to write your name on the sidewalk. Then we walked up and down the alley. And my name was still Eberts, back then."

"Mind like a steel trap, you."

"Yeah."

"I lost the rock."

"I know."

"You still have my aggy, don't you?"

"Of course."

"In your suitcase?"

"Yep."

"You amaze me, Miss Bean."

"I used to watch you."

"What?"

"At night. I'd sit across the street and watch you through the picture window."

"Little spy."

"I guess."

"What did you see?"

"You sat on the floor, playing with your Lego or Weebles or whatever. Your mom sat on the couch, knitting and your dad sat in his chair, reading the paper."

"Exciting."

"Sometimes, you sat on your father's knee. Sometimes, your mom brought the two of you tea and cookies. She'd stand behind your dad and put her hand on his shoulder. It looked nice."

"Why didn't you come visit?"

"I just liked watching you." I held his hand, "I think that you and I should grow old together."

He smiled. "We are growing old together."

LETTER FROM MATTHEW, BIBLE, AND MISTER GOD
THIS IS ANNA

In April, I got a letter from Matthew Guteleute offering to send me to Bible School with Elly — in England and Sweden.

I showed the letter to Goose. "The Christians," I said.

He read the letter. "They want to send you to Europe?"

"Yeah. To Bible School, with their youngest daughter."

"Cool. You wanna go?" he asked.

"Maybe. I went to Bible Camp once."

He laughed. "I remember."

"I liked it."

Goose nodded. "You felt safe there."

"What?"

"You wrote me about it. You felt safe there. You felt like you belonged — 'til they pulled that crazy *pretending you were in Russia* thing."

"Yeah. But Bible School?"

Goose waggled his eyebrows. "In England."

"Yeah."

"And Sweden."

"Yeah."

"I think you should go for it."

I applied. I had to write an essay about why I wanted to attend Bible School. Goose helped me write it. I got accepted but Elly didn't. The schools had a quota on how many people from each country they let in. I guess they figured Elly Guteleute was already solid in the faith department, and I needed all the help I could get.

For a while, I resisted. It didn't feel right for the Guteleutes to send me to England and send Elly to school in Caronport, Saskatchewan.

Rachael called. "You should go, Bean. It's a great school." Rachael had gone to England, Sweden and Austria the year before. She'd wanted me to go with her — but I had the scholarship to University. "My parents really want you to go."

"I know."

"It will make them so happy, to be able to offer you this."

"I know."

"So go."

I packed up my stuff.

Goose said I could leave the Samsonite with him, but I took it with me. He drove me to the airport. Prissy and Dee came along to see me off. Dee asked if I was going to be a Nun now.

"No Sweety, I'm just going to learn more about the Bible."

"Will you come back?"

"Of course." I hugged her.

Prissy and I didn't hug. "Be careful," she said.

"I will."

Goose gave me a huge squeeze. "Have fun," he said.

"I'm going to Bible School."

"OK. Not too much fun." He gave me a copy of *Mister God This is Anna* — one of my favourite books — a beautiful, magical, story about a ragamuffin girl and God. Anna's a girl after my own heart. She gathers up little pieces of beauty on the not so beautiful streets of East London. To Anna, these bits of beauty are bits of Mister God. When she finds a good bit, she makes someone *write it down, big,* and then she tucks it into a shoe-box. Goose hugged me again. "Ask real questions."

"Always." Anna's friend Fynn finds her standing up in bed one night, with tears streaming down her face, asking Mister God to teach her to ask *real* questions. Fynn thinks she's had a nightmare, but Anna tells him that she was just saying her prayers.

The Guteleutes sent me a book too — The *New American Bible*.

I boarded the plane and flew to England. I was gone for a year.

Shakespeare and Avalon

They searched my luggage at Heathrow.

The woman behind the counter scowled at my paperwork. "You're going to Bible School?"

"Yes."

She squinted at me — took in the ripped jeans, the leather jacket and the Rolling Stones t-shirt. "Go wait over there."

A man went through my bags. The backpack of clothes, notebooks, pens and the Bible was fine. The Samsonite was a different story. I watched him rifle through the books, pictures, bits of paper, and rocks. He held up the broken dog's head. "What is this stuff?"

"Ephemera."

"What?"

"Souvenirs." I smiled. "I collect things."

He found the bullet. "And what is this?"

"A bullet."

He closed the case. "How long you here for?"

"A year — at the outside."

He looked at my papers. "School up north for seven months?"

"Yes."

"And then on to Sweden."

"Yes. But I may come back here before I head home."

"You'll do well to leave this case behind when you're crossing borders. Raises questions."

I thanked him for his advice.

I rode the bus north through fairytale green and arrived at the school. It was a huge old manor house with arched windows and a fountain. *I'm not in Kansas anymore.* I found my way to my room. I was in the largest room at the school — sharing with nine other girls. I grabbed a bed in the corner.

It wasn't OZ but I was definitely a stranger in a strange land. First, I was in England — it was cold and wet; we ate custard, Yorkshire pudding and marmite on toast; and the toilet paper was thinner and stiffer than the pages of the Sears Catalogue. Second, I was living in a mansion. I had to share my room with nine others, but it was still pretty swanky for a North End gal. It was exactly how I'd pictured an international boarding school. We didn't have uniforms, but everyone dressed nice. The fresh-faced boys reeked of piney, sporty, cologne and the girls smelled of flowers. We attended lectures in a big hall and had our choice of three different dining rooms for meals. Nancy Drew would have fit right in. Bean E. Fallwell was a bit of an interloper, but I did my best to blend in. Third, and most disconcerting, I was at Bible School. The lectures were interesting — most of the time. It was the other stuff that got to me. I bit my tongue when, after watching Gandhi, one of my roomies said, "Isn't it too bad he won't be in heaven?" I learned to refrain from talking politics or rising to the bait when the Americans went on about their right to bear arms and Christianize the world.

I really did want to be one of these shiny people that were so sure about their place and purpose in the world, but it was tough. I spent a lot of time roaming the hills of England in the fog, screaming at God for bringing me to a place where all they seemed to want to do shove him into a tidy little box instead of asking the real questions that would lead us into . . . *Into what?* Into a fuller understanding of God and ourselves. Into *God's middle* as Anna would say.

I stayed sane by writing Goose. We wrote each other almost every day when I was in England. I asked him to keep an eye on Prissy and Dee for me. I told him about the wild things some of the students said. Things like, *Catholics aren't Christians because they have a priest who intercedes for them with God.* I wrote him about making an old lady lecturer cry because she was harping on and on about why people should stay married — for the sake of the children. He wrote me about school and his mom and dad. He wrote me about Prissy and Dee and passed my letters on to them. They were still moving all the time and I kept losing track of them.

Prissy never wrote me back.

Dee sent me drawings and her grade four school picture. She had a big old head of crimped hair and wore neon green. She was missing a tooth.

I also wrote Goose about Jonah.

I met him in the library, the first week of school. It was a big library. There were lots of books. Lots of *Christian* books. This guy, scanning the stacks, said, "No Nietzsche."

I nodded and, without thinking, I said, "No *Mister God this is Anna*, either."

He laughed, "Good point."

"You've read it?" I couldn't believe it. Anna's not exactly a best-seller.

"Sure. Have you read Nietzsche?"

"I have. Gives me a horrible headache."

He laughed.

I crossed over to him and stuck out my hand. "Bean E. Fallwell, Canadian. Agnostic Elvis worshipper by birth, with a tendency to explore churches. I like old movies, U2 and Mountain Dew."

We shook.

"Jonah Bartholomew Riley, American. Baptist by birth, with a tendency to stray. I like Bruce Springsteen, Coca-cola, and have a weakness for Pop Tarts." He was cute — in a big glasses, smarty pants kind of way. He had curly blonde hair and soft looking lips.

"Jonah," I said. "Really?"

He nodded. "Destined to be swallowed up by a whale, if I deviate from the path God intends for me. Bean a nickname?"

"Nope."

"Gotta love parents."

The next day we walked into town, found a used bookstore and bought some books to carry us through. He bought *Thus Spake Zarathustra* and some Herman Hesse. I bought *The Compleat Works of William Shakespeare* and *The Mists of Avalon* by Marion Zimmer Bradley.

I read the Shakespeare in class. It was a big old black book with gilt edged pages. Looked just like a bible.

I read Marion Zimmer Bradley in the bathtub after lights-out.

Jonah made me feel like less of a freak at school. I wrote Goose about our adventures — how we snuck out one night to see *Echo and the Bunnymen* at a local university, broke into the library to watch *Eraserhead* at midnight on the BBC, and raided the kitchen on a regular basis. Jonah started adding little notes to my letters home and then he and Goose started writing each other directly.

Goose sent us both care packages — Oreos, peanut butter, and two-ply tissue; books and booze; chocolate and these awful clove cigarettes that made us both sick.

Our little rebellions and my sessions of screaming at God kept me on an even keel, but in November, my nightmares came back.

One night, my roommate Judie tried to wake me from a dream and I punched her in the face — knocked her down and blackened her eye.

Jonah convinced me to go and talk to Morley about it.

Morley Channer was an ex-soldier with a Cockney thick as
week-old porridge when he got worked up. He stood five foot two,
had a brush cut and a tattoo on his arm so faded you couldn't
make out what it said. He smelled of malt vinegar and something
safe.

I liked Morley. He booked conflicting lecturers back-to back.
Drove the kids crazy. We'd hear one interpretation of a gospel
and then, the next week, something completely different about
the same book. *Think about it!* I wanted to scream when the
kids got confused.

I went to see Morley, but I had no bloody idea what to say
to him.

He asked me what the nightmares were about. I told him that
I didn't know, that I never remembered them. He pushed it, so
I finally said they were probably about my stepfather. That all
the, *God the Father this and, God the Father that* was getting to
me — having had no great father figure in my life.

He asked about my mother.

I said, "She has nothing to do with this."

We sat in silence until I asked Morley about the books in the
library. About why there weren't any opposing views.

"They'd never let me get away with it," he said.

"Who?"

"The Board."

I had *Mister God This in Anna* in my bag. I held it up. "How
about this one?"

He laughed and took the book, "Ahh, Fynn and Anna. A
good book." He handed it back. "It would just confuse them."

"That's no reason not to have it in the library. Maybe it would
clear some, *bits of glass* out of their eyes."

"Bits of glass?"

"Anna says people look at God through bits of glass, so they can see the God they want to see. They can't handle the whole picture."

"Right." He leaned forward. "I admire the strength of your faith, Bean."

"My faith?" I laughed. "I spend half of my time screaming at God."

"Exactly." He put his hand on my shoulder. "Their faith will be tested. It always is, right? Sometimes it comes early and sometimes it comes late, but the dark night comes to us all."

"You think so."

"I know it."

"They're so fucking righteous. Excuse my French."

Morley laughed. He leaned back.

I leaned in. "You know that they really believe that Gandhi won't be in heaven."

"Well, then. I suppose they're in for a bit of a surprise, yeah?" He winked. "What is it your gal, Anna, says about different religions?"

"She says we call it by different names, but to Mister God, we're all playing the same chord."

He smiled. "Smart little tich, isn't she?"

Morley was all right in my books.

Jonah wrote Goose about my nightmares coming back — told him I wasn't sleeping.

Goose sent more booze.

BLUESTONE

During the Christmas break, I hitchhiked to Stonehenge.

The circle had a simple rope enclosure, to keep tourists away. There was a man there when I arrived. We walked the circle, opposite each other. He was taking pictures. When I stood before the headstone, I put my pack down and offered up a prayer — to God, to the old gods and, for the first time, to the Goddess. I heard a screech and opened my eyes. A peregrine falcon landed on the headstone. I laughed. I heard a click. The man had taken my picture.

I hunkered down and watched the falcon tilt his head at me. When he flew away, I placed my hands on the earth to push myself up and felt a rock, smooth against my palm. I took it.

I gathered up my bag, and walked over to the trailer that sold tea and souvenirs. I bought two Stonehenge mugs, one for me and one for Goose. I sipped weak tea out of mine while I watched a tour bus pull up.

The Photo Man got a tea and leaned beside me, watching the tourists circle the stones. "I take your picture," he said, with a thick German accent.

"I know. It's all right."

"What is your name?" he asked. "And what do you know of Stonehenge?"

I couldn't resist. I smiled as I slung my pack onto my back, "Name's Morgan, and all I know is what the falcon told me." I sauntered back down the footpath to Amesbury with my scraggly old witch hair blowing in the breeze.

BRIGHID'S POUCH

In February, I met my first, self-proclaimed, witch.

Brighid had flame red hair, a butterfly tattoo on her left hand and a ferret named Bruce who lived in her knapsack.

The school sent us up to the Lake District for *Outreach Week* with two musicians from London as our fearless leaders. We held Coffee Houses. The guys sang Larry Norman tunes, we did a few skits, and then one of us would *witness* — meaning tell the story of how we came to the Lord. We were saving souls. Jonah was in my group. So was Judie, the roomie I'd punched out.

I met Brighid on the street in Penrith. She was playing with Bruce. I asked if I could hold him. He was restless, twirling round and round my hands. He leapt back over to Brighid, climbed up her arm and down into her knapsack. I invited them to the coffee house.

"Sounds dead boring," Brighid said.

"C'mon," I wheedled. "What can it hurt?"

"True nuff." Bruce crawled out of the knapsack and perched on Brighid's shoulder, nibbling her hair. They both looked at me. "Make y' a deal, Canada. I'll come to your party, if you come to one a mine." I hesitated and she smirked. "C'mon, then. What can it hurt?"

"All right."

"Brilliant. See ya later."

"Cool."

She headed off down the street. "Y' won't be savin' my soul though," she tossed over her shoulder. "It's not in need of rescuing."

I smiled.

Jonah and Judie came over. "Be careful," Judie said.

"Of what?"

She shrugged, "I don't know. She just gives me the heebies."

"You're just afraid of Bruce."

Judie wrapped her arms around herself. "No. Well yeah, I am afraid of rats, but it's more than that. It's her eyes." She shivered. "Feels like she can see right through me."

I shrugged. "Bruce is a ferret."

Brighid was true to her word. She came that night, sipped Earl Grey tea, and laughed at our skits. When Jonah got up to tell his story, she went outside for a smoke.

I followed. "Hey."

"Hey, ya," she replied. "Funny stuff that."

"Glad you liked it."

"Yeah, well. Don'tcha go mad with all that *God the Father* stuff, though?"

"Why would I?"

She stopped and looked at me. "You coming to my party?"

"Now?"

"Yeah."

I looked back towards the coffee house. "I have to help clean up."

"Tell 'em you were off saving my soul."

We walked.

She lit up. "Cig?"

"No thanks."

"Calm yer nerves."

"I'm not nervous."

She laughed.

I asked her where we were going.

"A friend's place," she said. "Just outside of town."

I stopped. "I can't. I can't go without telling them where I am. They'll worry."

"I bet." Brighid stopped and looked up at the sky. "Nice night for it."

"For what?"

"It's Imbolc."

"Imbolc." I'd heard that before. "Imbolc. The Festival of St. Brighid."

"There ya go. I knew you were a little witchy." She started walking again.

I caught up to her. "What?"

"You're a witch."

I huffed out a laugh and stopped again. She didn't say anything — just kept walking. I followed. "There's no such thing as witches."

She laughed.

"I'm not a witch. I know about Imbolc from a book and from . . . an old friend."

She pointed up, "Star."

"What?"

She grinned. "Falling star. You missed it." She kept walking.

I made her stop. "My friend's name was Star."

"Really?"

"The friend who told me about Imbolc."

She nodded, as if it was no big deal.

I sat on the curb. "Gimme a smoke."

We sat on the curb and smoked. Brighid asked me about Star. She asked if Star had given me a stone. She told me that, in England, they gather stones at Imbolc. I told her about Star's turquoise earring. Brighid told me that giving turquoise is a pledge of affection. That it protects the innocent. She told me that blue stones are good in general. That sapphire increases intuition. That the druids had used Preselli bluestone — dolomite from South Wales — to build Stonehenge.

I had Star's turquoise and Jack's sapphire in the Samsonite. The bluestone from Stonehenge was in my pocket. This chick was freaking me out. I asked her, straight out, what the hell was going on.

She laughed. "I see things. Sometimes I dream things. Runs in the family. My mom used to say I should just keep my mouth shut."

"Used to?"

"She died."

"Oh. Sorry."

"Yeah, well."

We smoked. She flicked her butt out into the street. Looked like a falling star.

I flicked my smoke out after hers. "I dream things, too."

"Yeah?"

"Nightmares mostly. Sometimes wolf dreams." I hadn't had a wolf dream in ages. "There's this wolf. Sometimes it's an old lady, but I know it's the wolf in a different shape. When I was a kid, she came to warn me about things. That must sound crazy."

"Not to me."

"You dreamt about me?"

She nodded.

"What did you see?"

"Not much. Your face. Star with her turquoise earrings. A blue sapphire ring. Stonehenge. Then, here you are, on the street in Penrith with a bunch of happy clappies."

"Happy clappies?"

"Evangelicals, yeah?"

I asked her for another smoke. I lit it and took a drag. "So. You are a witch. A psychic witch."

She nodded.

"OK then." I nodded back.

We smoked. Finally I said, "Why would this happen?" She asked what I meant and I said, "Why would you dream of me? Why would I come here? For what?"

"Dunno."

"That helps a lot."

Brighid shrugged. "Ask me something. Tell me something."

I asked her about the ring.

She asked me where I got it.

I told her it was Jack's and why I took it. I told her the story he'd told me about how he got the ring and what it could it do. "You think it's true?"

"That he can see things?"

"Yeah."

"Nah," she said. "He doesn't sound the type. Just likes making up stories."

"Yeah." The smoke was making me dizzy. "But he knew things. He knew everything we did. Everywhere we went."

Brighid shrugged. "Maybe people just told him."

"Probably. Charming ol' Guitar Man."

I asked Brighid if she did spells.

"Not really," she said. "I do rituals."

"For what?" I flashed on my room at school: a gnarled branch above the door, a feather or stone on every window ledge, a piece of bone beneath my bed with the Samsonite.

"Celebrations mostly," she said. "Marking the seasons and such — like tonight. I do blessings for people, make amulets."

"For luck?"

"Protection. Amulets ward off negative forces. Luck is Talismans. They attract things."

I rubbed the bluestone in my pocket. "So, you do believe in magic?"

"I believe we can affect the world with our intentions."

"What's that mean?"

She tilted her head, thinking. "I believe that we can call things to us, or keep them away." I felt woozy. She took my arm. "Y' all right?"

"Yeah." My stomach was churning. "I better go."

"I'll walk you."

"No. It's fine."

"What's the matter?"

"I gotta go." I ran. A few blocks from the coffee house I threw up. I was shaking and sweating. I told myself that it was from too many smokes.

When I looked up, Brighid was standing there. She took a pouch from around her neck. She emptied it out, slipped the contents into her pockets and hung it around my neck. It was beautiful. A small bag of soft tan leather with a B embroidered on it. "Here," she said. "It's for keeping stones in. The B isn't for Brighid or Bean, it's a rune — Berkana — means fertility, growth, the Mother. Wear it for balance."

I didn't know what to say. "Thank you. It's beautiful."

"Yeah, well. Be seeing ya, Canada." She turned away.

"You think so?"

She smiled over her shoulder, winked and sauntered off. Bruce was peeking at me through her hair.

POSTCARD FROM PARIS

Near the end of term, Jonah got all weird and distant — like he was pissed-off at me for something. I had no idea what was up, but I was worried. We'd made plans to travel together after we were done school in England. I was headed to Sweden and he was headed to Germany and then on to Upward Bound —a six-week program in Austria. It was just like Outward Bound except, amidst all the physical challenges and torture, you also got preached at. We had two weeks to travel. I wanted to see Paris. I wanted to see Paris with Jonah.

I finally just came out and asked him if he still wanted to travel together and he nearly chewed my head off. He asked if I'd *gotten a better offer.* He could be such a jerk.

I should have just gone on my own.

We went to France. We landed in Calais on Easter Sunday in a raging downpour. We got picked up by a guy named Fred and his huge German shepherd named Satan. I climbed in the front seat with Fred and made Jonah sit with Satan. Fred had a flat in Paris. He invited us to stay with him. We were there for a week.

I couldn't believe I was in Paris — wandering around the Champs-Élysées and Montmartre; looking at the Mona Lisa. I missed Goose. I missed Prissy and Dee. I wished Elly Guteleute had come to school with me and was there in Paris to sit on benches with and talk. Jonah and I were barely speaking to each other.

Fred thought Jonah and I were lovers. He found our sleeping arrangements peculiar. We slept in our very separate sleeping bags on the couch. I told Fred that Jonah and I were just friends and besides, we were fresh out of Bible School. He just thought we were fighting. I guess we were, only I had no frigging clue what we were fighting about.

On our final day in Paris, Jonah went off to the Museum of Modern Art and I sat on the steps of the Sacre Coeur and wrote Prissy a postcard. I had no way to mail the card — no *where* to mail it to. Goose had lost them. I knew he'd find them again, or I'd find them when I got back home, but I didn't know if I'd ever give Prissy the card. It was too honest. I told her how much I missed her — not because I was in Europe, but because I felt so far away from her even when we were sitting at the same table. I pulled out another postcard and wrote her again.

> *Hey Prissy,*
> *I'm sitting on the steps of the Sacre Coeur in PARIS — can you believe it?!!!!*
> *Just watching people, and thinking of you.*
> *One day I'll bring you here — to Paris and we will sit on these steps together and watch the people. Wouldn't that be great? Just you and me some bread and cheese and maybe even a bottle of wine. You can do that here — drink wine wherever you want.*
> *I miss you, Mom.*
> *Take good care.*
> *Love, Bean.*

I'd send her that one when Goose found them again.

After Paris, Jonah Bartholomew Riley and I went our separate ways. I never wanted to see him again. He went off to Germany, and I headed for Sweden.

HUWELIJKS CAKE (WEDDING CAKE)

Partway though my time in Sweden, Goose's letters stopped. When my letters started coming back, unopened, I called. His number was disconnected. I called his parents. Mrs. Peterson answered. She told me Goose had moved. She started crying, and hung up on me. I wrote Prissy. The letter bounced back with someone's handwriting on it — *Return to sender. No such person at this address.* I sent letters to friends from University trying to find out what was going on.

Goose's ex-girlfriend, Natalie, finally sent me a postcard. It was a stupid picture of the Legislative Buildings. "He's OK, Bean. Let him be awhile." That's all it said.

I had to let him be. I had no idea where the hell he was.

I started counting the days until I'd be home.

Near the end of term, the Head of the school went on a trip. When he came back, he announced that Upward Bound was full. *Who gives a shit,* I thought. I was ready to go home.

Then, I got a phone call.

I never got phone calls.

My palms were sweating as I picked up the receiver. I was sure it was about Goose.

It was the Guteleutes. "We're praying for you, " Matthew said.

I almost passed out with relief. "I'm praying for you too."

"We're praying for you right now. Everyone is here, at home, and we are praying for you."

"Uh . . . OK. Well, I'm fine. I'm good. Is everything OK? Why is everyone there?" I started getting nervous again.

"We want to send you to Upward Bound."

"What?"

"We'd like to send you to Upward Bound."

I told Matthew that it was full. That the Head of the school had just come back from some big meeting and announced that UB was full — that morning.

Matthew asked me to call and check.

I didn't want to call and check. I didn't want to go to Austria and run up and down the freaking Alps. I wanted to go home and find my best friend.

Matthew asked me to call and check. "We love you, and we really feel that God is telling us to send you to Austria."

My throat hurt. "I love you, too." I did love them. I do love them. "I'll check."

I called England praying — *please God, please God, let me go home!* The secretary, answered. I chatted awhile, mostly to avoid the question. I had a bad feeling. Finally, she asked me what I was calling for.

"Upward Bound is full right?"

"What?"

"Upward Bound is full, right?"

"Ahh."

"What?"

She had that crazy *God works in mysterious ways* glee in her voice, "We received a cancellation this morning, actually."

"Let me guess. Canadian Female." *Love that quota.*

"Yes indeed."

What could I do? "Sign me up," I said.

I still thought I could get out of it. The deal with the Guteleutes remained the same. They paid my tuition at school, but I had to cover the travel costs. I didn't have enough cash to even get to Austria. My plan was to head to Ilse's, my Dutch roomie's, and not say a word about being low on funds. I knew if I said anything, some crazy Christian would get me to Austria. I would stay at Ilse's and then, right before I was supposed to head to UB, I would let her know that I was busted and catch the plane home from Amsterdam. No problem. I had an open-ended return ticket. I could fly out, stand-by, whenever I wanted.

Everything went according to plan, until we went to Ilse's best friend's wedding. I didn't want to go. I told Ilse that I'd just end up sitting in the corner with some kid that wanted to practice English. Ilse convinced me go. I ended up in a corner with the eleven-year-old sister of the bride. She asked about Upward Bound and, being an idiot, I told her I wasn't going.

"Why?"

"No money."

"What do you need money for?"

"To get there."

"I be back." She took off and I got a sinking feeling.

She ran back in a few minutes and gave me a piece of wedding cake and the *good news*. Sure enough, her and her parents were headed out on a holiday to Austria. They could drop me off, right at the school.

I couldn't not go. It was *God's Will*, after all. I'd spent months screaming at Him to show Himself to me. To give me a sign, show me that He was in charge of my destiny. I asked for a sign and He sent two.

That's when I remembered that Jonah was headed to Austria. *Perfect.*

God is frigging hilarious.

Letter from Goose

The happy Dutch family dropped me off in Austria — the land of music, mountains and best chocolate in the world.

I was sitting on the school steps when Jonah arrived. He looked sufficiently shocked. "Bean?"

I stood. "Hey, man, how's it going?"

He tossed down his bag and pulled me in for a hug. "What are you doing here?"

I told him the truth. "God sent me."

We were up a mountain the day I got the letter from Goose.

Hey Bean,

So. Long time no write, I know. I'm sorry. Just couldn't find the right words.

Did you know that when opossums are playing possum, they aren't "playing"? They actually pass out from sheer terror.

I feel like I'm going to pass right the fuck out. I've started this letter a million times. I've finished it at least twice. I have a friend standing by, right this minute, to rush this completed epistle off to the mailbox so I can't tear it up again.

I have no idea why this is so hard. Why I am so afraid to tell you this.

I'm gay Bean.

Queer as a three-dollar bill. Or, as I'm told they say in the grand UK, bent as a nine-bob note.

My parents aren't taking it well.

I'm afraid you won't take it well either.

Please write.

I love you Bean. For ever and ever. Amen.

Goose

I ran. I got up and ran outside, into the dark. It was raining. I just ran. I stopped at an edge. I sat on the side of a mountain and I started to cry. I couldn't even scream at God. I just sat in the rain and cried. I hadn't cried since the night I'd sat at the Peterson's kitchen table and realized I'd left home.

Jonah found me. He sat. Near me, but not touching.

I snorted, trying to stop crying.

Jonah wrapped his arms around his legs and stared into the dark. "It's Goose, right?"

I nodded, unable to speak.

"He's gay, isn't he?"

I looked at Jonah. "How the hell would you know that? I didn't even fucking know. Did he write you about this? Has he been writing you this whole fucking time?"

"No. No no no. I haven't heard from him since we left England. He never said anything. I just wondered."

"Why the hell would you wonder if Goose was gay?"

Jonah shrugged, "Takes one to know one."

"What?"

He laughed a little. "I don't know. I don't know what the hell I am. Messed up, I guess. There was this guy at school in England."

"What?"

"We didn't do anything, but . . . That's why I was so weird at the end. That's why I was such an ass in Paris."

"What?"

"You were supposed to seduce me."

Click. Light bulb. Duh! "Of course I was."

"So?"

"So what? You want me to seduce you now?"

"No." He smiled. "So . . . what do you think?"

"About what?"

"About Goose being gay."

"I don't give a rat's ass who people sleep with."

"Then what's wrong?"

I could hardly get the words past the ache in my throat. "He said he couldn't tell me. What — he's afraid I won't be his friend anymore? How the hell can he even think that?"

"Look around, darlin'. We're at Bible School."

"So fucking what?"

"Did you write Goose about taking those guys up on the offer to start a mission."

"Yeah. So what? I write Goose about everything." The guys we toured with up in Penrith were starting their own mission, working in jails and drug rehab centres all over Europe, and they'd asked me to join them when I was done school. I considered it. A mission. A purpose. Saving Souls.

"You're a million miles away from him, Bean. For all Goose knows, you're about to go Kamikaze Christian at any moment."

"Oh for Christ's sake!"

"Exactly."

I had to laugh. "I love him. He is my best friend. How could he ever think that I would . . . That's just crazy."

"He's scared, Bean. It's scary."

"Christ."

"Yeah."

I looked at Jonah. He was staring out into the dark. I touched him. "Are you OK?"

"Yeah. No." He shrugged. "I don't know."

We stared out into the night for a long time. When we went back inside, I wrote a postcard to Goose at the address on the letter's envelope.

Hey Goose:

Did you know that a duck's quack doesn't echo? No one knows why.

All of my love, always.

Bean

Our letters back and forth resumed.

God Stone

Jonah and I both survived Upward Bound.

I even survived the solo — three days alone on the side of a mountain with nothing but a bottle of water, a sleeping bag, a tarp, and the Bible.

That's where I met God.

I didn't actually see him.

I heard him.

Really.

I couldn't tell, from the voice, whether God is a boy or a girl. My guess is neither.

The idea of the Solo was to set up a rudimentary shelter and then just sit there and pray, think, and listen for God. A vision-quest — Christian style. I set up a little shelter in the shade. I read, I chatted with God in my usual way, and I stared off into space, enjoying the silence and the break from running up and down mountains. On the third morning, I was stiff from sleeping on the ground. I did some stretches. I was wearing a big, baggy, burgundy sweater and black leggings. I loosened my braids; finger combed my hair, and rebraided it. For some reason, it felt like I was getting ready to go to rehearsal for a show.

Someone said, "It's not a rehearsal." The voice was not booming from the heavens, but it wasn't inside my head either. I heard it.

Three days alone can make you kind of squirrelly. *Did I say that out loud?* I thought. I looked around. I thought someone was goofing with me — Jonah maybe — sneaking around and spying on me. "Hello? Jonah? Come out, come out, wherever you are."

Nothing.

I kept looking. "Very funny."

The voice came again. "Be who you are."

I stood still. "Who's there? Come on. It's not funny."

Nothing.

I sat down.

I know that God the Almighty does not talk to people — out loud. If you scream at him long enough for him to show himself, he may reach down, pluck you up and set you right on the front steps of a school you don't want to be at, but he does not *talk to people* — and if he did, he sure as hell wouldn't pick me. I hadn't eaten in three days. I was obviously having aural hallucinations. *Be who you are? What the hell does that mean?*

When I was a kid, I had a very clear mission — taking care of Prissy Fallwell. First, Prissy and Ritter and then Prissy and Dee — but always Prissy. I went to Bible School to find a new mission. I so wanted God to tell me what to do, set me on a path. I really did want to be close to God, be sure of my place in the world, be part of His shiny happy family and a useful tool in His grand scheme for mankind. I wanted God to give me a new mission — so I stood up and yelled at Him. "If you're going to make a bloody appearance, you better tell me what the hell it is you want me to do!" It was crazy. Who the hell did I think I was? Joan of Arc standing on a mountaintop waiting for my mission from God?

The voice came again, "Be who you are."

I am definitely hallucinating. I thought. *I have not eaten for three days and I am hearing things. Simple.*

I sat back down. I closed my eyes. I felt warmth on my face. My eyelids went pink. The sun was rising.

Fine then, I thought. *I'll be who I am. I'll be . . . an actor.*

My heart slowed. I took a deep deep breathe and I felt calm and peaceful — like a weight had been lifted; like a final, irrevocable decision had been made.

I felt something soft brush against my cheek.

I opened my eyes and there were butterflies — everywhere. Monarchs.

I blinked. I stretched out my arms, and they landed on me. They walked on the palms of my hands.

I whispered to them, "I am going to be an actor. And I'm going to play Joan of Arc."

The butterflies flapped and lifted off — a cloud of orange, disappearing into the Austrian sky.

It was strange and unbelievable. It was magic. It was real.

I took down my shelter, rolled my sleeping bag and bible in the plastic, and drank the rest of my water. I picked up a smooth black stone and slipped it into Brighid's pouch around my neck, beside the bluestone from Stonehenge. When the sun hit its zenith, I walked down the mountain. I was ready to go home.

WANDER BALL

There's an old red rubber ball in my Samsonite. I tried to throw it out when I left home, but I couldn't. I'd originally put it in the suitcase to remind me never to leave Prissy.

Slim gave me the ball on a camping trip. I wandered off one night, following the bouncing ball all over a campground near Revelstoke BC. I was gone for six hours. When I came back, Prissy was a mess. She hugged me so hard I thought she'd break my ribs. She was shaking like a baby bird who'd fallen out of her nest. Once she knew I was really back and really OK, she smacked me across the head. I'd scared her. I promised never to wander off, like that, again.

I hated that fucking Wander Ball. It made me feel guilty for leaving home. But I couldn't throw it out any more than I could throw away GT's funeral announcement and pretend that he was still alive. They were part of me.

On the plane ride home from Europe, I stared out the window and thought about Prissy and Dee. I'd been gone for nearly a year. I'd hardly heard from them. I'd hardly written. I didn't even hug Prissy when I left. She didn't hug me. Anything could've happened. We could've died. I could've run off to be a missionary.

I will hug her. I thought. *I'll just march right up to Prissy Fallwell and I will hug her guts out.*

I landed at home with five dollars in my pocket. Luckily, Goose was there to meet me. He looked great. He'd always been a sharp dresser, which, in the land of mukluks and lumber jackets, should've tipped me off to the whole gay thing. He looked taller. I hugged him and told him that he looked amazing.

He grinned. "It's the hair care products."

Goose was happy. His mom had stopped crying. His dad was still silent, still mad or hurt or confused or whatever, but Goose hoped he would come around eventually.

We drove home to his place. When he swung the door open, I almost had a heart attack. The place was packed. Mrs. Peterson was there with people from the drugstore, Vera's, and school; Auntie was there; even Alden, Mr. Q, and Spuddy and Slim.

Prissy was standing at the back of the room.

Dee was scarfing chips. She ran at me, spewing crumbs from her mouth, "Bean!" She almost knocked me over. She was taller too. I hugged her, hard, and watched Prissy smile.

I took Dee's hand, walked straight over to Prissy and grabbed her. "Hey, Mom."

She was stiff in my arms, but I wouldn't let go and she finally hugged me back. "Hey, Kid, don't squish my guts out." She leaned back. Her eyes were shiny with tears.

"You remember that time I wandered off — in that campground?"

"Revelstoke."

"Yeah."

"I thought I lost you."

I kissed her on the forehead. "Never. I love you, Mom."

She gave me another squeeze.

Then it was hugs for everyone — shy or not. Alden introduced me to his wife and two little girls. I hadn't seen him in years. He looked happy too. Auntie had a new beau — a handsome man named Glen with a big belt buckle and an artificial arm. Spuddy almost smothered me with a hug and Slim blushed when I gave him a peck on the cheek. Mr. Q tried to shake my hand, but I gave him a good crushing instead. Mrs. Peterson hugged me lightly and patted my hair, "Welcome home, Honey."

I hugged, and laughed, and told stories about Bible School.

Dee curled up beside me on the couch. She held my hand. We watched Alden play with his girls. He looked like a good dad.

Dee patted my arm. "Hey, Bean?"

"Yeah, Dee?"

"Why don't you come and stay with us? For a while."

Dee's eyes are blue. The colour shifts, depending on her mood — a deep soft blue for sadness, hard turquoise for anger. Goose says my eyes do the same. Maybe that's why I rarely look anyone in the eye. They'd see too much. Dee was ten years old. She was ten years old, and her eyes were sad.

"I can't, Sweety."

"You can," she said. "We don't live with Jack anymore."

My mouth probably fell open. "What?"

"He's over on Pasqua. We left."

"Prissy left Jack."

Dee grinned.

I couldn't believe it. "Holy shit."

Dee giggled. "Thought nuns didn't swear."

"Holy hot spewing stacks of summer sausage! What happened?"

She shrugged. "Doesn't matter." She looked away. I didn't press it. I was in shock. Dee looked back at me. "So?"

"So what?"

"So, will you come home?"

I couldn't answer. My stomach hurt. "I can't." I watched my sister's eyes lighten to turquoise as she realized I was never coming back.

She got up. "I need a coke." She didn't talk to me for the rest of the night.

I don't know why I couldn't move back in with them. Maybe I didn't trust Prissy. Maybe I thought she'd go back to Jack. Maybe it was just because I already had a plan to move even farther away.

After everyone left, Goose and I had a few more beers and I told him about meeting God on the mountainside in Austria.

"That is wild," he said.

"Yeah. Well, I hadn't eaten in three days." I took a swig of beer.

"Still."

"Yeah. I heard him Goose. Heard her. Whatever."

"And what did he, she, say again, exactly?"

"Be who you are."

Goose looked thoughtful.

I nudged him. "What?"

"And you think that means, go be an actress?"

"Yes. I shall go forth and become a famous actress and I shall play Joan of Arc."

"OK then." He didn't look convinced.

"Whaaaaat?"

"Nothing." He shook his head. "If you heard God tell you to be an actress, then *you go girl*." He patted me and headed off to bed.

I did hear God tell me to go be an actress — so I went. To Toronto — the centre of the Canadian acting universe.

I was gone for five years.

Well, mostly gone.

Prissy and Dee kept calling me back.

JACK ROCK

Once I left home, fewer and fewer things went into the Samsonite. Time was speeding up. The world was slipping by and I had less of a need to mark things, to gather bits and pieces that would tell me who I was. I thought I had that all figured out. First, I left home. Then, I ran off to Bible school and tried to immerse myself in the happy Christian world. When that didn't work, I headed to Toronto and dove into the Theatre world. I was trying to achieve Escape Velocity, but the pull from home was too strong. I couldn't totally leave Prissy and Dee. Even though, by the time I hit Toronto, I didn't want to be the girl that the Samsonite told me I was. I didn't want to be a Welfare brat who was brought up in chaos, moving every few months, with stray men wandering in and out of my life. I sure as hell didn't want to remember anything about my time with Jack Vara. I wanted a whole new life — away from all that.

I met a boy and fell in love.

Lee Mathews was a Johnny Depp look alike from the wrong side of town. He was twenty-one, loved Vietnamese Food, Warren Zevon and rolled his own smokes. Lee had sad eyes, a quick laugh and hid his baggage well.

We met in a coffee shop. He was cute, and smart, and funny. He was an actor and a playwright. We were friends for a year before we finally kissed. Two weeks later, we were living together. We moved into a warehouse. It was groovy, but it had no tub. It had no separate rooms with a lock. It had a shower and a sink and a hotplate. We built a platform for the bed. We rode the subway. We acted in shows together — shows that made no money. We paid our rent waiting tables and working as temps. We ate Singapore noodles from the takeout place down the street. We bought each other *Happy Tuesday* presents from the Dollar Store.

Lee knew a bit about my family. Goose and I still wrote all the time and talked on the phone at least once a month. Prissy and Dee didn't write. I called them once in a while. I hated calling home. It made me tired.

Lee laughed once, after I got off the phone with Prissy. He said I talked funny when I called home. I asked what he meant and he said, "Well, I can't tell if it's Saskatchewanian or White Trashese — but you definitely talk weird when you talk to Prissy."

I told him that I hadn't noticed.

I had noticed. It bugged Prissy when I talked — normal. She thought I was being snotty. Normal was the way everyone spoke, wherever I was. I picked it up. I wasn't being pretentious, or using big words or anything, but something irritated Prissy about the way I talked when I was in Toronto. She thought I was trying to be a big shot, especially if we got into an argument. Prissy and I didn't argue much. Prissy and I didn't even talk much, but if we did get into a discussion, about Dee or whatever, the way I spoke drove Prissy nuts. I was — calm.

Prissy only called me when something was wrong. The calls always came in the middle of the night. They were always about Dee. Dee was failing classes. Dee was dropping out of school. Dee was in trouble with the police. Dee was in the hospital — again.

One night, I woke from a sweaty dream to the phone ringing.

It was Prissy. "Come home," she said. "It's Dee. I can't handle it."

When I hung up, Lee said, "Don't go."

I said, "I gotta go."

Prissy called, and I headed home. Like always.

Dee was in the Munroe Wing. The same place they put Ritter that time he shoved a knife in his gut.

She was slouched in a ratty green lazyboy in the patient's lounge watching *Cheers* when I arrived. I listened to the opening song and thought, *Not me. I hate places where everybody knows my name.*

I looked at Dee and ran the film noir voice-over in my head.

Dee-dee Fallwell was fifteen years old and as tough as her red acrylic nails. She had an impenetrable wall of bleached blonde bangs, smoked Export As, and had a chip on her shoulder the size of Jupiter.

Dee was mad. At me. She'd been angry for years. Angry that I left. Angry that I kept leaving. Maybe angriest of all that I kept coming back.

I remembered the day Prissy brought her home from the hospital. The day I promised to love Dee forever, to make sure she got enough vegetables to eat, and to keep her safe. I'd promised that I would never let anyone split us up — ever. I'd lied.

I leaned on the doorframe, unsure of what to say.

I slipped on my best Cliff Claven voice and said, "Did you know that laugh tracks all come from the Red Skelton show?"

Dee turned her head. She smiled, at least.

I walked into the room. "They say it all goes back to 1953 when the *Laff Box* was invented by a guy named Charles Douglass." I plunked down on the couch beside her lazyboy. "According to legend, most of the laughs we hear today came from Red's old Freddy the Freeloader bits. Mime. No disturbing dialogue to interrupt the laugh."

"Cool," Dee said, and turned back to the TV. She looked tired. Gloomy. She looked sullen. I took her hand. She let me. We watched TV.

Dee had been in and out of the Munroe Wing for a year. She'd made seven suicide attempts: each one worse, according to Prissy; each one better, according to Dee — closer. She usually took pills.

The first time Dee tried to kill herself, I'd taken all my money out of the bank and flown home. She was asking for me, but when I got there, she wouldn't talk to me. I stayed until she was released from the hospital. I tried to talk to her, find out why she'd done it. She wouldn't say. Finally, I just went home. To Toronto.

The next time Dee hurt herself, I took the bus.

The last few times, I'd just called her on the phone.

She'd never say much. I just tried to make her laugh, cheer her up. We took to calling the psyche ward *The Spa*.

When we talked, Dee mostly said she couldn't handle it.

I didn't understand. "Handle what?"

She couldn't tell me. It was — everything. She dropped out of school because she couldn't handle it, but then she couldn't deal with having to go out into the world and get a job and whatever. Dee couldn't handle growing-up. She couldn't handle life.

I didn't understand. To me life is life. You just get on with it.

Dee kept saying, "It's so easy for you."

Things went OK, for a while. Dee and Prissy both said that they were glad I was *home*. Dee got released from the hospital. She seemed calm. Her and Prissy told me funny stories from the Spa — like the time Dee escaped and went running down Broad Street in a hospital gown, butt to the breeze.

I listened. I realized that Dee actually liked spending time at the Spa. She felt safe there. They took care of her.

I decided to stay a while. I watched Dee. I listened to her. I tried to figure out what the hell I could do to make her stop trying to hurt herself.

I had no idea.

One night, a week after Dee got out, Prissy and I went to a baby shower for some friend of hers. Dee was supposed to come along but, at the last minute, she said she wasn't feeling well. I offered to stay home with her. She brushed me off — told me that she was fine and just wanted to be left alone; told me that I had to trust her. So. We went to the shower and left Dee at home. Alone.

In the middle of the stupid games, I decided I wanted to escape so I whispered to Prissy that I was worried about Dee. We headed home. When we walked in, the stereo was blaring Guns 'n' Roses. All the lights were on. Dee was in the bathroom. I turned down "Welcome to the Jungle", and put the kettle on, for tea.

"Hey, Kid, you want some tea?" I yelled. She didn't answer, so I went and tapped on the door. I thought she was in the bathtub having a soak. "Dee?" No answer.

Something's wrong. I try the door. It won't budge. *Shit.*

"Prissy?"

"What?"

"I can't get the door open."

Prissy comes into the hallway. "Open it."

"I can't.

"I took the lock off," she says. "Open the damned door."

I try. I can't budge it. "She must lying against the door."

Prissy takes a few breaths. "Dee?" She moves to knock on the door. She steps back again. "Dee. Open the door."

We wait.

I state the obvious, "She's not answering."

Prissy flies at the door, smashing it with her fists. "Wake the fuck up and open this door!"

I send her to call the ambulance. I keep pushing at the door.

Prissy yells from the livingroom, "What did she take? They need to know what she took!"

"I don't know. I can't get in the fucking door!" I throw myself against it again and again, yelling for Dee. I finally manage to shift her enough to squeeze in. She's naked and the room reeks of strawberries — her favourite shampoo. I toss the pill vials into the hallway. I yank Dee up. I try to make her sit up. I yell at her. She slugs me in the face. I slap her back. "Wake the fuck up!"

The paramedics arrive. They get her on a gurney. She's crying. She's asking for her bathrobe. They start rolling her out. "She's just trying to delay," one of the guys calls over his shoulder. I run out after them with the robe. I climb in the ambulance and cover her up.

Prissy is standing in the street, her arms wrapped tight over her chest. She looks tiny. "I'll meet you there," she says. Prissy hates ambulances.

We squeal off. The siren's blaring and Dee starts fighting with the paramedic. She's screaming. She just keeps screaming and the lights are flashing and the siren's shattering my head and it's like a bloody nightmare and I slip out of myself and up to the ceiling, but the jangly steel guitars can't drown out the screaming and I drop back into my body. I pull back inside. Watch from behind my eyes. Dee's mouth screaming. Paramedic Man trying to calm her. I am trying to calm her. I'm talking but I don't know what I'm saying. The paramedic has brown eyes. Dee's hair is still wet. She's painted her nails. *She wanted to look pretty.* Her robe has butterflies on it. *Like that old robe Prissy used to have.* There's a cigarette burn on her robe. Right on a butterfly wing. *That's so sad.* I feel the robe. *Silky.*

"Monarch's fly all the way to Mexico every year," I say. "Only the women go though. Only the women go and they never make it back. They lay their eggs on milkweed plants and then they die, leaving the eggs to survive on their own. The young Monarchs never know their parents. They grow up alone, on poison weeds, and then they fly all the way back here. They come home. They finish the journey of migration with their intergenerational memory to guide them." *Intergenerational memory. What do we hold, little sister? From Prissy. From a*

Grandmother who ran off with a traveling man? I look up at Dee's face. She's still screaming. *What the fuck am I talking about butterflies for? Doesn't matter. No one's listening anyway.* "Milkweed is poison," I say. "Baby Monarchs eat poison — but it protects them from predators. It protects them."

At the hospital, Dee almost escapes when they try to transfer her to a table. There is no way she's going to let them pump her stomach. My sister is screaming and screaming and she looks right at me and her eyes are huge and hard — they flash blue-black. She stops screaming. She stops fighting. She stares into my eyes. She speaks, low. "Let me die, you fucker!" She blinks, and she starts to fight again.

It takes six people to strap her down.

When she is silent, I go outside. I bum a smoke off a guy standing there with an intravenous pole. *I was here. I was right here and it didn't matter at all.*

Prissy arrives with Spuddy and Slim. They bring me coffee from Tim Horton's. Spuddy and Slim have hung in with Prissy this whole time. They still come over every Christmas. They still send me birthday cards. They bring us coffee at the Spa when Dee is trying to kill herself.

When Dee is in her room, I go in. She won't open her eyes. There are tears running down her face, so I know she's awake, but she won't open her eyes. She turns her face to the wall.

Spuddy and Slim drive us home.

The next day — every day — I go to the hospital. I buy Dee smokes. I start smoking. Something we can do together. We don't talk much.

She's on intravenous for a few days. She looks tired, big dark circles under her eyes. She sees a psychiatrist, Dr. Schlusser, once a week. She says he smells of mothballs and Listerine. She tries a few escapes. She tries to get her hands on a knife. After she escapes into the laundry and drinks bleach, Doctor Mothball suggests that she needs Electro-Convulsive Therapy.

I go with Prissy to meet the Doctor. "Are you mental?" I ask him. "Jesus!"

"It's not as bad as it sounds," the *good doctor* says. "It isn't exactly like *One Flew over the Cuckoos Nest* anymore."

"Really? Good to know. What the hell is it like, exactly?" I ask. "What the hell does it do?"

He actually sits there and tents his fingers, leaning forward to explain it to me. "ECT seems to help with depression of this sort. The patient, say your sister, gets herself into a state where she has tunnel vision — where all she can think about is killing herself. The ECT literally shocks her out of it. We think it erases the short term memory and thereby the patient is no longer in the tunnel."

"Erases her memory? No way. No way no way no way. You are not gonna fuckin' fuck with her fucking brain. Sorry about my language, but you have no idea what ECT actually does to the brain, do you?"

"As I said," he croons, "we've seen great progress with ECT in similar cases." He leans towards Prissy. "If we don't do this, Deirdre will succeed in killing herself," he says. He leans back in his leather chair. It squeaks.

Prissy looks at me.

So. Dee is signed up. She undergoes a program of eight electro convulsive shock fucking treatments over two weeks. She has headaches. She loses a bunch of weight, because she's so frigging nauseated all the time, and by the end of it — she can't remember why she's in the hospital. I guess it worked.

While Dee is recovering, I get to know the other patients. They bum smokes off me. There's an old guy named Arnie, who I figure drank himself into the Spa; a couple of older women who don't talk much; and Frankie. The nurses tell me that Frankie is schizophrenic.

One day, Frankie grabs me by the arm and drags me to the padded room, where they put patients on suicide watch. The nurses call it the safe room. The inmates call it the Bunny Hole. Dee was in there twice, before the ECT. Frankie just got out. He was in the room for forty-eight hours, and he's written all over the walls. A whole world. I can't take it in. I stand there a minute thinking, *I hope Dr. Schlusser reads this. The answer must be here, in these symbols, in these words. It could be deciphered.* Frankie's standing beside me, holding my hand. I pat him. "That's great Frankie, good job." He lets me go and I hurry off to Dee's room. Sarah, a nurse's aide that Dee's chummy with, had called me at Prissy's and told me to come right over.

Dee isn't in her room. She's in the lounge, watching TV. "What's up sugar-puff?" I ask.

"Hey," she says. She doesn't look at me.

I sit. Watch *Wheel of Fortune* for a while. "Sarah called me,"

"Yeah?"

"Yeah. Seemed like she wanted me to come right over. She here?"

"Off shift."

"Oh." Vanna flips a letter. "Anything weird happen today?" Dee finally looks at me. "Gotta smoke?"

"Indeed I do."

We go outside and light up.

Dee takes a few drags of her smoke. I wait. Finally, she says, "Sarah gave me a book."

"Yeah?"

"Yeah."

We smoke.

I ask her what book.

She squints at me. *"Don't."*

I exhale. I go cold. I know that book. *Don't: A Woman's Word* by Elly Danica. A book about child abuse. About sexual abuse. *Don't.*

Dee watches me. "You've read it."

"Yes. I have." I sit down.

"I guess that's why I'm trying to kill myself, eh?" She says it just like that. Matter of fact.

I can barely breathe. *Damn it. damnit damnit. Shit. Say something.* "I guess." *Damn it.* "Dee. I . . . " *Shit.*

"I didn't remember," she says. She takes a drag on her smoke. "They say sometimes people don't remember. They block it out. I guess I blocked it out." She butts her smoke. "Gotta go. I've got group."

She leaves me there.

I smoke another smoke. And another. I go over to the donut shop. I drink coffee and I smoke. The sun goes down. I drink more coffee and I smoke. I have a book with me. I do not read. I do not talk to anyone. I drink coffee and I smoke 'til the pack is empty. I go next door, to the store, and buy a new pack. I go to the phone booth on the corner. I find his address. There he is, right there in the book. Listed. Right here in this town. Not far. I start to walk.

Forty-five minutes later, I'm in front of Jack Vara's house. I walk around the block. I stand in front of his house, across the street. I watch a light go off. I have a rock in my hand. *What am I going to do, smash a window? Smash him? Son of a bitch.* I put the rock in my pocket. It will go in the Samsonite. Another marker. Another bit of our fucked-up life.

I walk back to the donut shop. I drink coffee and I smoke.

At 8am, I go back to the hospital. It isn't visiting hours, but no one stops me. I go to Dee's room. She's eating breakfast. I stand at the door. I say, "Jack."

She nods.

I say, "I'm sorry."

On my way out of the ward, I pass the Bunny Hole. Frankie is standing there, staring at the walls. It's all white again. His world has been washed away. I ask the nurse on duty if Schlusser saw it.

"What for?" she asks.

I walk across town to Prissy's. She's still in bed.

I crawl into the closet and I stay there for three days. It's a big closet. I drag in the mattress from the rollaway, my backpack, and the Samsonite. *Don't leave home without it.* I close the door, and I tell Prissy to leave me alone. She threatens to call the loonywagon. I say, "I just don't feel good. Leave me alone." There's a light in the closet, but I leave it off. I like the dark. I just want to be in the dark. *I've gone down the Bunny Hole.* I giggle.

Prissy tries to lure me out with food, with drink, with cigarettes. She calls Lee. I let her slide the phone into the closet.

He tries to talk me down, talk me out, talk me sane.

"You sound weird," I say.

"I sound weird?" he says. "You're in a closet."

"It's a big closet." I tell him. "What's wrong with you?"

"Nothing's wrong with me."

I wait.

He finally says, "I can't make rent. We're losing the place. You have to come home."

Home? I think. *What's home? Our apartment? Here? Who's my home — Lee or Dee? Prissy? Goose? I miss Goose.* I tell Lee that I need to talk to Goose.

"What?" He sounds mad.

"Nothing." I can't talk to Goose. Goose is incommunicado. Goose is on a trip around the world. Goose stayed in school. Goose didn't fuck off to study the Bible or move to fucking Toronto. Goose stayed in school and then got a job as a speech-writer for the NDP. He saved his pennies and took off on a trip around the world. *You should have gone with him. You should have gone and never come back.*

I hang up on Lee.

I stay in the closet.

I keep hearing things, seeing flashes of things when I close my eyes. I hear Jack calling Prissy a stupid slut. I feel him hitting me. I see him bouncing Dee on his knee that time I came home to pick up something for rehearsal. As I was leaving, I heard him call her *Babycakes.* I went back and told him not to call her that. "She likes it," he said. I left. I went to rehearsal and left them alone. *Where the hell was Prissy?*

I see myself, bouncing on other knees.

I smell rye, rum, tobacco.

I taste blood.

I curl in on myself. I taste soursalt. I gag.

Flashbacks. I'm having flashbacks.

I know this because I've read the books. I've read everything. Because that's what I do. I read.

I know what this is. I know what is happening to me, but I refuse it. *This is not happening. I am fine. I have always been fine. Shit happened, but it doesn't matter — because I am fine.*

But the flashbacks keep coming.

Shut up shuddup shuddup, I sing in my head. I start the guitars jangling. *I can just lie here — die here. Lie? Lay? Stay. I can just stay in here and never come out — ever. I can just cover up my head and disappear. I can. Dark and warm and safe in here. I don't ever have to come out.*

I can slip down the Bunny Hole.

I fall asleep.

I dream that I'm at the edge of a pool holding on to the top rung of the ladder and my arms are tired. My arms are so tired and the water is so warm and I think, *I should just let go. Just let go and sink to the bottom of the pool and watch the lights play along the water. Like I did at the pool in Hamilton — with Lola, the one eyed girl.*

I think, *This is what it's like to go mad. It's just — letting go. Hand opening. Slipping backwards. Going under.*

I think, *it will be warm there. I will fall back inside myself, and watch — like in the ambulance; like I've always watched — but from an even safer distance. I will never speak. I will just stop speaking. What's to say anyway? What on earth is there to say?*

I will retreat.

And people will take care of me.

I suddenly understand the appeal of the Psych Ward. You don't have to do anything there. You have food and shelter and people are mostly kind to you. You don't have to make any decisions at all. You can rest.

I need to rest. I'm tired. I'm tired of making decisions. Making a life. I'm tired — of struggling. Struggling to get out of bed. Struggling to pretend that everything is OK; that I don't do weird shit like leaving my body; like I don't have nightmares. Struggling to smile and smile and smile when I can't even fucking breathe — when I smell that dishsoap smell and the hole opens up inside me; when the Mean Reds come.

It's too hard. I think. *And I am too alone. And I get so tired.*
So tired.
So tired.
So tired.
I would like to stop now.

But my hand won't let go. My hand is still clenched on that rung. I'm half-in half-out of the water.

I look down, and the water turns to sludge. It's sucking at me, and I know that if I let go it will pull me under and fill my eyes my ears my mouth my lungs and there will be silence and darkness and cold and I will be cold and silent forever and there will be no dancing lights and there will be no watching — there will be nothing but blackness — not even memories replayed. Nothing.

Silence
and
Cold.

My hand is on the rung.
My hand is on the rung.
My hand is on the rung.

I wake in my mother's closet. My fists clenched tight. One of my hands is holding the Samsonite. I don't know if it represents the rung, or what will drag me under.

My Auntie Lip came over on the fourth day. She brought me tea. She came into the closet and closed the door. She sat on the end of my mattress. "It's not really so bad in here," she said. She turned on the light. "It's like your own little room."

"Yeah."

"When Priss said you were in the closet, I thought you'd flipped. But this ain't so bad. More of a pantry actually."

Yes. I nodded. *I've taken to living in the pantry.*

She pushed my hair out of my eyes. "You OK, Kid?"

"I'm always OK."

She smiled. "You are."

"I'm not."

"I know. You're scaring Prissy."

Like I care.

"Are you mad at her? Did she do something?"

I almost laughed. *Oh, where to begin.* "Dee didn't say anything?"

"About what?"

"Jesus fucking Christ." I opened my mouth. I couldn't say it. *Fuck.* "C'mon."

We left the closet.

Prissy was in the kitchen — making cabbage rolls.

I went to the sink. I ran the water cold. I drank a glass, slowly.

Prissy kept rolling cabbage rolls.

I stared into the sink. "Jack molested Dee."

I heard Auntie take a breath.

"No." Prissy said.

I looked at her. She was staring at the layer of cabbage rolls in the roaster. Her hands were shaking. "Yes."

Prissy wiped her hands. "It happens to lots of kids."

"It happened to your kids."

"Well," she said. "We've been through hell and back, but at least we still have our insanity."

I laughed — inside my head — I laughed like a fucking lunatic. "Sanity," I said.

"What?"

"Sanity. At least we have our sanity."

"That's what I said."

I had nothing else to say. "I'm leaving."

Prissy nodded. I knew she wanted to say, *What about Dee?* She didn't say it.

My hand was on the rung.

Goose from Goose

I stayed in Toronto for one more year.

I went into therapy.

Things got messy, quick.

Lee and I broke up.

Goose called. "I hear you've come out of the closet."

I laughed. "How'd you know I was in?"

"My mom writes me, Poste Restante. Prissy tried to find me when you went mad."

"Poste Restante, I should have thought of that." I hadn't written Goose since he left on his big adventure.

"No biggy." He paused, probably to figure out what the hell to say. "So. How's it going?"

"I'm in therapy."

"No shit?"

I laughed again. "Piles and piles of shit, actually."

"You OK?"

"I will be."

"You want me to come there?" He meant it. He sounded worried.

"No. I'll be fine. Where are you, anyway?"

"Morocco. You wanna chuck it all in and meet me in Marrakech?"

"Love to, darling. But, no."

"You working?"

I laughed. "I am actually. I've become quite the Ibsen heroine." I was finally getting real work in the centre of the universe. I was paying my rent without waiting tables.

Goose laughed. "Ah Hedda, you'll be fine."

"Yeah. I know."

"No guns around the place?"

"Funny. Guess what my next part is."

"Hint?"

"Shaw."

"Not Joan?"

"Yeah. Can you believe it?"

He giggled. I knew he'd clap his hands if he wasn't holding a phone. "Will you cut your hair?"

"To the scalp if they want."

"Ah, Bean. You'll make a lovely saint."

"Thank you."

"God must be very proud."

"Wouldn't know," I said. "We're not speaking."

Goose blew out some air. I know he wanted to say something about that little tidbit, but he switched tacks. "Good therapist?"

"Yeah. She's tough, but good. Keeps asking me what I'll do when Dee succeeds in killing herself."

"Jesus."

"She wants me to write about my feelings."

"Oh Lordy."

"Yeah. I told her that I have no feelings and that I sure as shit never put anything in writing."

He laughed and then went quiet. I waited. He asked if I ever saw Lee.

"Wow — you know everything."

"Prissy's not the best at keeping secrets."

"I didn't think she even talked to your mom."

"Who knew?" He chuckled. "What happened? With Lee?"

"I got weak."

"What?"

"I started having nightmares again. I felt . . . broken. I got needy." I started laughing.

"What?"

"You know what he said when he left?"

"What?"

"He said, *You're not as strong as I thought you were.*"

"That is a son-of-a-bitch thing to say."

"He was right."

"No he wasn't."

"I tried Goose, I really did. I thought I was fine. I didn't even know I was pretending. Now, I'm a fucking mess. I cry all the time, like some kind of sucky-tit psycho baby."

"Good."

My throat hurt. "I hate crying."

"I know."

I blew out some air. "God, it's good to hear you."

"You too. You really OK?"

"I will be. You?"

"I'm fabulous."

"Good. Tell me some stories."

Goose told me some of his adventures. Made me smile. Just before he hung up, he said, "Watch your mail, there's a present coming."

He sent me a carving of a goose, made of Sunstone, from Tanzania. The note said:

Bandele, the very handsome carver of this gem, told me that sunstone chases away our fears and protects us from destructive forces. He says Geese are lucky. I know this Goose is. I stayed with Bandele for a week.

Kisses and all of my love, as always

Goose

I carried on — acting, and working on my *issues*.

Acting was easy. On stage, I was in my body, and the words were all thought out for me. The rest of the time, I watched the world from some calm, floaty, place behind my eyes. It felt like there was a sheet of glass between me and the rest of the world. I smiled and smiled. I watched the dances people do. Watched actors court Artistic Directors at opening nights, in bars. The soft touch on the arm. The flattery. I listened to heated debates about Mamet and what the hell George F. Walker was up to. I admired Judith Thompson and Linda Griffiths from afar. They looked so strong.

I floated on the edges of the world.

I talked with my therapist. When she asked about Prissy, I told her about the Husky and the happy movie I dreamed us into — just me and Prissy Fallwell. When she asked about Dee, I cried.

She finally got me to write some things down. She wanted me to write about Prissy and Dee. I wrote about Jack. I let her read it and then we burned it.

I got another call — middle of the night — from Dee this time. "I'm pregnant. Please come home."

I packed up the circus trunk I'd found at St. Vincent de Paul. I shipped the trunk and three boxes of books to Dee's place. I carried the Samsonite with me on the Greyhound.

I didn't think about it. Dee needed me, so I went.
I had another chance.

BLUE FEET, BLUE HANDS

I got an apartment across the hall from Dee and a job at a café down the street. We took Lamaze classes together.

Goose was back in town, working for Roy Romanow. When Dee had a middle of the night craving, Goose and I drove to almost every 7-11 in town until we found some Quaker Instant Oatmeal.

"Who craves oatmeal?" he'd said when I called him at 3am, but he came. Goose drove us everywhere — to doctor's appointments, Lamaze classes, shopping, and to the hospital the night Dee went into labour.

She had a baby boy. She named him Cody. He was perfect. His birth was the most amazing thing I'd ever seen. Dee was amazing. She was so strong and determined — red in the face and pushing. She had a baby. She was a woman. *She'll be okay now,* I thought.

The first time I held Cody, he grabbed my finger, tight, and smiled at me. Made my chest ache. "You did that too," I told Dee. "You did exactly that."
Dee was bleary. "The nurse says it's just gas."

The day we brought Cody home, Dee and I made cards with prints of his tiny hands and feet in blue finger paint. I mailed them to everyone I knew.

For a few months, we were all thick as thieves. Prissy, Goose and I were over at Dee's every chance we got — vying to hold the baby, rock the baby, walk the baby. When Cody fell asleep, the four of us sat around and played cribbage.

Sometimes I stayed over, to feed him in the night, so Dee could get some sleep. We'd sit by the window and I'd show Cody the Lady on the Moon. I'd whisper stories to him — fairytales and the stories GT had told me, about sailors and adventures on the high seas. "You will grow up to be a hero," I whispered.

Then Milo came back.

Milo, the asshole who knocked Dee up and disappeared. He just showed up one day, and moved back in. Dee said she didn't know what to do.

I told her to kick his ass out.

"I can't," she said. "He's Cody's father."

Milo made Dee move away from me a few weeks after he moved in. He told her he didn't like me *hanging around so much*.

They got married.

Dee wanted me to be her maid of honour.

I said I couldn't.

She was pissed off, but I just couldn't do it.

She said I should support her. She said it was her life and that she was doing what was best for her and Cody. She said that I never supported her — that I was always judging her. That everything was always so easy for me. That I didn't understand.

Goose came with me to the wedding. He wanted to sign the card *To Darling Dee and Assface*. He never could remember Milo's name.

I told Goose what Dee said about supporting her. He said, "Your sister can be a real bitch. Let's wear fabulous outfits." We sat at the back.

I hated going over to Dee's place after she got married. I didn't like Assface Milo and he didn't like me, but if I wanted to see Dee and Cody, I had to see Milo, too. I tried to be civil. I tried to keep an eye on Dee and Cody, but it got harder and harder. Dee started showing up at my place with black eyes and bruises. I tried to convince her to leave him. She wouldn't.

I didn't know what to do — so I did nothing.

I went back into therapy.

I saw Dee and Cody and Prissy less and less. But I didn't leave town.

I stayed in Regina, and I worked at the café.

Goose asked me why I wasn't acting anymore. I didn't really know. I didn't really want to think about it. I was happy working at the café. It was simple and social. It paid the rent.

Time passed. I wrapped myself in the *cotton wool of daily life* and four years went by.

I watched Cody grow.

Cody Fallwell had big brown eyes, eyelashes like a giraffe's and a lunatic woodpecker laugh. He smelled of cinnamon and sandwiches.

I had fantasies about running away with him — to a cabin in the woods, to a houseboat, to the Badlands — somewhere that no one would find us. In my day-dreams, it was just me and Cody. I brought him up. I taught him about wild plants and herbs, how to ski and sail and dance, how to cook. I taught him things I didn't even know how to do in reality. I raised him up to be a gentle man.

As if I could ever *raise anyone up.*

I babysat Cody sometimes. Until I let him eat cigarette butts. He escaped while I was hunting for socks in his dresser. He found an ashtray under the couch and, by the time I caught him, he had a soggy butt in his mouth. I couldn't tell how many he'd swallowed. He ran around like a maniac for about fifteen minutes and then lay down on the floor. I called Goose and we rushed him to the hospital.

Dee and Milo didn't let me babysit much after that. Couldn't blame them.

I was unfit.

Prayer Card for Ritter

Ritter was still living in Regina. I ran into him a few times. He was still driving cab. We never managed to get together.

On Father's Day 1995, I went out with Goose to see *Boys on the Side*. When I got home, there was a message on my machine from Jacqueline.

Ritter was dead. I hadn't sent a Father's Day card.

Ritter's daughter, Kyla, found him in the garage, lying on the front seat of his cab, with a Johnny Cash cassette in the deck. He killed himself.

Goose came with me and Prissy to the funeral. We sat at the back. It was an open casket.

I went up. Prissy tried to come with me, but Goose held her back.

Ritter looked good. Peaceful.

They'd put makeup on his right hand.

I flashed on a memory of him lying in the backyard, in Moose Jaw, with a towel over his window arm trying to even out his taxi driver tan.

I started crying. I cried and cried and cried and cried all the way through the service. Great hulking silent sobs. Goose passed me tissues. Prissy stared at me like I was some kind of freak show. Later, I asked Goose why I couldn't stop crying.

"He was your Father."

"Yeah, but he was . . . It's not like I ever saw him or anything. Hardly ever."

"So?"

I sniffled. "Prissy was sure freaked. I thought her eyes would pop out of her head."

Goose stayed serious. "When was the last time Prissy saw you cry?"

I shook it off. "Let's go for a beer."

Cody's Hand

That Christmas, I went to Dee's. I got there just after eight. Prissy was already there. We slept over at Dee's every Christmas Eve, so we could be there for Cody in the morning. Milo, was out.

We watched *It's a Wonderful Life*, like we did every year.

Cody fell asleep on my lap and I put him to bed around 10:30. He woke up as I was tucking him in. "I love you, Auntie."

"I love you too, kid. A bizillion times a million."

Milo showed up around 1:30 — pissed to the gills, and looking for a fight.

All my therapy went to shit.

I froze.

Milo stood there, screaming at Dee, and I didn't say a word. I stared into the middle distance. I waited for the move forward, for the hit. *If he takes one step toward her,* I thought. *If he takes one step toward her — I will be able to move.*

Milo didn't take the step. He ranted and raved but he didn't take the step.

Dee just sat there. She didn't rise to the bait like Prissy used to. She didn't try to soothe him or to defend herself. She just sat there.

We all did.

Prissy stared at the floor. *Make him stop,* I thought. *You're supposed to be the mom.* As if.

I sat there while a drunken asshole raged at my sister and I did nothing.

I didn't slip into jangly steel guitar land. Therapy had taken my guitars away. I didn't leave my body anymore. I just retreated inside myself, slipped behind the pane of glass. I watched from there. I didn't listen to what Milo said. It was all the same old shit. I listened to the flashing mini-lights around Dee's picture window that played carols. *Jingle Bells, Jingle Bells* . . .

After an hour or so, Milo threw his wedding ring in Dee's face and stormed out.

We sat there awhile listening to the lights. *Silent night, Holy night* . . .

I got up, went to my bag, pulled out a mickey of Wild Turkey and poured us all a drink. "Don't suppose there's any use in locking the door, eh?" I asked.

We laughed. Hysterically.

We drank and Dee started talking. She told me all the stuff she'd been holding back — the beatings I didn't know about, the jealousy. How, when they'd first started going out, Milo stormed home from work one day because he called home and Dee didn't answer. He thought he was going to catch her screwing around. She was in the shower. She'd just finished painting their bedroom.

"Didn't that raise a flag?" I asked.

"What do you mean?"

That he's a frigging lunatic and you should have run for the hills right fucking then? I thought. I thought it, but I didn't say it. There was no point. I'm the runner.

Then Dee said, "At least Cody's asleep."

"You're kidding, right?" It was out of my mouth before I could stop it. I knew better, but I couldn't stop. "Dee, you know he's lying in there listening to every word. He's probably wet the bed, like you used to."

She started crying.

I felt like shit.

"You don't understand," she said. "Milo loves us. He doesn't mean it when he gets this way. It's just the booze talking. He's frustrated at work. I upset him earlier today. It's my fault."

I wanted to yell, *Bullshit!* Instead, I hugged Dee and said, "I'm sorry, Sweety. You're right. Cody's asleep." *And I'm a fucking useless coward.*

"He's a really sound sleeper."

"Yeah."

Dee and Prissy went to bed about four. I sat on the couch, smoking, waiting for Milo to come back.

I thought about the first time I saw Jack hurt Prissy. It was before they were even married. She was pregnant with Dee. They were arguing about something. I was under the kitchen table. She told him to shut up, and turned away to go into the basement to get something. He kicked her, hard, and she went down the stairs. It was so sudden, and so violent, I froze. Prissy'd been with hitters before. She'd gotten fat lips, bruises, and arms sore from twisting. This was something else. This was crazy.

He left.

I went to Prissy.

She said, "I'm OK."

"He kicked you down the stairs."

"I'm OK."

"You're pregnant."

"We're OK."

Jack came back with pizza, and it was like it never happened. They laughed, and she sat on his knee and he told stories about how we'd move out to the country one day and I would have a pony and he'd teach me how to ride. They laughed and laughed. Like it never happened.

Two days later, I had to pee when Prissy was in the shower. She got out to dry off and I saw the bruises on her back.

It did happen.

Cody got up around seven. I gave him his stocking, made fresh coffee and hauled Prissy and Dee outta bed. "Merry Christmas!"

Cody was over the moon with the sled I'd bought for him. He gave me a plaque. It was a plaster cast of his hand.

"Me and Mommy made it and we painted the hand blue. You made blue pictures of my hands when I was a tiny baby, right?"

"That's right."

"See how big my hand is now?" He held up his hand and I placed mine against it. "I'm almost as big as you, Auntie Bean."

"You sure are." I touched the palm of the blue hand; ran my finger over Cody's hand. *So small. He's still so small.*

Cody tilted his head. "Are you crying?"

I sniffed. "Nah. Thanks, Honey. It's the best gift ever. Get your coat and I'll take you for a ride on your new sled." I dragged him around the yard while Prissy and Dee cooked the turkey and cabbage rolls.

Spuddy and Slim showed up around ten. Auntie couldn't make it that year. Milo arrived in time to eat. He laughed and joked with Prissy and Spuddy and Slim. Dee and Cody sat on his knee while he opened his presents.

I helped Prissy with the dishes, hugged everyone, and left. I didn't have to hug Milo. He was having a *nap*.

I decided never to see Milo again. I didn't make a big scene. I just started seeing Dee and Cody over at Prissy's.

Dee and Prissy didn't even notice, but Cody did. "How come you don't come play at my house anymore, Auntie?"

I didn't know what to say, so I said nothing. I tickled Cody and told him I'd just been busy at work.

The accident happened in the spring of '96.

I woke in a sweat. The telephone was ringing.

It was Prissy.

Cody was dead.

I took a cab to the hospital.

After I talked to Prissy, and saw Dee, I called Goose. He came to the hospital. I met him outside. He looked pale and his hair was mussed. He was still wearing the sweats he slept in. "What happened? Bean, tell me what happened."

I was smoking. I was cold. It was a nice night, but I was freezing cold. My voice sounded funny in my head — echoey. "Milo was drunk. He was drunk and pissed-off. Driving fast to scare Dee, as if that would work. He was drunk and he was roaring down an alley and he hit something and the car spun into a fucking wall and the side of the car was crushed and Cody is dead." I looked at Goose. My eyes were weird. He seemed a million miles away. Like I was looking through the wrong end of a telescope. "Cody's dead."

Goose reached for me.

I stepped back, away from him. I was so cold. I was cold and I couldn't breathe right. I couldn't cry. "What the fuck is wrong with them? No car seat. They didn't even have Cody in a fucking seat belt. And Dee . . . Dee is in there, drugged to the tits and crying — about Milo getting arrested."

"She's in shock."

"She's a retard."

"You're in shock, too."

"I'm fine."

"Bean. You are not fine. Why are you pulling at your sweater like that?"

"The neck's too tight. I can't breathe right."

Goose reached for me again, "Let me — "

"I'm fine." I shook him off. "I should've taken him."

"What?"

"I should have taken Cody."

"Bean."

"I should've. I could've taken him, Goose. We could've gone anywhere."

"You couldn't. Dee would have died."

"Bullshit."

"Having Cody saved her life. You told me that she — "

"I told you a lot of bullshit. Dee wouldn't have died." I felt dizzy, like I was drunk. "You know what? You know what she would've done? She'd just have another kid. She probably will have another kid . . . and another and another — "

"Bean. Stop it."

"Dee won't kill herself. If she really wanted to die, she'd get it right. Cut down, not across. Take the pills and go lie down someplace where no one will find you. Pick a high spot, over concrete. It's not that fucking hard. I can fucking show her how to kill herself!"

"Bean stop."

"And Prissy. She just . . . I hate them, Goose. I hate them."

"You don't."

"I do. I can't . . . " I started laughing. "They wanted me to come home, right? For what? I came back and it didn't make any fucking difference. I was right here! I stayed right fucking here and it doesn't matter. It doesn't matter, Goose. I can't do anything. They just do whatever the fuck they do. Doesn't matter if I'm here or not. They'll be fine, y'know. They'll just carry on. This will just be another fucking awful thing that happened to them. Another thing that some bad man did to them. They... They won't . . . I fucking *envy* them. Isn't that hilarious? It never gets them — not deep down. I keep thinking something will break through and they'll — I dunno. Maybe they'll have to go to therapy. Can you see that — Oh fuck I would pay big money to see that. Then maybe they'll see how fucking easy it is for me. Fuck. Oh fuck. What is wrong with them? They don't feel anything. Why can't they feel anything?"

Goose looked stunned. "Dee feels things."

"Oh yeah, right. She feels things and then she runs off and pretends to hurt herself so she can go to the fucking Spa. But she won't *deal* with anything. She just... What the hell is wrong with her?"

Goose reached out for me again.

"Don't touch me!" But he did touch me. Goose touched my arm and I finally started to cry. "What the fuck is wrong with me, Goose? Why didn't I take him?"

"You couldn't."

"Why didn't I take her?"

"You couldn't."

"No kidding, right? I can barely take care of myself. I'm a fucking nutter, just like Ritter."

"Bean."

"It's true Goose. I'm fucked. I am so fucking fucking fucked."

Goose pulled me into his arms. "This isn't your fault."

I felt like I would die from the pain — sobbing and snotting all over Goose's pretty blue jacket. I pulled back and looked into his eyes. He was crying too. "Whose fault is it?"

I didn't die.

We had a funeral.

I watched from behind my pane of glass.

Jack came. He had a whole new family. Dee clung to him and cried. He hugged Prissy. He didn't approach me.

I watched Prissy. She sat beside Dee. She reached over and brushed Dee's bangs back. They held hands and cried together. They knew how to take care of each other. Prissy and Dee were together and I was a million miles away.

Milo went to jail.

I did what I always do. I ran.

I left the suitcase with Goose, and I went to the desert.

Goose drove to the bus depot. He gave me a copy of *Breakfast at Tiffany's* — the movie.

"What am I supposed to do with this?"

"Carry it. It's light."

"Could've given me the book."

"I like the movie better," he said. "She stays."

I gave him the key to the Samsonite, and climbed on the bus.

Four

Record *vt* to set down in writing or other permanent form; . . . to make a recording of, to mark, indicate; to bear witness to; to put on record (an offence, ect) without taking further measures against the offender; to register (as a vote or verdict); to celebrate; to call to mind (*Archaic*); to get by heart *(*Obs*)*; to go over in ones mind (*Spenser*); to repeat from memory *(Spenser)*; to narrate, set forth *(archaic)* . . . [OFR *recorder,* from L *recordari* to call to mind, get by heart, from *cor, cordis* the heart]
— *The Chambers Dictionary* (Standard)

Recordar: (Spanish) To remember; from the Latin word re-cordis, to pass back through the heart.
— Eduardo Galeano, *The Book of Embraces*

RED ROCK

Getting on a Greyhound makes you feel like you're going somewhere — even if you aren't. The sound of the tires on the highway soothed me. I stared out the window. I drank bad coffee in truck stops. I watched people. I sat alone — my backpack a barricade on the seat beside me.

I didn't really have a destination. Figured I'd go check out the VLA — the Very Large Array west of Socorro, New Mexico. I wanted to walk among all those crazy radio dish antennas aimed up at the sky — listening for messages from space.

By the time I hit Albuquerque, Gene Wilder and the Oompa-Loompas had invaded my dreams. They don't give you headphones on American buses. They just play the movie at full volume. They all play the same movie. I'd seen *Willy Wonka and the Chocolate Factory* five times. I decided to get off the bus and hitch the rest of the way.

A blue pickup pulled over just outside of Albuquerque. The sign on the side said *Moon River Organic Goat Cheese*. There was a red-headed woman driving. I climbed in.

I was doing up my seatbelt when she spoke. "Hiya, Canada."

I took a better look at the driver and gawped like a carp. "Brighid?" She looked exactly the same. Some crow's feet — but the same far-seeing eyes. She was smiling.

Brighid had been living in the States for seven years. She offered me a place to stay. She ran a goat ranch near Pie Town, New Mexico. How could I resist?

I bunked out in an old trailer, up the hill from Brighid's cabin. The first night I was there, a feral cat ate her dead baby on my bed — while I was in it. The crunching sounds woke me. I let the cat finish her meal. I got up and relit the wood stove. The wood smelled like incense — pinon and mesquite.

Brighid came into my trailer at dawn. She stood beside the bed with a steaming mug. "Drink this."

I thought it was tea. It wasn't. Something salty and strange. "What is this?"

"Miso. Drink it." I did. I got dressed. Brighid tossed me a big burgundy sweater. "Put this on, it's dead cold out."

It was cold, but I didn't really feel it. I didn't really feel anything. I put the sweater on. "I had a sweater like this once." *In Austria.* "I lost it somewhere."

We stepped out of the trailer into a Georgia O'Keeffe painting — ragged red and black. The clarity, the edges of things, hurt my eyes. I took a breath. I was surfacing but I still couldn't get out. I'd locked myself inside. Brighid was watching me. I exhaled a cloud of white. "I thought the desert was warm."

"High desert," Brighid said. "We could still get some snow." She took me to the barn. She showed me how to milk the goats. When we were done, she told me to round up the kids. "They don't go out with the herd yet. Put them in that pen." Then she left.

Goats are not sheep. They're smart. They're mischievous. The kids didn't want to be separated from their mothers. They ran. They hid. I chased them, slipping in the goat shit. By the time I'd penned them all, I was laughing my ass off and I was back in the world. The pane of glass had melted.

Brighid was watching me from her deck. "You hungry?"

"Starving."

"Open the gate and let the mothers out."

I did. Two big white dogs rounded them up and they all headed out into the red. I looked at Brighid. "Don't we have to go with?"

"No. The dogs handle it. They're Maremmas," she said. "From the Italian Alps. Bred for wolf control. The male stays with the goats. The female circles the herd and looks for predators."

"And if something attacks?"

"The female takes care of it. Come and eat."

An omelet — goat cheese and green chilies. Strong black coffee. First food I'd had in weeks that didn't taste like sawdust funeral sandwiches.

Brighid watched me over the top of her coffee mug. When I finished, she set down her cup. "So. How ya doin', Canada."

"I'm good."

She poured me some more coffee. "What are doing here?"

"Don't you know?"

"Meaning did I have a dream?"

"Yeah."

"You've floated through my dreams, but no, I didn't know you were coming. I got a flat."

"What?"

"I was dropping off a load of cheese in Albuquerque. I was supposed to have left town an hour earlier. I got a flat tire. I had to change it."

We laughed. Neither of us believed in coincidences.

Brighid leaned in. "Why are you here?"

"Just decided to take a trip."

"Bollocks."

I told her about Cody.

She told me about her mother dying. "I was just a kid. Went a bit doollaly, they say. I slipped away — inside somewhere."

"Behind the pane of glass."

She smiled and nodded. "That's it. That's exactly what it felt like. I could see things and hear things, but I couldn't get out." She traced a wing of the faded Monarch tattoo on her hand. "My old auntie told me this story about a butterfly. Old story. About dealing with grief. Some say this butterfly lost a lover; some say a sister. Way my aunt told me — the butterfly lost her mother to a stormy sky. The butterfly was sad, yeah? So, she plucked off her wings. She packed them up in a little kit, and pissed off on a trip. She went all around the world and she kept her eyes downcast, on the ground, stepping on each and every stone. Then one day, as she was crossing a river, she actually *looked* at a stone — I mean really saw it, y'know — and that stone was so beautiful that it healed her. That butterfly put her wings back on and she danced."

"Nice."

"I got this tattoo to remind me to pay attention. To really look at what's right in front of me. That's how I stay out from behind the glass. Two things I know: one — it's hard to play a sad song on a banjo, and two — it's impossible to stay out of your body, or locked away inside it, when you're chasing a kid through goat shit. You have to pay attention."

I stayed on the goat ranch for forty days.

Brighid had never seen *Breakfast at Tiffany's*.

I asked her if she'd read the book.

She laughed. "I'm more of a *Hitchhiker's Guide to the Galaxy* kind of gal."

"But your place is called Moon River."

"So?"

We watched the movie — and cried.

Holly Golightly is a lost soul. She's beautiful, charming and entirely forlorn. She sees herself as a wild thing that doesn't belong anywhere or to anyone. Capote's book ends with Holly still on the run, searching for her perfect place — a place like Tiffany's. In the movie, she's saved by love. In the rainy final scene, Paul tells her that people do belong to each other and that belonging to someone, with someone, is our only chance of happiness. Brighid sat on the floor with her arms wrapped around her legs, knees up to her chest. "Tell me about Goose."

I told her the story of how we met; about playing spy; about watching his family; about the Ouija Board and Gloria Arella's grave. I told her about the book he gave me for graduation and how his family took me in when I left home. I told her what it felt like when he sent me the letter at Bible School — when he was afraid that I wouldn't be his friend anymore.

Brighid shook her head. "Silly prat."

"Yeah, but I can see what he was afraid of. I really did want to be a . . . good Christian."

"You wanted to be close to the Big Fella, you didn't want to be a happy clappy."

"No. But I envied them."

"And now?"

"Now, what?"

"How's that going?" she rolled her eyes heavenward.

I couldn't lie to her. "Not so good." I changed the subject. "Hey. Why is your place called *Moon River*?"

Brighid told me about Gavin, the boy she'd come to New Mexico with. "He named the place." She chewed on her thumbnail. She smiled, sadly. "He sang me that song."

"What happened?"

"He left." She shrugged. "I guess he still had some drifting to do. He got bored, out here, with me. I dunno. He had to go and I couldn't leave. Not yet. This is my place, for now."

I told her about Lee.

Brighid and I took out our memories and turned them over like stones in our hands — looking at each one. We worked — milking goats, making cheese — and we told each other the stories of our lives. Mine, except for Lee, were all connected to the items gathered and tucked into the Samsonite.

My keepsakes of Lee and Toronto were still in a separate box. I hadn't sorted through them yet.

I told Brighid about the Napkin Kiss and the Elvis scarf. I laid out the happy movie I'd made in my head of the time when it was just me and Prissy Fallwell. Then, I told her the truth.

There were only four years between Ritter and Jack. In my mind, I'd made it longer. I made it my whole childhood. *Happy times.* I told Brighid that it was never just Prissy and me. There was always a guy around, and the guys were mostly losers — even Keith, the hippy guy who gave me the Buddha necklace, the *best guy Prissy ever dated.*

"He was the Earthquake man," I told Brighid. "He had this cute little Earthquake game he liked to play. He'd lay on the floor and I'd sit on him, and he'd quiver and shake, bounce me around like an earthquake — on top of his erection. The others weren't as subtle. They came into my room when Prissy was asleep."

Brighid asked me if Prissy knew.

I shrugged. "I never told her."

"Why?"

"I don't know."

Brighid nodded. "You should tell her."

"Yeah, well."

I told Brighid about Jack — the bad and the good. I told her about the bullet and the Nosoy-Nopoy killer. I told her about all his little girlfriends. I told her about Dee. I told Brighid the truth about Jack, too. "Jack Vara was an evil son of a bitch. But he never touched me, sexually. It was the others — Prissy's boyfriends, one night stands. My father, Ritter. Just once. One drunken night when I was six. Jack never touched me."

Brighid asked me how that made me feel — Jack with all those young girls and never once trying anything with me.

I told her I felt lucky.

She went really still, and then she said, "No. Not how does it make you feel now. How did it make you feel, then?"

We were sitting on the red rock. We'd followed the goats out that morning so I could see some of the desert. I felt a rush of heat on my skin. I looked at Brighid. She met my eyes and held them. I started to shake. I felt water in my mouth. "Oh shit. Shit." I scrambled away from her and threw up. She came and held my hair and rubbed my back while I puked and puked and sobbed and puked.

When I was done, she passed me a bottle of water. "Rinse and spit."

I did. I told her I was sorry.

She smiled. "For what?"

I laughed.

We talked about Cody and Dee.

I told her that I was afraid that Dee would start trying to kill herself again. "She only stopped because she got pregnant. Some cop convinced her that if she tried to kill herself while she was pregnant, he'd charge her with attempted murder."

"Could he do that?"

"Probably not. She believed him though. When Cody was born, she had a reason to live. She had someone to take care of. Now that he's gone . . . "

"You're afraid she'll kill herself."

"Yeah."

Brighid nodded. "And that whole — killing herself thing — is your fault."

"Yes."

"Why?"

"Because I didn't kill Jack Vara when I had the chance."

Brighid thought a while. "You stopped because Dee was screaming. Yeah?"

"What?"

"You told me that you were calm when you picked up the gun. You knew the law. You knew you'd get off. You stopped because Dee was screaming."

"Yeah. So?"

"You told me that Dee never screamed. She never made a peep, no matter what was happening. She saw you and Prissy getting kicked to shit and she never made a sound."

"Because of me. I always told her if she stayed quiet she'd be OK."

"So — why do you think she screamed that night?"

"I don't know. To stop me."

"Why?"

"I don't know. I should have killed him. Then he never would have . . . "

"You don't know when it started, Bean."

"I should've known."

"Just like your mother should have known about what happened to you."

"That's different."

"It isn't."

My throat started to ache. "That's the night I left them."

Brighid looked confused.

"The night of the bullet. The last time Jack Vara hit me. That's the night I left them." I'd told Brighid my big brave story. How I stood up and stood up and stood up. How Jack beat me until there was blood running out of my ear and then never hit me again. "Jack didn't stop hitting me because I was some big hero or had some power over him. It was because I disappeared. I went to school early and stayed late. I wandered the streets at night. When I finally left home physically — they didn't even notice. They only found out I was gone because Dee was home when I went to pick up my fucking curling iron — two weeks later. Dee was there and she begged me to stay and I had my little *take her take her take her* battle with myself. What a joke! I'd left her and Prissy behind years ago." Brighid tried to speak, but I cut her off. "And you know what? I have the fucking *temerity* to miss them! I took myself away. I abandoned them and now I'm all sad and lonely because I feel this . . . gulf between us . . . this distance. This *chasm* I fucking built with my own two hands." I started laughing. I could feel the edge of hysteria in my voice. "For a few months, after Cody was born, I thought we were coming back together — me and Prissy and Dee and Cody. Like the old days, when Dee was a kid, when we had funerals for dead gerbils. Then Assface Milo came back and I left them again. I was there physically, but I ... stepped back. Nothing I could do, right? Dee's gonna live her life — doesn't matter that I'm right fucking *there*. But, am I there? Was I there? I keep myself separate, somehow, like — I have to protect myself from them. From getting sucked back into that world and . . . " I stopped. I took a few breaths and the tears came. "I miss them Brighid."

She took hold of my hands. "I know."

"I had to leave."

"I know." She wiped a tear from my cheek. "They can leave, too."

"What?"

"They can leave, too. You found the door. They saw you go through it. They've watched you build a different life for yourself. That's all you can do."

"I never thought of it like that."

Brighid shrugged like it was no big deal.

It was a huge deal.

When I headed to New Mexico, I wasn't sure why I was going, or what I planned to do when I got there. I was thirty. I had an uncontrollable urge to leave town. The desert sounded good.

Once I got to the red rock, I knew why I was there.

When Jesus went to the desert, he wrestled with Satan. I went there to wrestle with God.

We hadn't spoken since I went into Prissy's closet.

I told Brighid about what happened on Solo in Austria. I told her I needed another sit-down with the Big Kahuna. She dropped me off in the middle of nowhere with a sleeping bag, a tent and three bottles of water. I didn't need a Bible.

Things didn't unfold the way I thought they would.

I envisioned a soul-cleansing screaming match. I'd let God have it. Open the gate and rail at Him. He'd send a raging storm to crush me for my defiance and I'd stand in the teeth of the wind and scream, "Is that all you've got?" I would fight God and win. The storm would abate and the clouds would part and the butterflies would come. They'd bring me another message — a clearer message — about where I should go from here.

That's what my inner drama queen was hoping for, but it's not what happened.

I sat — like a radio antenna west of Socorro. I sat on the red rock for three days and I waited for a message from God.

Nothing happened.

I got up, packed my shit, and sat back down.

I closed my eyes.

I said, "Please."

And He came.

God came and She whispered in my ear.

Brighid picked me up an hour later. "He came," she said.
I nodded.
"You've got a new mission."
I smiled.

The next morning, I gathered up four things: a sand scoured red rock with a hole straight through it, a jet black feather tipped with silver, a twisted piece of pinon, and a tiny bleached jawbone. New magic.

Brighid gave me a ride to the Albuquerque bus depot. She hauled my backpack out of the truck and handed it to me. "See ya around, Canada."

We clenched hands, chest high.

I leaned in. "So long, and thanks for all the cheese."

She was still laughing as I climbed aboard the bus.

Epilogue: Coming Home

I called Prissy from Cheyenne Wyoming. "I'm coming home."
"Good," she said.
I asked how Dee was.
"She's OK. She'll be OK."
We weren't sure what to say to each other. I took a breath and
let it out. "I have some stuff to tell you. Old stuff."
"OK." We went quiet again, and then Prissy said, "Bean, are
you happy? I don't mean right this minute. I mean . . . in life.
In your life. Are you happy?"
I heard a woman laughing behind me. I looked over to the
counter, and there was a waitress in a uniform that was just a
little too tight across the hips. She looked tired, but she was
teaching a kid how to make a spoon stick to his nose. *Prissy at
the Husky.*
I thought of all the stories I'd told Brighid.
I thought about what God whispered in my ear out on the
red rock.
I smiled into the phone. "Mostly."

NOTES

Bean and Prissy Fallwell originally appeared in a short story in *The New Quarterly* (Issue 86 Spring 2003).

Excerpts have been previously published in *spring* (Volume Four, Oct. 2005) and *Transition* (Fall 2004).

GT's dictionary: Definitions Bean looks up are from *Funk & Wagnalls Standard College Dictionary* (Canadian Edition), Fitzhenry & Whiteside Ltd. Toronto, 1963.

Definitions outside of the narrative are from *The Chambers Dictionary*, Chambers Harrap Publishers Ltd. Edinburgh, 2003 and *The Book of Embraces*, Eduardo Galeano, W. W. Norton Co. N.Y., London, 1989.

PAM BUSTIN's play *Saddles in the
Rain* won the John V. Hicks award
in 2002, and was published by
Playwrights Canada Press in the
anthology *The West of all Possible
Worlds* in 2004. Her other stage
plays include *barefoot* and *The
Passage of Georgia O'Keeffe*. Three
of her radio dramas have aired
on CBC and her short fiction has
appeared in *The New Quarterly*,
spring and *Transitions*. Pam
Bustin was raised in a host of small
towns across the prairies and lives
in Saskatoon, Saskatchewan. This
is her first novel.